Fiesty Tee

I am so glad to
hear about your spiritual
growth. Stop claiming stuff.
Glad you liked the book.
Yourig is so Powerfull I know!
C.C.

To my son Zaybien,
you are a little inspiration, who taught me how to dream.

Fresty,
you do have to put it, to get it!
curguasm
onest comments. watch the guse pumps!
Sassy

Fiesty,
I am happy that you
have "grown" spiritually
Vibrint

ACKNOWLEDGMENTS

Searchable Whereabouts took about four or five years to complete, mostly do to procrastination on my part. It is actually my third book I've completed, but my first to be published. I especially wish to acknowledge the following:

To my son, Zaybien—dear to my heart and keeps me on my toes every single day—you are my world, son, and I know you are going to grow into a responsible and empowered young man.

To my husband, Ron, I love you. Thanks for dealing with my multiple personalities and time away as I slaved away on the computer for days and nights. You are a wonderful husband and I appreciate you every day. Sometimes when I felt as though no one believed in me, you reassured me, and that kept me strong.

To Jessica Tilles, my publisher and friend. Thank you so much for taking me under your wings. You believed in me and I thank you for that. Your hard work is appreciated in so many ways. I am so grateful to you.

To my ASA family (www.freewebs.com/asanetwork.com). I am so happy I met you all. You all are an inspiration and I wish you much success with your careers.

To my mom and dad, I love you both. I can't wait 'till the day I can take care of you both and pay you back for all the care you've given me. Well, I guess I could never pay you two back, but I can try.

To all my friends who supported and believed in me. Friendship is so important, and I am blessed to have friends. Thank you.

Searchable Whereabouts

A Novel

Chapter 1

Sluggishly, I pulled myself up and sat on the side of the bed, remaining motionless for a minute, almost certain it was not going to be a good day. It was my son's birthday. Matthew died three years ago. Every year, around this time, I would feel depressed. I hated when I did this to myself. Sometimes, I really believed my depression was self-imposed. Thirty-three years old, no life, no Matthew and, dare I mention, no sex with a man in damn near two years. Not even a real relationship since my ex. I'm not a bad looking woman. At least, that's what I'd assured myself.

Slipping my chilled feet into my furry slippers, I moved toward the window and drew open the blinds. Peering out the window, the sky wasn't looking very promising for the sun to shine much today. A cloud, in the shape of a long-stemmed rose, emerged with a faint image of Uncle Leon's face beside it. If I see another image in the sky, I don't know what I'd do.

Sighing heavily, I stretched my fingers across my hips and exhaled. "At least today, it's a decent one, considering the occasion," I mumbled to myself.

Contemplating taking off from work, keeping as preoccupied as possible, was something I needed to do. Grabbing my pack of cigarettes off the dresser, I ambled into the bathroom. Standing in the mirror, I lit the cigarette that dangled from my lips, drew in deep and blew the smoke at the mirror, forming a hovering cloud. My hair looked wild, coming very close to looking like a frizzy afro, sticking out every which way, and my ends needed to be trimmed.

Normally, my hazel eyes would be my best feature, big and bright, but instead they were red, droopy and tired. Inhaling another puff of smoke, I grabbed my plump cheeks, and blew it out right away. I squeezed my cheeks, took my other fingers and pulled the skin under my eyes down. Damn, that was a pathetic sight. What I was trying to accomplish, I had no idea. I pulled off my white and red heart pajamas and jumped into the shower.

Dressing in blue scrubs and brushing my hair back into a ponytail, I headed downstairs. Opening the front door, I stepped onto the porch and picked up the newspaper, before waving to Mrs. Jenkins across the street, pulling weeds out of her yard. I always thought she was a little weird, an older Irish woman, maybe in her late sixties. In the summer, she wore boots and pretended to shovel snow in her yard. During the winter months, she would turn on the sprinkler and water the front yard, at times watering snow. For ten years I've lived in this house, I don't believe I'd ever seen any family visit her. During the holidays, I'd made it a point to bake a tray of cookies, or some kind of desert, and take it to her, with a card. She would never say thank you, but I knew she appreciated it. If it got too late in the day, on a holiday, she would knock on my door and ask if I was coming over.

Opening the paper, I turned directly to my favorite section: Your Daily Horoscope, which I usually read everyday. There was a time when I was hooked on psychic readings. It fascinated me so, but Mama always said I should leave that stuff alone or else something bad could happen. Mama had tendencies of putting fear in me, so I hadn't been up on the psychic thing as I used to be.

Moving my eyes through the paper, I scrolled down to the sign of Aries. It said: *When searching for what you want, the answer lies in front of you, directly in front of you, and comes to light when you least expect it.* I pondered for several minutes, trying to tie the horoscope into my life, but I didn't really know.

Tucking the paper under my arm, I stepped inside the house and into the kitchen, to fix a bowl of cereal. Dropping the paper on the kitchen counter, I turned on the television and looked over at the green digital clock on the stove: 8:10 a.m. Good, I still had time. I was in no rush to get to the nursing home, where I worked, anyway. In general, I liked my job, but some of those old people just plain got on my nerves.

I knew I shouldn't have come to work. Not really feeling being here, and after working for six hours, I left the nursing home early. I wasn't feeling well anyway, and I couldn't work a complete day. Besides, time was ticking away and what I dreaded was getting close. I felt anxious, nervous and sad all at once. Thinking of Uncle Leon, I realized I never called him back yesterday. I thought about calling him, but I didn't want him to hear the sadness in my voice. That would be all I'd need.

At times, it was so hard hiding my emotions, even when I tried to. Uncle Leon was more of a father to me, than my own father had been. When I was little, he always told me that I was his daughter in a prior life. He'd given me a necklace, with a black marble at the end of the chain. As a child, I wore it a lot, but now I kept it in my jewelry box for sentimental reasons.

It was the end of July and, in a couple of months, summer would be over. I met up with Janetta for a late lunch. I knew I could count on her to make me feel better. But, honestly, I think I wanted to feel miserable. I didn't want to be happy today—that self-imposed depression—I guess.

Janetta was a cool friend. She and I go way back. She was my best friend and really one of my only friends to be exact. I lost a lot of friends over the last few years. This was mostly because my dealings with my ex, who was shot, the death of Matthew in a car accident, and my drug and alcohol addiction.

Janetta didn't take a lot of mess from anyone and she told you like it was. She could be as ghetto as she wanted to be or an angel with a little bit of an attitude. She was overweight, but beautiful. That girl could dress her ass off, with her hair hooked up in one of her many unique styles. Janetta had two obsessions in life: food and men.

I pulled into the garage and entered the house through the side entrance. I tossed my purse on the kitchen table and went upstairs to change out of my scrubs. After slipping into a pair of jeans, and a T-shirt, I grabbed my purse and cigarettes, sat on the front porch and waited for Janetta. Lighting a cigarette, I tried to think good thoughts like flowers, trees, the water sprinkler in the back yard, kids playing, and summer. Summer made my spirits feel good. With closed eyes, I rocked back and forth in the rocking chair, with tightly clenched fists. Then the horn blew. In an instant, I snapped back to reality. I stood, with a smile on my face, when I saw Janetta pulling up in her Land Rover. Seeing Janetta, bouncing her head back and forth to an old school jam, briefly took me back down memory lane.

It was 1986, our senior year in high school and it was graduation time at Northwest High School. With plaid green pants and a silver blouse,

11

you couldn't tell me anything, with my hair mushroom-shaped with the shag in the back. My eyes wide as can be with my thin lips painted with a light purple lipstick. Our school colors were green and silver, so I did my best to coordinate. Janetta wore a black skirt with a silver blouse as well.

We both planned to wear a skirt, but I chickened out at the last minute. I told her my legs were too big.

"Well, mine are, too," she debated, "you think I care?"

I wasn't sure if I was going to graduate or not, because I missed a lot of days hanging out with the wrong crowd. I always wanted to fit in and never quite thought I did. I always managed to date the creepy guys who wanted nothing but sex. Janetta was smart and never cared about what anybody thought of her. That was what I always admired the most about her. We have been friends since the ninth grade and, I must admit, she was always there for me.

Although Janetta was a big girl, that never stopped her from enjoying life. She would call herself F.A.T, *Fabulous and Thick*. That was her way of putting a positive spin on something others may look at as negative. In high school, we were the same size, but different height. I was five-seven and dark-skinned, while she was light-skinned and five-foot-three. That was until I lost weight from all the stress, and drug and alcohol abuse. It's strange though; looking back, it seemed like I was happier at a size twenty, than I was at my present size eight.

Calling out to me, Janetta snapped me back to reality. "Hey girl, I know what day it is, but we are going to get through this day, okay? I'm taking you to your favorite restaurant."

I leaned back, looked at her and smiled, with a raised brow. "What, the Fondue Palace?"

Janetta nodded and licked her lips.

I slid into the passenger seat. "That place is expensive; you don't have to do that, Janetta."

"Don't tell me what I don't have to do. I know I don't have to do anything but be proud, black and die. But, today is a special day, maybe a hard one to deal with, but a special day. Let me see a smile on your face, right now," she demanded. Then she looked at me and placed her finger under my chin, and turned my face toward her.

I stuck my tongue out at her.

"Okay, that's what I'm talking about," she chuckled. "That's much better."

"How's Steven?" Janetta dated a lot, and if I was sure of anything, it was to hear all of her men stories.

"Girl, Steven is history. He's a cheapskate. Do you know he wanted me to give him gas money at the end of our date? And, on top of that, I couldn't even order my own meal. He ordered for me. And, ordered like the cheapest thing on the menu. What am I supposed to do with a big piece of broccoli and chicken staring back at me? I ain't on no damn diet."

I laughed. I thought that was too funny.

There was a long silence.

"So," Janetta said, breaking the silence, "when are you going to the gravesite today?"

I knew I was going, but I didn't want to think about it. Not yet, anyway, even though I had to. "Probably around six. Mama and Sierra are going with me."

"Well, I have a teddy bear I bought for Matthew, if you can take it with you." Janetta reached in the back seat and pulled out a small, baby blue bear. It was so cute. I tried to hold back the tears, and surprisingly, I was successful.

"Thank you, Janetta, it's beautiful." I was happy Mama and my youngest sister, Sierra, was going with me. Last year, they were out of town for Sierra's seventeenth birthday, so I went alone. That was a big emotional mistake.

After lunch with Janetta, I felt better. However, as soon as I inserted the key into my front door, I suddenly felt bad again—out of control as each second passed—so I paced the living room and chain-smoked one cigarette after another. I thought about calling Sarah, an old friend. I guess not a friend; you really wouldn't call someone a friend if all you did was snort up white crap together.

Before I changed my mind, I grabbed the phone and dialed. Someone answered, but my words lodged in my throat. I hung up and visualized my therapist asking me if I really wanted to make that call. It's been a little over a year since I have been totally clean. I can't, I thought to myself, and smoked another cigarette instead. After a few minutes, I put it out, as I eyed the bottle of gin on the top cabinet in the kitchen. Finally, and as much as I tried to restrain myself, I opened it. I took a long swallow, and then another, and then, one last swallow.

Standing in the middle of the kitchen floor, I wiped my mouth with the back of my hand and imagined Matthew in the living room, playing with his Legos. I ran to him, he looked up at me. He was so happy, and as I reached out to him, his image disappeared. Then instantly, I saw another image of Uncle Leon and it scared me. I looked down at the bottle of gin and hurled it across the room. Chips of glass scattered everywhere. I dropped to my knees, wrapped my arms around myself and cried profusely.

Unable to stop the downpour of tears, one would've thought I had just buried my son, but it was three long, pain-staking years ago. Matthew would be eight if he were alive. So many thoughts ran through my head. I missed him so much. On my hands and knees, I crawled up the stairs to the top. Standing, I reached out and wrapped my trembling hand around the doorknob. Inhaling deeply, and exhaling slowly, I opened the door to his room, which I rarely went into. Nothing had changed. The room remained the same way for the last three years. I didn't touch much of anything when I went in. I closed my eyes and breathed in deeply, wanting to smell him once again.

On his bed was a picture of him I placed there three years ago, that I looked at whenever I mustered the nerve to visit his room. That's what I thought of my infrequent pop-ins to his room, a visit. But this was the last picture I took of Matthew riding his new bike I bought him. Standing in the middle of his room, I embraced the photo and looked around.

So vividly, I remembered the day my precious son died. I suppose it's a day I will always remember, well into eternity. I was driving. Nevilla, Uncle Leon and Matthew were in the back seat. I'd bought a new television for Matthew's room, which was in the front passenger's seat. We were on our way home from McDonald's. It was raining so hard that day. We'd stopped at the gas station. I thought Matthew had on his seatbelt, but I learned later, that he hadn't. The car flipped several times as I swerved to avoid a semi-trailer that I thought was coming toward us. When the fire truck, ambulance and police arrived on the scene, Nevilla, Uncle Leon and I were still in the car, buckled in. I was unconscious. The day after the accident, I learned that

Matthew was thrown several feet into a field, where he died on impact. From that day forward, my life had been one complete mess after another, and the feeling of guilt grew from a molehill into a mountain. Had I strapped my baby in, he would still be alive.

In the middle of Matthew's room, I sat down on the floor and rocked myself to sleep to later awake by the ringing telephone. I knew it was Mama. She was probably crying too. I looked up at the Mickey Mouse clock on his wall. After three years, it's still running like the first day I bought it. It was almost time to go to the gravesite.

Closing Matthew's bedroom door behind me, I noticed the newspaper on the table in the hallway. I picked it up and read my horoscope, again, aloud: *When searching for what you want, the answer lies in front of you, directly in front of you, and comes to light when you least expect it.*

I still wasn't sure what that meant, so I tossed it on the bed in my room. My head was pounding, so I went into the bathroom, drank some water and took two aspirins.

Chapter 2

Besides working at the nursing home, a few days a week, I also worked part-time at Uncle Leon's leasing company. He owned a few rental properties. I helped him with the accounts payable, filing, processing applications and run errands—going to the bank—or whatever he needed me to do. Janetta also worked there full-time as the receptionist. Uncle Leon paid both of us very well.

Although Uncle Leon was fun to be around, he was a private man who didn't like a lot of people in his business. After spending a year in the military, he was dishonorably discharged. At least that's what Mama told me, but that's a sensitive subject, and I've never heard him speak on it. And, now that Sharon, his daughter, and me were grown, he was especially close to my niece Nevilla, Sharon's daughter. Nevilla loved that man, and Uncle Leon would do anything for her.

Lately, at the leasing office, I noticed Uncle Leon having a lot of meetings, mostly with Franklin, his business partner and a family friend. Not sure, what they were talking about, but Janetta said that there sure were a lot of people calling for Uncle Leon. I'd been filing like crazy and even helping Janetta out at the front desk.

Franklin and Leon had known each other for a long time. Franklin's business wasn't going well, and Uncle Leon thought it would be a good idea if Franklin became his business partner. At first, he hired Franklin as the office manager, but within a few short months, Franklin became his partner and co-owner.

The leasing office also employed five other employees and two temps: Emily and Jessica. Then there was Rob who worked as a Leasing consultant, but he mostly worked out of his home and was only in the office a couple of days a week. Then there was the housekeeper, Martha, and sometimes her two daughters, Gracey and Gina, who worked as the receptionist whenever Janetta needed a day off.

For a Wednesday, it wasn't that busy, or at least I wasn't feeling as rushed to get everything done. But, I had to admit, Janetta had done a lot around the office. Janetta made eighteen dollars per hour, not bad for a receptionist.

Once in awhile, Uncle Leon would let me organize his bills and accounts. As I was going through his files, I ran across a few loans he secured. With current outstanding loans, I couldn't understand why he needed new loans. Putting those to the side, I found a mortgage payment to the CEO of an investment company, my uncle sometimes talked about. The payment was for ten thousand dollars, which seemed weird considering he hadn't dealt with them in years; and it was paid to him in cash, which made it appear even stranger. I remembered him telling me he stopped doing business with that investment company because they'd moved out of state. What property was this payment for?

I called Janetta at the front desk. "Hey can you look up a name for me, and tell me what the property address is on this person?"

"Sure, who is it?" Janetta was chewing loudly on something. I loathed when people chewed like cows in my ear.

"Donald Hamilton." I looked at the date on the receipt: July 16, 2002. I tried to remember what took place on that day. I looked at the desk calendar. That was only last Tuesday. Actually, Uncle Leon was out of town, but it showed that he signed for it, and stamped it with our front stamp. I thought that to be strange.

"The address is 123 Kings Drive. So when are we going to get some lunch, I'm starving girl? And plus, after work I have to meet up with Craig for a quick booty call." She was still smacking on that damn gum.

"I'll be up in a minute, and who is Craig? Never mind I'll be up there." I think it was the same address, but I wasn't quite sure. I put everything back the way it was. I would have to finish looking at it when I return from lunch.

After lunch, Franklin was in the back office where the files were. The door was cracked. He was a big man, who breathed hard, as if he had a bad case of asthma. Sometimes I wanted to ask him if he needed a breathalyzer.

His back was turned towards me, but he quickly turned around as soon as I opened the door.

"Hi Rahkel, how's it going?" He gasped for air. I swear…

"I'm fine." What was he doing back here? I sat behind the desk and continued what I was working on before lunch, and I noticed the file for Donald Hamilton was gone.

"Did you see a file lying on the table?" I searched on and around the desk. "I was looking at it before I went to lunch." I lifted a pile of file folders.

"Oh yeah, I have some work that's not finished on the Donald Hamilton file, if that's the one you're talking about." Franklin lowered his reading glasses. "Why were you looking at it?"

I didn't really know what to say. Besides being nosey, there really was no reason for me to be looking at it. "I was filing it, making sure everything was in order," I said quickly. I wasn't sure if that made any sense, and wasn't sure if he believed me or not.

Franklin closed the file cabinet, pulled out a pocket watch and glanced at the time. "Oh, okay. Well, I'm about to go. If Leon stops by, tell him I need to talk to him." Franklin wobbled as he turned around and walked towards the door.

"Okay." I picked up his hat and gave it to him on his way out. What was so important about that file? I finished up some other paperwork before visiting with Janetta at the front desk.

Chapter 3

It was Saturday and I was at Mama's house, with Janetta and Sierra, preparing for her birthday. Up all night, we cooked everything but the kitchen sink: chicken, spaghetti, ham, greens, mac and cheese, candied yams, potato salad and, not to mention, the appetizers I sent Sierra to get from the store. One would've thought it was Thanksgiving, but without the turkey.

My cousin, Sharon, and my niece, Nevilla, took Mama to get her hair and nails done. She was going to be so surprised. It's such a coincidence that Matthew and Mama's birthday were in the same month. When Matthew was alive, he and Mama did their traditional thing: go to the park, to a movie and out to Show Biz Pizza. I know Mama missed that. The whole family was here, well almost. My sister, Kareena, who was eight years younger than I am, and her husband and daughter came out from North Carolina. Tony flew in from California. My brother, Tony was working on his Master's degree in Education, and I am so proud of him. At thirty, he's really got his life together. I think Daddy wished that for me, but things didn't turn out that way. I believed this was a big reason why Uncle Leon and I were so close. He never judged me and always wished me the best.

Looking back, when I met Matthew's father, life was not too good for me. He used to beat the crap out of me and Matthew witnessed it on more than a few occasions. I'm embarrassed to say, but he really made me feel like I couldn't get anyone else besides him. It was definitely a mental thing, and my mind was in his control.

However, Matthew's dad, Carlos, was shot one night, at a dance club, by some gang member because he owed him money. This was only shortly after Matthew died. I hate to say it, but I felt free after Carlos' death, but at the same time, I was depressed. Carlos' sister called me one morning. It was so strange, because when she called, I sensed something was terribly wrong. That morning, when I woke up and Carlos hadn't come home yet, I looked out my window and saw a picture of a gun in the sky and then Uncle Leon's faced appeared in the sky next to it. It frightened me to say the least. He didn't like Carlos, but none of my family did. But who's to blame them. I can't believe I was so naïve and stupid. However, Carlos was always into drugs, gangs and anything that involved trouble. So it wasn't the biggest surprise for me. I was glad he didn't really bring it into the house.

I sent Sierra to the store to pick up the cake—chocolate cheesecake— Mama's favorite. Unfortunately, my brother, Jacob, will not be able to join in the festivities. He said he'd call though. He was sentenced to five years for drug possession charges. He should only have a year left on good behavior, I'm praying. Mama's house was getting packed. I was happy. A few of Mama's friends from her church were here as well, including her Bingo partners.

"So how are you doing, Sister Jackson?" I asked one of Mama's good friends who was sitting on the couch next to Nevilla, with a glass of wine in one hand and a cup of tea in the other.

"Oh child, well this arthritis has been kicking my butt, but other than that, I'm good child, with God's will, of course. How's Jacob doing?" She sat her cup of tea down and sipped her wine.

"Jacob's in prison and he probably won't be getting out anytime soon," Kareena blurted out. That girl had the biggest mouth and was very loud and insensitive. A real bitch, and believe me when I say that. We'd always said she came from a different family. Jacob and Kareena were twins, and they never got along growing up. But then again, Kareena always thought she was better than anybody and everybody else, so she really didn't get along with anyone. She was very high maintenance. Her six-year-old daughter, Shawntel, was a mini-Kareena all the way.

If it wasn't for her rich husband, Fred, she wouldn't have much of anything. A CEO of his own contracting company, Fred was tall, slim and fair-skinned with that good hair. He's also very intelligent; a nice man—very low key and humble—but I don't know how he puts up with my sister's attitude.

I looked over at Kareena and rolled my eyes. "Kareena, Sister Jackson knows Jacob is in prison," I snapped with an intended attitude. "But anyways." I returned my attention to Sister Jackson. "He should be out in about a year. He's actually been reading the Bible while he's been in jail." It wasn't true, as far as I knew, but it sounded good.

"Well that's good, dear. Next time you talk to him, give him my blessings." She handed her wine glass to one my cousins for a refill.

Graciously I smiled, and headed toward Janetta, but not before rolling my eyes at Kareena. I swear, sometimes, she can really work my last good nerve. Janetta's plate was full of food. I wasn't surprised. She introduced me to some guy named Melvin. He was nice looking, tall and slim. After the introduction, I pulled her to the side, after she handed Melvin her plate.

"So what happened to Craig?"

"Didn't I tell you he was a booty call?" She spoke through clenched teeth, and then she looked back at Melvin and smiled. He returned her smile, still holding on to her plate. Janetta was too much. I looked the other way and laughed.

I saw Uncle Leon on the couch, drinking his favorite drink: beer. Making my way over to him, I sat beside him.

"How's my favorite niece?" Uncle Leon was looking spiffy, with a fresh haircut and dye job. It was neat and clean. He dyed his hair often, so it was all black and very low cut. He was probably the only fifty-eight-year-old black man who paid regular visits to the hair shop, to get his hair washed, conditioned, cut and dyed. And, his feet and nails aren't neglected.

"Uncle I'm good." I was tired and needed to rest my feet. I laid my head on his shoulder.

"My sister is going to be so happy. Baby, you went all out for her this year. But she deserves it." He kicked a balloon to some boys on the side. He put his beer and shot of rum on the end table, and reached in his vest for a cigar and lit it.

"Yea, this has been a bit of a rough month for us all. So I wanted to let her know how much we appreciated her. You only get one Mama."

"Yes you sure do, don't you, Sweetheart?"

"Uncle Leon, I wanted to ask you about a receipt I'd found yesterday, when doing your books." I figured this was the time to bring it up.

"Yea what's that?" Standing up, children running around in the kitchen diverted his attention. "You boys get from over there, away from the food. Watch out, and stop running." Uncle Leon sat back and blew out the smoke from his cigar.

"Well it was a ten thousand dollar receipt to Donald Hamilton. I thought he moved."

Uncle Leon placed his hand over his forehead, and then looked my way. "Girl, don't worry your mind about that. It's just business." Uncle Leon looked at his watch. "I need to make a call, let me know when your Mama gets here." He sat up, downed the last of his rum and went into the back room with his can of beer.

I released a sigh and pulled myself up from the couch. I saw Tony heading in my direction. He brought some girl with him from San Francisco, and I wanted to know all about her. I heard he was serious about this one. She was definitely his type: short, big breasted with long hair. She was really cute and nice. Unsurprisingly, when I looked up, I saw Kareena making her way toward us. Oh no, I hope Kareena doesn't hurt her feelings too much. I giggled because Tony already knew how Kareena was. He grabbed his date by the hand and took off in the opposite direction.

It was getting closer to the time; Sharon called and said they'd left from the beauty shop. Soon after, Sierra pulled into the driveway.

I hurriedly opened the front door. "Come on. Mama, Sharon and Nevilla should be here soon." I was glad I was having this party, because in addition to Mama's birthday, Sierra was going off to college soon and I knew that since she was the baby, Mama would miss her.

Tony, Kareena, Sierra and I stood in the middle of the living room, holding the cake, while everyone gathered behind us. As soon as Mama opened the door, we all yelled, "Happy Birthday!" and then the phone rung. The expression on Mama's face showed it all. She looked so happy and in total disbelief. I would do anything to keep that smile on her face. I rushed to answer the phone; it was Jacob. I handed Mama the phone.

I looked around for Uncle Leon. Tony must have known I was looking for him, because he pointed downstairs. Following Tony's direction, I found Uncle Leon in a back room talking to Franklin. The door was cracked, and I don't think they saw me, but I sure wanted to know what they were discussing.

Chapter 4

The next morning, I stopped by Sharon's house. Uncle Leon was there and Sharon was cooking breakfast. Sharon was the only daughter Uncle Leon had. Her mom, a white woman, was actually cheating on her wealthy husband with Uncle Leon.

"Hey cousin!" Sharon stood in the kitchen wearing a silk robe, with four pans on the stove: eggs, bacon, pancakes and grits. This I had to stay for, because Sharon *never* cooks. Her hair was down around her shoulders, which was a surprise since she always had it up in a ponytail or hair clip. It was getting long, a little past the middle of her back. She wore daffy duck slippers, as she paced from the refrigerator to the stove; it looked like the foot of her shoe was talking with each step she took. Nevilla was sitting in Uncle Leon's lap, wearing a pink Barbie doll gown. Her hair was so pretty, black and full of curls.

"I'm good; I just thought I'd stop by to see how you two were doing. Hi Uncle Leon, are you going by the office today?" I hoped he would say no.

"No, I have some business to take care of. Janetta said she'd work today, so you don't have to go in."

I looked down at Uncle Leon's military vest. I watched as he and Nevilla played chess.

For the last few weeks or couple of months, he seemed more stressed than usual. I wanted to ask him about it. Something didn't sit right; between all the meetings and him hardly ever being at his own company, I didn't know what was going on. Janetta and Mama always said I worried too much. But I guess when you don't really have a life, worrying becomes a hobby.

"Well I guess I'll stay since Sharon's cooking. How many opportunities do we all have for this?" I looked in the kitchen hoping she heard me. She did and gave me the middle finger.

"Well, Tony and Kareena said they were coming over. So I want to make them feel at home. Know what I mean?" she said without looking up from what she was doing.

"Please, it don't matter what you do. Nobody can impress Kareena's uppity ass." We both laughed.

Uncle Leon's cell phone rang. He looked at the caller ID. "Excuse me, baby girl, I gotta take this call." Uncle Leon sat Nevilla on the side of him and went into the bedroom. I went out front on Sharon's balcony and smoked a cigarette. I looked out into the city. I thought about Matthew, wondering what he'd be doing right now. I pushed that thought out of my mind, the last thing I wanted do was cry. I looked at my hands. I think I'll get me a manicure. After a little while, I went back inside.

I went into the kitchen with Sharon. "So what's going on with Uncle Leon?" She was pulling a plate from the cabinet.

"What do you mean? He's fine." Sharon gave me a look of confusion and continued what she was doing.

"What do you mean, he's fine?" I couldn't believe she's acting like she hadn't noticed how he'd been behaving. Of all people, Sharon should know when her father was acting strange. "I don't think so, he's been under a lot of stress, and I do mean a lot. I think it has something to do with his office. I don't know."

"No, he can handle it." Sharon gently pushed me to the side, and looked into the living room. "Nevilla come in here and help me set the table please."

"Okay Mommy." Nevilla looked a little tired. She was so precious to me. I loved that little girl. Matthew and she were best friends. Being the same age, they were so cute together.

Later, while everyone was up front stuffing their bellies with food, I went back to the bathroom. I'd noticed Uncle Leon was, once again, in the back room. He was sitting on the bed. I tiptoed to the door and put my ear to it. I could overhear Uncle Leon talking to an attorney. I knew it was an attorney, because he said, "Well if you represented me as your client, I wouldn't be in this mess. It's going to unfold. I can't let this go any further. I'm starting to get worried."

I pulled away from the door and played over in my head what Uncle Leon had said, and then I plastered my ear against the door again.

Nevilla crept up behind me. "Auntie, what are you doing? Granddaddy is on an important phone call." She scared the living daylights out of me. I hope he didn't hear us.

"Don't you pay no mind, Nevilla," I whispered. I put my arms around her shoulders as we walked back towards the living room. "I was trying to find your Granddaddy, that's all. Let's go back into the living room, so you can tell me all about your new school."

Soon after his call, Uncle Leon left, and so did I. I wanted to go to the office. I didn't care if I was being nosey. I just wanted to find out what was going on.

When I arrived at the office, I saw Rob pulling off in his car. I waved at him. Rob was a cool funny white guy. He was newly married and performed stand up comedy at a local spot downtown.

As soon as I walked inside the office, Janetta grabbed me by the arm and took me to the side.

"Girl what's going on with your Uncle?" She looked concerned.

"What do you mean?"

"There were two men here looking for him. One man, his name was Donald Hamilton, the same guy you had me look up an address for you. I remember that. Well anyway, he looked very angry, and said that Mr. Leon Wilson had a week to respond to him or else. Now I don't know what that means, but on the streets, that type of talk means trouble."

I immediately went back to Uncle Leon's office. "Damn, the door is locked." I tried again. I went back to the front where Janetta was. "Do you have a key to Uncle Leon's office?"

"Hold on, child, I'm trying to work here and you asking me unrelated questions." Janetta turned back to the customer who was waiting impatiently for his rent receipt. "Thank you, Sir, and here's your receipt. Next time you are going to be late with your rent, there may be attorney charges involved. I just thought you should know. And have a good day." Janetta turned around and blurted out, *"That asshole."* I sure hoped he didn't hear her. I turned around and the man looked back with disgust and pissed written all over his face.

I looked passed the man and saw Uncle Leon pull up in his black Lexus.

"Damn, I'm not supposed to be here. Let me hide under your desk." I quickly moved Janetta out the way and sat with my legs folded beneath me, under her desk.

"What, you're not supposed to be here? Girl you gonna get me in trouble messin' around with you. Don't move." Janetta sat down and scooted in her chair. She rolled over my finger, and I let out a slight moan. I wanted to scream. I moved her chair back and pulled my finger from beneath the wheel, and shook it like crazy, hoping the pain would cease instantly. I put the straps of my purse in my mouth, keeping me from letting out a horrified scream. I could hear the small bells attached to the front door jingle when the front door opened.

"Hello Janetta. How's everything?" Uncle Leon's voice sounded little distant. I knew he was going to the back of the office.

Janetta pushed her chair away and stood up. "Leon you got a message. Two men came by today. One was Donald Hamilton." Janetta moved around to the other side of the desk, and gave him the note she'd taken. "He sounded sort of upset."

"Damn, okay, well, I'm gonna step out again. If he comes back, just tell him I'm out of town for a week, and I'll call him sometime next week. I'll be in my office for a few minutes, I have some paperwork to catch up on, but if anybody comes by just tell them I'm not here and take a message."

"Okay, whatever you say Leon." Janetta returned to her chair and sat down.

I pulled on her skirt. "What the hell is going on?" I whispered.

She shrugged her shoulders.

I must have sat under that desk for almost twenty minutes. I would have left, but I didn't want to leave yet. Finally, Uncle Leon came out of his office.

"Janetta, if you don't hear from me by next Tuesday, give this guy a call by the end of the day and have him pick up this box. Just call him at this number." Uncle Leon handed Janetta a box. I peeked out a little, and then quickly pulled back when I saw Uncle Leon's head. I was so curious to know what was in that box. "Look, Janetta, everything is fine, just some business mix up, but do me a favor and don't mention any of this to Rahkel. You know how she can get."

What did he mean by that? Just how can I get?

"Okay, Leon, so should I tell anyone that's looking for you that you're out of town on business as well?" Janetta was filing her nails. How could she be filing her nails at a time like this?

"Yeah that's perfect, just tell everyone that, and if you need help with anything, Rahkel knows a lot about running the office, and you can always call Franklin. If you call that number just leave a message, it's a voice mail, so no one will answer." I could hear him open up the front door. "Okay Janetta, see you when I get back. Oh yeah, I almost forget, when you leave the message, just say something like, this is Mr. Wilson's assistant, the box is ready for you to pick up. And one more thing, if no one comes and gets the box by the end of the business day, mail the box to this address." He pulled out his note pad and jotted down an address.

"Okay Leon, see you. Be safe," Janetta said.

As soon as I heard the bells jingle from the door closing, I pushed Janetta's chair back and stood up. I took the box from her. It was locked, but I took a letter opener from her desk and opened it within minutes. Inside was a bundle of receipts, with amounts and dates, no other information. It was strange. As I shuffled deeper into the box, I found a business card with no address, only a phone number and the initials T.D., and a CD with no label. There was a key inside as well. What was all of this?

Janetta pulled out each receipt, examining it. She looked as puzzled as I did.

"Well I'm going to figure all this out, and I'm going to figure out where Uncle Leon is going." I looked at Janetta's calendar to see what day next Tuesday fell on, which was a week away.

"Janetta, I'm taking this stuff. If Uncle Leon contacts you between now and then, call me immediately."

"You better not get me in any trouble. The last thing I need is to get fired over yo' crazy ass." Janetta sat down, opened her desk drawer and pulled out a Snickers and a can of pop.

"I'm not, don't worry. But I have to find out what's going on with my Uncle."

Chapter 5

I got up early and dropped Tony off at the airport. He begged me to come to California next summer to visit.

"I'm not sure, Tony, I'll try."

"Dad's been asking about you."

"Well why hasn't he called me, if he's been asking about me?"

Tony drew silent, not knowing what to say.

I really don't have a problem with my daddy being gay; it was just how he did Mama; and all those years of keeping a secret. Maybe he thinks I don't accept him, but I think it's the other way around.

Kareena and Fred, of course, rented a car so they left a few hours after Tony. I hugged my sister goodbye and told Shawntel to be a good little girl.

Shawntel looked up at me, and with a cute little proper voice, she said, "I am a good little girl, Aunt Rahkel. I listen to everything my mother tells me." She even had the hand motion with her finger.

"That's my baby," Kareena said. They both gave each other quick pecks on each other's opposite cheeks.

"Oh boy," I said to myself. Personally, if she does listen to everything Kareena tells her, then I'm going to be very worried that there will be two Kareena's in the world. Lord, help us all.

Later that afternoon, I met up with Sharon and Nevilla at the park. Getting out my car, I smelled something in the air. I dropped my cigarette butt I'd been smoking on, and smashed it into the ground. I know that smell oh so well. As I looked closer, I saw Sharon and Terry sitting at the concrete bench and table smoking on a joint, most likely laced with Ecstasy or something.

Terry was sitting on top of the table and Sharon was sitting on the bench, between his legs. They were hugging and kissing each other, while getting so high it was ridiculous, considering Nevilla wasn't that far from them. I'm not proud to admit it, but Sharon and I used to do drugs all the time together. However, at the time, I think I was more hooked then she was.

I didn't like Terry too much. Sharon met him at a bar years ago, and he's been in and out of her life ever since. She introduced him to my brother, Jacob, and they always hung out. I blamed Terry for sending Jacob to prison. I found out, through the grapevine, that he snitched on my brother. After spending six months in jail, Terry was paroled, while Jacob had been in there for almost two years. It pisses me off that Terry was out enjoying his freedom, when he should be sharing a cell with Jacob.

Jacob was angry about it too, of course, especially since they had become such good friends. But, even before all this happened, I warned Jacob about Terry. And, to have Sharon still messing around with him after knowing he got her own family member locked up…well that just made me sick…

Terry was nothing but a thug. Everything about him was thuggish—not that I am totally against thugs—his lifestyle and his drug problem, was what I'm against.

"Hey what's up girl? How's Rahkel doing these days?" His slanted eyes were blazing red. He threw up a gang sign at me.

He had the nerve…. I looked at Sharon who was high as a kite, as well, and giggling out of control. I threw my hands up in frustration and dismissed them both as I walked to the playground to Nevilla.

Nevilla looked down as she sat in the swing. Her hair was in pigtails, wearing white sandals. I sat in the swing beside her.

"What's the matter, my little princess?" She loved it when I called her that.

She looked up at me and smiled, then frowned again. "Well Mommy said she'd take me to get ice cream, but that idiot, Terry," she pointed over to him, "is here and now she won't."

"Yeah, he is an idiot, isn't he?" I thought about what I said, but it was too late to take it back. "Well, how about Auntie Rahkel taking you to get some? How about that?"

Nevilla perked up. "Okay, lets go."

"Okay in a minute. I want to ask you something first. Have you or your mom heard from Uncle Leon?"

"Um, no. Well, I think he might have called, or at least his number came up on the caller ID, but he didn't leave a message." She got off the swing and pulled a dandelion from the ground. "Some man called our house looking for Granddaddy."

"A man?" I paused for a moment and turned toward Nevilla. "When was this?"

"I answered the phone yesterday. He said he was a good friend of Granddaddy, and if he came by to give him a message."

I looked over at Sharon and Terry. They were still sitting on the bench, getting high. I saw a police car drive by and Terry placed the joint behind his back. After the cruiser passed, he hit the joint long and hard, blowing round holes of smoke, before passing it to Sharon. I shook my head in disgust.

"What was the message, Nevilla?" I was concerned.

"Um, let me think." She looked up toward the sky. I could tell she was thinking hard. "Oh, I remember. He said, 'Tell Leon he has forty-eight hours to clean up the trash.' That's exactly what he said. Let's go, Auntie, I'm ready for ice cream." Nevilla took off running toward Sharon and Terry. I stood there for a moment. What she said kept running through my head.

As I walked closer toward them, I heard Nevilla asking Sharon if I could take her to get ice cream. I glanced up at the sky, only for a moment, and saw an image of a teddy bear I used to own as a little girl. Startled, I hurried toward Nevilla.

Sharon stood up and looked down at Nevilla, and then back at me. "How about we ask Auntie Rahkel if you could spend the night as well? Doesn't that sound like a good idea?" Sharon grinned.

"Oh yeah! How about it, Auntie?" Nevilla jumped up and down.

How could I resist. "Sure, what time are you picking her up tomorrow?"

"I'll be there by noon, maybe." She and Terry walked off. He still had a small piece of joint in his left hand. Shamefully, I wanted to hit that joint so bad.

Sharon stopped and ran back to Nevilla and gave her a kiss on her cheek. "See you tomorrow, sweetie. Be good for Auntie Rahkel."

"Okay." Nevilla took me by the hand and we headed to the car. After getting ice cream, we went to the movies. By the time we got home, I practically had to carry Nevilla to the bed. I woke her when we reached the steps. She was too heavy for me to carry up the stairs. I think if I'd taken another step, I would have broken my back. I led her to the spare bedroom next to Matthew's, took off her shoes and jacket, and tucked her in.

Inside my room, I rummaged through Uncle Leon's box. I reached inside the drawer of the nightstand, pulled out the calculator and added up all the receipts that were in the box. They totaled over $30 million. I was still puzzled. There wasn't any clue if they were paid to Uncle Leon or someone else. Why were there only dates and amounts? However, I did notice that the dates on the receipts ranged from a period over the last three years.

I picked up the CD in the box and examined it. I wondered what was on it. Finally, I went over to my laptop on the desk and inserted it into the CD drive. The first thing it said was that the CD was protected and I needed a password to access it.

"Damn!" I said out loud. I pushed my laptop, out of frustration, and reclined in the chair and released a long sigh. This really had me even more anxious. What the hell was on this CD? Well, if anyone had a password, it must have been both Leon, and whomever this person was that he wanted Janetta to leave the message for. I examined the phone number. Then I looked at the address on the other piece of paper Uncle Leon had given Janetta. It was a post office box located in, Naperville, Illinois. What or who was in Illinois? I looked at the name on the business card: D.L. I spoke the initials out loud. What could that stand for? I dialed the phone number and, indeed, it was a voice mailbox. All it said was, *Leave your message or press two to leave a phone number.* I gave up. I put everything back in the box and placed it on the dresser. I took off my clothes, slipped into my nightgown, wrapped a scarf around my head and climbed into bed.

Chapter 6

The next morning, I woke up to Nevilla standing only a few inches away from me, staring me in the face. That scared the shit out of me. Her arms hung by her side, with a blank expression plastered on face. There was something about her eyes. I immediately sat up. She didn't budge, didn't even blink.

I shook her. "Nevilla, wake out of it."

She blinked a few times before coming around. "Sorry Auntie." She gave me a hug and headed downstairs. "Can I have some cereal," her voiced echoed as she was halfway down the stairs.

That weird child. I stretched my arms high above my head, climbed out of bed, went downstairs and fixed her a bowl of cereal. I turned on the Cartoon Network for her, and went back up stairs to take a shower.

After my shower, I joined Nevilla and sat in front of the television. Before I knew it, it was noon, and of course, Sharon hadn't called or come by.

Out of the blue, Nevilla turned toward me. "Did you know that Granddaddy is a genius?" she asked, while eating her bowl of cereal.

"A genius, huh? Why do you say that?" I flipped the channel on the television, and then looked down at the time on my cell phone.

"He can make people disappear." Nevilla giggled.

"Disappear?" I looked at her with a raised brow.

"Yeah, we were playing a game with my toys and he made them disappear."

"Oh really? Well what if I start to make you disappear?" I tickled her. She laughed, kicking her legs. "Come on let's get you in the shower, so we can go, you silly." I was starting to collect a lot of Nevilla's clothes in my closet, as I was looking for Nevilla an outfit.

I decided to go by Mama's house. On the way, we stopped by McDonald's and then I stopped and got a newspaper to read my horoscope. I looked in the back seat to see if Nevilla had all her food. I smiled at her and turned back around. I thought about Uncle Leon and the contents in that box.

"Auntie, I have a question." I was about to turn onto Mama's street. "Is my Granddaddy going to die?"

I swerved and pressed hard on the brakes, stopping in the middle of the street. I whipped around and looked at Nevilla who was about to put a French fry in her mouth. "Nevilla, why would you ask something like that?" I eagerly anticipated her response.

"I don't know. Sometimes people die and plus, in a dream, there was this man." Her eyes looked so innocent, before that crazed look from this morning, as she stood over my bed, reappeared. She stared at me and there was a long silence.

I snapped my finger at her. "Earth to Nevilla." She blinked her eyes. "What man from last night are you talking about?"

"The man in my dreams, Auntie. I had a bad dream last night. I dreamt some man came into my room and took me by the hand and led me into the woods. He just kept saying that my Granddaddy was hurt." Nevilla looked down at her food.

"That's alright, honey. Sometimes we all have bad dreams. Don't worry about it. Finish your food, okay?" I took my foot off the brake and drove off. I was a little concerned about Nevilla. This was way too bizarre.

When I pulled up to Mama's house, a police car was parked out front, with its lights flashing. I pulled up behind the cruiser, and saw Sharon's car across the street. At that moment, I had the worst feeling. I felt my muscles tighten up, as I walked around the car to the sidewalk. I waved to Nevilla to get out the car, and I took her by the hand. We walked up to the front door and I used my key to open it.

Mama was standing at the table, in the kitchen, crying profusely. Sharon was in a corner with her face in her hands. I stood still, holding

Nevilla's hand. I looked at the two officers, one standing by Sharon and the other standing in the kitchen next to Mama.

"That's my daughter," Mama said, in short breaths as she cried.

Nevilla released my hand and ran over to Sharon, asking her what was wrong.

The police officer that was in the kitchen approached me. "I'm sorry, Ma'am. There's been a terrible accident. We found your uncle's car in a lake not far from Blue Spring Road. It's a couple of hours or so from here. We are trying to identify the body, because it was badly burned."

I don't remember what else, if anything, the police officer said, because after that, a deadly silence blanketed me. I leaned my head against the wall. I felt sick to my stomach, and light headed, an all too familiar feeling, when Matthew died. I ran out the door and dropped down onto the grass. I could hardly breathe; my heart ached. That's when I looked up at the sky and saw different colors and everything around me was spinning. For some reason, the different colors reminded me of the ice cream sprinkles Uncle Leon used to buy me when I was a little girl. I felt nauseous. I wanted to pinch myself, hoping this was all a bad nightmare and Uncle Leon would be walking up the street any minute. I saw Nevilla run outside. She came over to me and stared down at me. I tried reaching out to her, but pain shot through the left side of my body and that's when I collapsed and passed out.

When I woke up, I was in the hospital. They said I had a mild stroke. Mama was standing beside the nurse. She hugged me so tight. I was only thirty-three, how could I have had a stroke?

"Where are Sharon and Nevilla?"

"They're in the waiting room." Mama cried. "I can't believe Leon is gone. Who would do this to him? He was a good man."

"I don't know, Mama, but I'm sure the police will find out," I assured her, even though I didn't believe it, but I didn't know what else to say. It was so unreal. I didn't want to believe he was gone. I couldn't believe it. I sat up in the bed, and noticed an IV in my arm.

The nurse came on the other side of Mama and took it out. "How are you feeling, Ms. Williams?"

"I feel fine. When can I leave?" I wasn't at all comfortable in the hospital.

"Well, we just need you to sign some papers and you can be on your way in about an hour. I'll be right back." As the nurse was leaving, Sharon and Nevilla came into the room. Nevilla ran up to me.

"How are you doing, Auntie? I was scarred when I saw you lying on the grass." She put her hand on my arm.

"I feel fine now, my little princess. They're about to let me go in a few."

Several minutes later, the nurse returned, I signed the release papers and shortly after I was out of there. Mama drove Sharon's car. I looked at Sharon in the back seat, and she looked so pale. She hadn't said much at all. She didn't even ask how I was doing. She was looking out the window, with her thumb pressed up against her lips. I looked at Mama, and she had tears in her eyes. Nevilla had her head on Sharon's lap. The ride back to Mama's was complete silence.

When we got to the house, Mama went into the kitchen and sat at the table. Sharon went downstairs and Nevilla sat on the couch and turned on the television. to watch Cartoons I decided to go into the kitchen with Mama.

Sitting at the table, beside Mama, she took me by the hand. "They told me I need to come down to identify the body. They say his body was burned. I won't go down there to see any of that. I just won't. You will probably have to go, Rahkel." Mama rested her head on the table.

That didn't sit very well with me. I ran my fingers through Mama's thick black hair, and placed my hand on her shoulder to comfort her. I looked back out into the living room at Nevilla.

"Okay, well, if that's what I have to do. I'll also help out with the funeral arrangements." As I thought about Uncle Leon's body being burnt, I felt sick to my stomach, again. I quickly changed my thoughts, and looked out into the living room, above the fireplace, on the mantel where Mama kept all of her pictures. I looked at a picture with me, Sharon and Uncle Leon in the middle. We looked so happy, and I remember that day. It was when he took both of us to the amusement park when we were little girls. A deep sadness came over me. Then I thought about Nevilla's dream. My sadness turned into fear.

Chapter 7

I never went through with it. I couldn't identify Uncle Leon's body. If I would have seen that image of him, it would have stayed with me forever. Besides, why would the coroner do that to a family anyway? Was the world heartless or what? I wanted to remember Uncle Leon as the wonderful and caring man he was. I loved him so much. The doctor called and finally told us that Uncle Leon's dental records showed that the body they found in the car was indeed him. That was some of the hardest news. Although I had already known, but the confirmation made it harder to swallow.

I met with Detective Edgar Matters. He took me into a room with a mirrored glass, like you see in the movies. We were seated at a metal table, across from each other. He was a nice man actually, and I appreciated him telling me that he would do everything in his power to solve the case. I gave him the name of Donald Hamilton and told him about the phone call between him and Janetta. I also told him about the possibility of Donald Hamilton calling Sharon's house and having the phone call with Nevilla. I didn't know if it was right to assume that the caller was in fact Hamilton, but I wanted him to check it out anyway. Detective Matters reassured me he'd check into it. When he gave me his card, I made it perfectly clear to him that I wanted him to stay in contact with me every step of this investigation. What I didn't tell him, however, was that I'd be doing a little investigation of my own. He assured me, again, that he'd be on top of it. I failed to mention the box that Uncle Leon gave to Janetta, because I wanted to see if I could find out more information. I figured I'd give it to him eventually.

Detective Matters thanked me for my time, and indicated that he wanted to talk to Sharon, but that she wasn't returning his call. I was surprised and told him I'd talk to her. I shook his hand and left. When I got home, Janetta showed up at my door. She hugged me and came in. We talked for a while.

"So what are you going to do about the company?" Janetta asked. She sipped on Mint tea.

"I guess help run it. We still have Franklin you know." Actually, the company was the last thing on my mind.

"I can't believe someone would do this to him. If anything it was probably over money."

I thought about what she said and I did believe that to be true. After Janetta left, I smoked a cigarette and stretched out on the couch, in front of the television. I passed out after drinking a few shots of Tequila and wine.

Chapter 8

It was the day of the funeral and I was filled with confusing emotions. I was also sad, but I'd already made up my mind I wasn't going inside the church. I didn't' care how it looked to anyone else, I couldn't do it. I told Sharon and Mama; they were upset about it, but that still didn't change my mind. When I arrived at the church, I pulled up to the curb on the other side of the street.

I arrived late on purpose. I didn't want to see them carry him in. I rolled my windows down a little and looked around, so many cars. I glanced up at the sky and wondered if God made the sky look a certain way whenever there was a funeral in progress. I'd actually thought about this before. Ever since I was a little girl, there'd always seemed to be something strange about the clouds. At first, I thought it was because I was at, or near, a funeral. Now, I don't really think that's the reason. Up until now, I've never told anyone. I'd lived with the fact that I saw images in the sky.

I picked up the newspaper from the passenger's seat and read what my horoscope was for today. It read: *Chances are, today you will find out some disturbing news, but this is only the beginning, be prepared for a new learning experience.* I thought about that for a moment and laid the paper to the side.

I pulled a notepad from the glove compartment, and jotted down my thoughts. I don't know why, maybe to make the time go by faster or maybe to keep me from crying. I wrote: *I'm here at Uncle Leon's funeral, in my '98 Blue Caprice with tinted windows, across the street from the Rose Baptist Church.* I stopped. *What the hell am I doing?* I threw the pad and pen in the passenger's seat. I looked back up at the church.

My head was starting to hurt and my neck was stiff, so I reclined my seat a bit, and took a cigarette from the pack. Ever since Matthew was born, I'd promised myself I would quit smoking, but within a couple of days, I'd always start back up. I lit my cigarette, blew it out and I looked in my side view mirror. We all gotta go someday.

I looked around to see if any of the cars looked familiar to me. I know Mama and Uncle Leon had a lot of family, some I'd never met. Mama had mentioned it to me, that some of those family members would be here today. I saw a car with two men sitting in it down the street. *Maybe they were friends of Uncle Leon's*, I thought, *or maybe not*. I sat up in my seat, and peered into the side view mirror, to get a closer look. They were just sitting. I wondered if those men were ever in the office. I really couldn't tell. Maybe I had seen them at Uncle Leon's office in a meeting or something. I contemplated driving up to the car, to take a closer look, but I changed my mind. Uncle Leon knew a lot of people; that was for sure. I turned on the radio. The idea of someone killing Uncle Leon really scared me. Death period didn't sit well with me.

The clouds were very gray, and kept forming as two sets of eyes, whenever I would look up into the sky more than a few seconds. So, I avoided looking up as much as possible. A few drops of rain hit my windshield and within minutes, it was pouring. I put out my cigarette and turned up the volume on the radio. Even the trees looked somewhat tired, as the leaves hung over lazily, swaying back and forth.

I dozed off for a while, but when I woke up, I realized I'd been sitting in the car for almost an hour, still waiting for everyone to come out. I felt bad; here I was at my beloved uncle's funeral, sitting outside in the car sleeping. I cried, but quickly got a hold of myself. I immediately tried to think of something else. When I was in therapy sessions, the therapist taught me to think of something positive when I was feeling negative, claiming that would help me transform my emotions. Jan Glover was her name. I owed that woman a lot. She really helped me get through my drug addiction.

I changed thoughts, and began remembering my first image I'd saw. I was a young girl, about eleven years old. It was my Grandma Ethel's funeral, on my daddy's side, before Mama and Daddy divorced. I remember so well when my parents went through their divorce. She'd found out that Daddy was cheating on her with a man. I remember Mama was five months pregnant with Sierra when they divorced. Even to this day, Daddy was still with that man. I don't talk to him much. I might as well not be his daughter. It was more his choice than mine.

About Grandma's funeral and my image, I remember we were in a large boat out on the Mississippi River, spreading my grandma's ashes over the water. I was with Daddy, Tony, Kareena and Jacob. Daddy's brother, Alfred, and Uncle Leon were also there. On the other side of the boat were more family members.

The sun was setting, sort of fast, I might add, and, I swear a cloud passed over my head that resembled a tombstone, with Grandma's name printed on it, and Uncle Leon was digging her grave. A vision of Grandma appeared in a cloud, and I will never forget what she said: "Baby, take care of the family. They will, one day, look up to you. They will, one day, really need you." My eyes followed that cloud, and right when I was trying to get Mama's attention, so she could look at the cloud too, it disappeared. But, I have a feeling that even if she had looked at it, she wouldn't have seen it anything.

The second funeral was with Kareena. We were going to one of her friend's funeral; Tina I believe was her name. I loved that woman. I remember I was sitting in the funeral home with Kareena and a cloud passed outside the window, with an image of three old women, and they were each reading books. The third woman looked very similar to Uncle Leon. I could have literally reached out and touched them if the window was opened. I turned away, and when I looked out again, they were gone. Pretty much that's why I don't like going to funerals, but either way, I still see images in the sky.

Okay, time to focus on something else. I looked up at the front door of the church. I glanced down at the digital clock on the car radio, and then back at the door. Just when I was about to lay my head back, the first person walked out of the church. I'd seen him before, hanging out with Uncle Leon, every now and again. I think his name was Gerald. His hair was wavy, which he always kept in a ponytail. He had to be at least twenty years older than me. I reminder being attracted to him; he was tall and kept good care of himself. He actually didn't look that bad, considering his age. But, I didn't like the idea of dating anyone more than ten years my senior. This was when I was down and out. I probably would have slept with him at least once, if Uncle Leon hadn't ruined my chances by telling him I was too young for him.

Searchable Whereabouts

Every time he'd come to the office, I remembered hearing him from the back room asking Uncle Leon about me; if I had a man yet. Finally, Uncle Leon told him yes, although it wasn't true. I watched him, as he stood right outside the church, in the rain and smoked a cigarette. He managed to stand under a covering. He took a few puffs and flicked it on the sidewalk and left. Then Franklin came out. He had on a black suit with a red shirt underneath. Janetta walked out with him. Her hat was almost covering half her face. And it didn't make it even better with the sheer black scarf draping down over the rim, covering her face. They gave each other a quick hug and Franklin departed quickly through the rain around the back of the church. Janetta went back inside. Suddenly, I had a funny feeling that didn't sit right in my stomach about Franklin.

I watched the rest of the people come out a few minutes later. A lot of people either had an umbrella or a jacket of some sort over there heads as they rushed to their cars. Finally, I saw what I came for. I watched four men in black suites carry a beautiful cream and gold colored coffin. Following them was my Mama, Kareena, Sierra, and Tony. They all got into a black limousine that was behind the Hurst. Again, here we all were, and to think they'd just left a few weeks ago. Janetta exited the church, again, with a male friend of hers I hadn't seen before.

Tears formed in my eyes, when I saw them place Uncle Leon's coffin in the back of that Hurst. A deep sadness came over me, and this was the point of realization that I knew Uncle Leon would be gone forever. It finally hit me that I'd never see him again.

I turned on the engine, rolled down the window just a crack, and lit a cigarette. I reached for my black shades in the glove compartment. I remember Uncle Leon bought me those shades last year for my birthday. They had my initials engraved in gold on one side. I pulled my hair back in a hair clip. I hated how it got so frizzy whenever there was a lot of humidity in the air.

Just when I was about to put my car in reverse to leave, I saw Sharon come out of the church. She was holding Nevilla's hand. She had on the black jacket with silver buttons I'd bought for her yesterday. Before Sharon left my house last night, she told me how hard this was going to be for her. Before she got inside the limousine with everyone else, she looked around.

41

I knew she was looking for me, and then her eyes zoomed in my direction. She had a disturbed look on her face.

Sharon was a year younger than I. As long as I could remember, Uncle Leon had always treated us like sisters. Sharon and I used to be closer than my own sisters at times.

When we were little, I remember having to look after her, especially in school. Uncle Leon would always tell me that when we were little, I would get into so many fights because of Sharon. Girls were jealous and always seemed to start fights with her, and of course, I was always there to kick somebody's ass. Now instead of just taking care of Sharon, I'm always looking after both Sharon and Nevilla.

What was actually a few seconds seemed like several minutes, as she stood with the door opened, looking my way. Her face looked a little pale, and her eyes were definitely tired. She'd told me she had gotten her hair washed and pressed last night, so it was straight today. They put highlights in her hair, I noticed. The rain was making her eyes blink, so finally she got into the limousine. I waited a few more seconds. I pulled off shaking my head, thinking about everything- Uncle Leon, my son, and my life in general. Could it really get any worse? I tried, but I couldn't hold it back any longer, so I let the tears stream down my face. I followed behind the limousine to bury Uncle Leon, while wondering what the future held for all of us now.

Chapter 8

It's been almost three weeks since Uncle Leon's funeral. It was raining again, and boy was it was coming down. I sat on my bed watching the news; a bad thunderstorm was heading toward Indianapolis. I looked out the window and saw an image of an umbrella with a question mark on it in the sky. I studied it for a moment, and then it disappeared. I got out of bed and went downstairs to open the front door, and quickly retrieved the newspaper from the front porch. I waived at Mrs. Jenkins who was across the way. She was getting into her car about to leave. I had my long blue robe on, with my hair up in a scarf. I went back into the house, put on some coffee and reached for my pack of cigarettes. I could hear the drops from the rain pounding on the rooftop.

"Let's see what today is talking about." I plopped on the couch and lit my cigarette. My robe revealed my long legs as I stretched them on the edge of the table. I frowned, covering my legs back up from the site of them, because I really did need to shave.

My horoscope read: *Take a chance and be more outgoing. It might surprise you.* "Yeah, sure you're right." I was doubtful, but in the back of my mind, realizing that was true. I took another puff on my cigarette and went over to the window in the living room. I looked out and saw Sharon, surprisingly. She was getting out of a red car I didn't recognize, running up to my door. Loud muffled music came from inside the car. Opening the door, I wondered why she was here. I hoped everything was all right.

Sharon stood with her hooded raincoat on, dripping wet. She was looking at me with her eyes big and wide, her eyebrows neatly arched. I looked past her at the waiting red car. I stepped back and invited her in, closing the door behind her. It looked like she'd been crying. She took off her wet raincoat and hung it on the coat rack that stood behind the front door.

"So, how are you doing?" she asked me. I thought that was a weird question. I really should have been asking her that.

"I'm okay. What are you doing over here? And, who is that out there? Are they waiting for you?" I took another puff from my cigarette.

"Terry. He's in a rental." *Oh Lord*, I thought, *I should have known*.

Sharon sat down on the couch. She had no makeup on. She hardly ever came out the house without makeup. I looked down at her sandals which were completely drenched. She formed a small puddle of water on my floor. I was trying to be patient, waiting to see why she was here. She sat in silence for a moment.

I left her sitting there, went into the kitchen and poured us both a cup of coffee. I returned with the cups of coffee and sat them on coasters. I stood in front of her, leaning on one foot with my hands on my hips. She took a few sips, trying not to acknowledge me with her face toward the floor. Finally, I broke the silence.

"Sharon, what the hell is going on? If you have something to say then damn it, say it."

She eyed me warily. "I'm pregnant," she said in a low calm voice.

"Oh God, please tell me Terry is not the baby's daddy." I threw my hands up in frustration.

"Yes he is. Terry is not that bad. You just never gave him a chance." She looked up at me with a sad face and then back down at the floor.

"Gave him a chance?" I shouted. "Terry is the reason why Jacob is in prison." I paced the floor in disgust. "Why would you go out and get pregnant by that loser? He's got five other kids and don't barely take care of them. Yes maybe you don't need him financially, but do you really want to bring a child into the picture with him?" I thought about what I said, and maybe I shouldn't have said that. I turned around and looked at her; she had her head lowered, nervously folding a piece of paper, back and forth, in her hand.

"Well, I should have guessed this reaction from you." She looked up at me. "And plus, maybe I won't have this baby. Abortion is always a choice." She got up and went into the kitchen. She opened up the refrigerator and looked inside. She pulled out an orange.

I decided to go upstairs and get the metal box. When I returned, Sharon was sitting on the couch. I sat it next to her. She looked down.

"What is this?" She opened the box, picked up a receipt and read it.

"Well, this is what Uncle Leon gave Janetta before he died. She was supposed to mail all this stuff. I don't know if these are receipts given to Uncle Leon or what, but I do believe it has something to do with why he was murdered."

She pulled more receipts out and looked through them. I sat down next to her. "Those receipts add up to about thirty million dollars."

Sharon looked at me with disbelief in her eyes. "Thirty million? What are they for?"

"That's the thing, I have no idea." I put the last of my cigarette out and lit another one. She grabbed the pack and pulled out a cigarette for herself.

"You're pregnant. You better start taking care of your health."

She shrugged her shoulders at me. Sharon's phone rang. I'm sure he was probably wondering what was taking her so long.

For some reason, I thought about Matthew's death. I had no idea why. I didn't allow myself to remove the thought either. I don't think the pain of losing him will ever go away. And, what made it worse was the guilt of knowing that I didn't buckle his seatbelt on that horrifying day. I would give anything if I could rewind back to that day.

Then my focus shifted to Uncle Leon's last words I heard when I was under Janetta's desk. Sharon was talking to me but I wasn't really listening to her.

"Girl, do you hear me talking to you?" Sharon shook me by the shoulders. My eyes immediately focused on her.

"Yes, I hear you." I got up from the couch, stood in front of her and exhaled smoke from my mouth.

She continued. "The police called me talking about they want to question me. I know they don't think I would have anything to do with my own daddy's murder. I can't deal with this. As soon as they called I thought about my baby girl Nevilla." Sharon leaned back and shook her head. Then she sat straight up and looked at me with sad eyes. "Who on earth could murder my daddy?" A shrill from deep within escaped her.

I tried to comfort her, but she pulled away. "They don't think you did it Sharon. I talked to them already. They're just trying to gather information. Hold on." I ran upstairs and returned with Detective Matters card. "Call him. This is the detective I talked with."

She took it and slid the card into her purse. "I talked to Franklin at the funeral. He's really been supportive. He had flowers delivered to my house and assured me he's going to keep Daddy's company running. And, I know he'll take care of Daddy's company. I just don't want Daddy to lose everything." Sharon finished half of her cigarette and put the rest out into the ashtray.

Well isn't that nice of him. "What else did Franklin say to you?"

"Well he gave me his condolences. What else was he supposed to say?" Sharon looked up at me and signaled that she wanted another cup of coffee. "Well, he also said Daddy's financial situation wasn't that good, but he'd take care of it."

I thought about that for a moment. That didn't sound right. I was having a bad feeling about Franklin. Family friend or not, I was going to see what was going on.

"Sharon, do you think Franklin would have something to do with Uncle Leon's murder?" I finally got it out there, to see what Sharon would have to say about that.

"What! Franklin? How could you say that? He's a part of our family." Sharon stood up paced the living room floor with her hands on her head. She let out a few sighs. Maybe it was a long shot, but I'm sure she thought there could have been a possibility.

Sharon came to the couch and stood in front of me. I could see tears forming in her eyes again.

I leaned toward her.

"Do you remember when we were little girls?"

I put my cigarette out. "What do you mean?"

"So you don't remember?" Sharon reached for her unfinished cigarette in the ashtray and lit it. "Never mind, it's in the past anyway."

I stared up at her. I was confused. Her brown eyes looked darker than usual. I decided to go back to what we were talking about before. "Look, I'm not blaming Franklin. But, what we do know for a fact is that someone

46

murdered Uncle Leon. And I want to find out who." I was very adamant about it.

"Let the police do their jobs, and then we'll have an answer." Sharon stood in front of the mirror hanging on the wall, next to the front door. She combed her fingers through her hair. Sharon walked back over to me. "Let's just drop the subject about Daddy. He's gone and there's nothing you are me can about it."

I was shocked at her sudden attitude.

Sharon looked at me and shook her head slowly. She walked into the kitchen, aimed straight for the freezer and pulled out the half-filled bottle of Tequila.

I followed behind her, trying to figure out what she was doing. I snatched the bottle from her. "What the hell are you doing? Have you forgotten that you're pregnant?"

She snatched the bottle from me and drank the little bit of liquor that was left and slammed it on the kitchen counter. She wiped her mouth with the back of her hand and laughed, wickedly. I was completely baffled by her behavior. I stood, with one eyebrow raised, staring at her. Then she looked at me. It was almost like she was a different person.

"Shit! I ain't never gonna see my daddy again," she cried, as she pounded on the wall a couple of times with bald fists.

Standing a foot away from her, I watched tears stream down her face and fall to the floor. I went over to comfort her, patting her on the back, while thinking in my own mind what was going to come of all this. I looked out the window with a vague and confused look pasted on my face. Terry's car was still out front.

I watched as Mrs. Jenkins across the street was watering her grass with the sprinkler in her hand. She looked up at me in the window for a brief moment, with her gray hair, pink housecoat and pink slippers on. Her pale face reminded me of my grandma's face many years ago when she was in that coffin. It finally occurred to me that it's October, and Mrs. Jenkins was watering her grass. She looked away and continued watering the grass.

I spent a few brief moments, and thought about what Uncle Leon was going through and what he thought of during his last few moments of life. I put my head against Sharon's shoulder, while I kept my eyes locked on Mrs.

Jenkins watering her front yard across the street. I didn't blink, as fearful tears formed in my eyes. I have to get to the bottom of this. I just have to. I have to know what happened and I don't care what it takes to find out.

Chapter 10

The next day, Terry called, of all people, looking for Sharon. She told me he had gotten drunk after they'd left here. She decided to leave her own apartment and come to my house. I told her she should have kicked his ass out and made him leave. But, really, who am I to talk? I was doing the same thing four years ago, except I was getting my ass kicked. As far as I knew, Terry had never hit Sharon, and if he ever does, I will not hesitate to call some of Jacob's old gang banging friends to fix him right on up. And, believe me; they would come in a second.

I looked over at the clock and it was seven in the morning. I told him to hold. I went downstairs, tired as hell since me and Sharon sat up all night talking. I saw Sharon wrapped up in a blanket, on the couch asleep. I told them to sleep upstairs, but she didn't want to move Nevilla.

I looked over at Nevilla, who was across from Sharon, in the reclining chair, with a Mickey Mouse gown on, asleep as well. Her long black curly hair was almost touching the floor as she slept there with her head on the armrest. It baffled me why that girl's hair grows so fast, even though her Mama's always cutting it, but I knew one thing, I wanted the secret.

I shook Sharon on the shoulder and handed her the cordless phone. I pulled the cover up on Nevilla and went back upstairs. As I walked up the stairs, I looked back and saw Sharon press the 'Talk' button which hung up on Terry, then she placed the phone on the side of her and went back to sleep. I shook my head.

I tried to go back to sleep but I couldn't. I sat up in bed and thought about that metal box. I took it from off my dresser and looked through it again.

I was surprised I haven't heard much of anything from Detective Matters. I pulled out his business card and decided to give him a call, but all I got was his voice mail, so I left a brief message. He should have called me by now with something, anything. However, I was hopeful.

I decided to call into work and take another week off. I told them since Uncle Leon's death, I needed more time off to recover. They understood. I was glad to get away from them crazy old people at the nursing home anyway. But I had to admit, between working at Uncle Leon's office, which he paid me pretty well, and the nursing home, which both were easy, I was making good money.

Sharon had her own apartment, which Uncle Leon paid the rent each month. I guess now Sharon may have to get a job. Then again, maybe not depending on what Uncle Leon left her. I'm sure she'll get something since he's no longer with us. I never understood why Uncle Leon spoiled Sharon to death. Because he supported her, her whole life, she has never really had a real job. When he was alive, once a month, he would deposit $3,500 into her bank account, and that was not including her rent and car payment he also paid for. It was almost as if he was doing those things because he owed her. If anything, Sharon owed him.

I was worried about Sharon. Since the funeral, it seems as though she's fallen into some weird type of depression. She still hasn't figured out what she's going to do with the baby. What ever she does, she needs to decide quickly, she's already seven weeks pregnant. And, she hardly eats anymore. But maybe that's due to the pregnancy. Sierra said Sharon and Nevilla came over Mama's house a few days ago for dinner and Sharon ate a half a piece of bread and then said she was full.

Mama even said the day after the funeral, she, Sierra, and Nevilla watched as Sharon got up from the dinner table and said she was going to call her daddy. They all stared at each other. Then Mama said, "Honey, your daddy's no longer with us." Then Sharon looked at them and laughed, saying "Oh yeah that's right."

When Matthew died, I was a nervous wreck. Along with Mama, Uncle Leon was there to help me. Sharon and Janetta were also at my house a lot. Janetta practically moved in for a month. For a moment, while going through all that, I didn't want to live anymore.

My three-bedroom house was big enough, so I told Sharon and Nevilla they could stay at my house for as long as they wanted. I heard from Mama. She said Uncle Leon had $500,000 for Sharon in trusts and bonds. However, at this time, Sharon didn't need to be by herself, and I was more than willing to let her live with me.

I went into the kitchen to brew coffee. While waiting, I got the paper from the porch, lit me a cigarette and headed back to the kitchen.

I stood by the sink and looked into the living room. From where I was standing, I could see Nevilla tossing about in the recliner. I figured she'd be waking up soon. Then a few seconds later, almost as soon as I turned to grab a glass of out the cabinet, Nevilla let out a horrifying scream. It startled me so bad, I dropped my glass on the floor and it broke in half, shattering small pieces across the floor. I quickly put my cigarette in the ashtray and ran into the living room.

"Wake up!" I shook her, but not too hard. "Nevilla, honey." I shook her one last time and before she sat up, her eyes were wide open.

Sharon sat up and looked at us.

"Are you alright, Princess?" She stared at me. "Nevilla?" I called out.

"I had a bad dream. I'm alright." Nevilla got up and went into the kitchen. I looked over at Sharon. She frowned and then put her head back down. I looked into the kitchen and my eyes grew big.

"Stop!" I yelled loud into the kitchen. Nevilla turned around and gave me a look of confusion. "There's glass on the floor." I took a deep breath and walked into the kitchen, grabbed a broom and dustpan. I moved Nevilla out of the way. "What did you want? I'll get it."

"Can y'all lower your voice? Somebody's trying to sleep in here," Sharon yelled from the living room.

I walked to the edge of the kitchen. "Excuse the hell out of us. Your daughter just had a nightmare."

Sharon didn't utter a word.

"Can I have some milk Auntie?" Nevilla asked as she stood out of my way.

"Sure." I poured her a glass of milk and she went back into the living room and turned on the television.

I finished cleaning up the kitchen and then decided to mop it as well. I picked up my cigarette and lit it again. After I was done, I poured me a cup of coffee and went into the living. I sat beside Sharon who was still asleep, and watched television with Nevilla.

I rolled my eyes as I glanced over at Sharon. For a moment, she made me think about Angie.

Angie was Sharon's mother. I remember the stories Mama used to tell me about her, how Uncle Leon met her at a strip club where she'd worked. About the affair, Angie had on her rich husband, which led to Sharon being born. Angie was only nineteen at the time. After her husband found out about the pregnancy, he divorced her.

Sharon really hasn't seen her mom much. The last we heard, she remarried another rich man and moved to Canada to be closer to her sister. No one in our family really liked her anyway. Uncle Leon raised Sharon with the help of Mama.

I remember Mama telling me that Angie had the nerve to try and go after Uncle Leon for child support when Sharon was about eight. I'm guessing her money ran out. My only real memory of Angie was when she came to the house late one night. I'd spent the night with Sharon, and there was this loud knock on the door. I looked over and Sharon was up too. We looked at each other and then cracked the bedroom door and tiptoed to the stairs to see what was going on. It was Angie. She was drunk as hell and was banging on the door for Uncle Leon. It was a mess and she looked a mess too.

Mama would always refer to her as "That stank, alcoholic white girl." Come to think of it, I don't think Mama ever called her by her real name. It's been about two years since Sharon has last seen Angie. Maybe guilt got the best of her, because she paid Sharon and Nevilla's way to Canada to visit her and her new husband.

I took a sip of coffee from my mug, and looked down at my feet, which were cold against the wooden floors. I slid my feet into my slippers and looked over at Nevilla. She smiled at me and was almost done drinking her milk. I put one leg out in front of me and examined it. *My legs are starting to get sort of big,* I thought. I'll have to start back at the gym, but I needed to renew my membership first. I put out my cigarette in the ashtray sitting on the coffee table. I think I had like ten ashtrays around my house.

I asked Nevilla if she was hungry. She nodded her head so I got up and looked in the refrigerator to see what I could make for breakfast. The light was coming in from the shade and it lit up Sharon's fair face. She squinted a little and pulled the blanket over her head.

Then it dawned on me that the metal box was never mailed. I wondered what would happen now. I can't believe Janetta didn't remind me. Damn, I wonder how important it was anyway. If all fails, then I'll just turn it over to the police.

I looked at the calendar on the fridge. After cooking breakfast for Sharon and Nevilla, I decided I wanted to go visit my brother, Jacob. I try to visit him at least once a month. With everything that's been going on, it's been about four or maybe five months since I'd last seen him. And plus, it had occurred to me that in Jacob's last letter he mailed to me, he told me that Uncle Leon paid him a visit, and how strange he was acting. I now wanted to know why. For as long as he's been locked up, Uncle Leon had never visited him. I had to find out more.

Besides the one time Sharon, Sierra and Mama came with me, I was the only one who visited Jacob since he's been locked up at the Indiana State Prison. Mama prefers to write Jacob and talk to him on the phone, in addition to helping me put money on his books. The two-hour drive wasn't so bad, but now that winters coming, it's going to be rough.

Actually, there was that one time when Tony used to live in Atlanta, when he first started school. He came out here to visit and both of us went to the prison to visit Jacob. I know Jacob really appreciated that.

I went upstairs, jumped in the shower for a few minutes, pulled out a pair of jeans and a light sweater. It was slowly, but surely, starting to get a little cool outside. Winter was definitely on its way.

Back downstairs, Nevilla was already propped up with a bowl of cereal in her lap. Her legs were dangling over the arm of the recliner.

"Hey Auntie Rahkel." She waved at me, and then turned back around. She was watching *Tom & Jerry*.

"Didn't we just eat breakfast, Nevilla?"

"I know, Auntie, but I'm hungry again." She shoved another spoonful of Cheerios in her mouth.

Sharon must have already taken her shower in the bathroom downstairs, because she was dressed, makeup and all.

"So did we get enough beauty sleep?" I asked sarcastically.

"Sure did. Where are you going?" She pulled out a compact and applied more lipstick.

"I'm going to visit Jacob. Wanna go?"

"Nah, not this time. Let me know the next time you go." She got up and went upstairs.

"Let me use your curling iron." She said, half way up the stairs.

"You know where it is." I yelled back.

I looked over at Nevilla again. She wasn't eating her cereal, but was staring out the window. I walked up to her, and she didn't blink, almost mummified staring at something that held her captive. I looked out the window and didn't see anything, except a tree. I waved my hands in front of her face and still nothing. After calling out her name a couple of times, she broke her gaze and began eating her cereal again, as if nothing was wrong.

"You alright sweetie?"

"Yeah, Auntie." She picked up another spoonful of cereal and laughed at the television

That girl has been acting a little weird lately, but maybe she was going through a phase, I thought, especially since Uncle Leon was no longer here. Maybe this was her way of dealing with his death. I went over to the coat rack, by the front door, and grabbed a cap and placed it on my head. This would work, especially since I didn't feel like combing my hair today.

"Sweetie, I should be back by one or two. Call me on my cell if y'all need me." I grabbed my purse, keys and shades and headed for the door.

"Okay, Auntie. Tell Jacob I said what's up." Nevilla picked up the remote and changed to another station. "Hey Auntie, next time you go, I wanna come, Okay?"

"Sure, baby girl." I blew her a kiss and closed the door. I loved that little girl to death. I treated her as if she was my own. Sometimes I think about things Matthew would have liked to do and wanted me to buy for him and then I'd buy it for Nevilla. I know that's strange. Let's just say she now likes playing video games and basketball. I guess it was my way of keeping a part of Matthew alive.

Chapter 11

After driving for an hour and a half, I stopped at McDonald's for a snack. I ordered nuggets and a small fry. When I pulled off from the drive-thru, my phone rang, and it was Kareena. What did she want? Since she didn't work, she helped her husband with paperwork for his job sometimes, but that was about it. If she wasn't doing that, she was, for sure, shopping.

"So what mischief are you into? You better not be smoking those cancer sticks," she scolded me. "Girl I just found these cute high heel red shoes. They are going to go perfect with my red dress. Fred is taking me out tonight. I saw a nice yellow moo-moo for you, if you want me to mail it to you," Kareena said laughing.

"Um, first off, I probably will smoke soon after I get off the phone and secondly, fuck you. I'm no longer big in case you haven't noticed." *Why did I answer the phone*, I thought.

"Just joking, girlfriend, but I actually found some nice black dressy shoes with a small heel that I want to mail you. Because those run down three-year-old heels you had on at Mama's, that was just plain pathetic." She pulled the phone away from her ear, but I could still hear her talking to the cashier, handing over her credit card. I cannot believe this bitch. She really had her nerve. I was actually glad she'd left. I can only take so much of Kareena. *Thank God she lives in another state*, I thought to myself, as I waited for her to get back on the phone so I could respond.

"Anyway," I continued as she called my name. "My shoes are just fine. Just because you buy the most expensive shoes almost everyday, doesn't mean I have to."

"Rahkel you take things too personal. But, anyhow, expect those shoes in the mail in a few days. So what are you doing anyway?"

"I'm on my way to see Jacob." I took a bite from a nugget and jumped back onto the highway. I looked up and was glad the sky was clear.

"Well tell him I said hello. I should have stayed an extra day while I was down there to see how my twin was doing." I knew she was lying. Kareena never went to see Jacob in prison or even asked too much about him. She was so much like Daddy. Daddy's favorites had always been Tony and Kareena. I remember him buying both of them brand new cars for there high school graduation. The only thing I got was a card from Daddy asking me if I had plans for college.

Although I would never tell Sierra, but she's Daddy's third favorite. Jacob and I always seemed to have been the outcast in Daddy's eyes, but I think I was Mama's favorite, or at least second favorite. It might be a tie between Sierra and me.

As the conversation went on between Kareena and me, I started to wonder why she was really calling. Then I found out.

"Anyways," Kareena continued. "I was calling 'cause I wanted to know what Mama was gonna do with Uncle Leon's house in Florida. I talked with Sharon at the funeral when I was up there, and she said I could have it if I wanted it. We could use an extra vacation house in Florida. We're going there next spring to take Shawntel to Disney World."

I couldn't believe this girl. Uncle Leon has only been dead a couple of months and here she is being as selfish as possible.

"*Bitch,* I know you *ain't* called me to ask me about no damn house. And, how could you ask Sharon that? Her Daddy is dead, she probably didn't know what she was saying, and you had the audacity to *ask* that?" I let her have it.

I was so pissed off. See, this is a prime example of how I don't believe she belongs to our family.

"Hey, no need to get salty, and that's *queen bitch* to you. I loved Uncle Leon too. I just want to put my two cents in on his belongings. Just to let you know, I did help you and Mama pay for his funeral expenses, so he could be laid to rest in luxury."

She had her nerve again. "Kareena, Fred paid for that! You don't even work."

Then she went on about this business she was thinking about starting.

Oh my God, the more she talked, the more she was pissing me off. If she was in arms reach, I would have slapped the weave out of head. I really wanted to hang up on Kareena because I was on the verge of cursing her ass out.

I really don't know how Fred can put up with her. It seemed like she bossed him around and, like a fool, he accepts it. It's probably all that ass she be *shakin'* that got him so whipped.

I remember their wedding. It was right before Kareena found out she was pregnant with Shawntel. Kareena didn't want Fred's sister in the wedding, because she was too overweight, wearing a size twenty-four. She said it would look too awkward since all seven bridesmaids were a size twelve and smaller. Although he was a little ticked off, he finally gave in only to please her. Kareena told Fred's sister that the dress didn't come in her size. What a bunch of bull.

I almost slapped Kareena upside her head on her wedding day, with her 'sadity ass' when I found that out. Fred's sister really wanted to be in the wedding too. Kareena has always been smaller than me, much smaller. We both grew up being about the same height, but she was slim with a big ass, and I was fat with a big ass. And, she had all the boys and growing up; and that went straight to her head. Of course, my being a big girl at the time, I definitely wasn't in the wedding. But that's alright, me and Kareena had never really been that close. She had a tendency of judging people by their weight. Well actually, she had a tendency of judging people period.

Another call was coming in. It was Mama. I cut Kareena off in mid-sentence. "Hold on Kareena, Mama's on the other line." I clicked over. "Hey Mama, what's going on?"

"Rahkel where is Sharon?" Mama asked with panic in her voice.

"Mama, she was at my house the last time I saw her. What's wrong?" I wondered becoming concerned.

"Well, Nevilla is over here right now. She ran over here crying, talking about she saw vomit in the sink, in the bathroom, and she don't know where her Mama is. She say she *ain't* nowhere in the house, so now she's here." Mama lived about eight blocks from me.

Damn it, I thought to myself. *I can't believe she threw up in my sink and left it for me to clean up.* "Well, I don't know Mama. I'm on my way to see Jacob. Did

57

you call her on her cell?" I was not about to turn back now, unless somebody was dying. I forgot I had Kareena on hold. "Hold on Mama, Kareena's on the other line."

"Kareena, I gotta call you back," I said. "Mama and Nevilla are looking for Sharon. I'll talk to you about the house later." That was enough of her.

"Well call me later on tonight. Real quick, did I tell you that Fred bought me another diamond bracelet? Girl, that man is always spending money on me. Just the other day…." *click*. I hung up on her. I was definitely done talking to her.

"Mama, this is Sharon's new cell phone number. Nevilla should already have it." I waited for Mama to get a pen. "555-1234." I repeated it again. "Call that number and then call me back."

I hung up with Mama and focused on the road while finishing up my McDonald's that was getting cold. I decided to let Sharon tell Mama she was pregnant. But I'm sure Nevilla will tell Mama that is if she even knows yet. I can't believe she just left Nevilla at home. What the hell is wrong with her?

I found myself accelerating on the gas peddle. I thought about calling Sharon, but then I wanted to wait to see what Mama would say when she called me back. I looked at my speedometer and it was reaching ninety miles per hour. I looked to each side of the highway. I wasn't too far from Michigan City. I pulled out a cigarette and lit it.

Jacob's parole was coming up early next year, I was praying to God nearly everyday they'd let him out. I needed my brother out. He used to keep me sane.

Chapter 12

I was sitting on a metal stool, looking through a large glass window, waiting for Jacob to come out. I glanced around and noticed a woman and her daughter seated a couple of windows down from me. The little girl glanced at me a few times and smiled. She had red pigtails and wore a dingy white T-shirt. I remembered seeing them a few times before. Jacob had told me a while back, in a letter, he'd written me, that her husband was on death row for shooting and killing two police officers while robbing a convenience store, and then stealing a police car and running over two young boys while trying to get away.

Sometimes the waiting room made me feel nervous. I could smell the metal from the bars in the air. I always glanced around at the people waiting and then watched what inmates would come out to greet them. I saw the woman's husband come out. He was a scrawny man, with long hair, dirty and stringy. His beard had grown the last time I'd seen him. His wife stood up and they kissed each other through the glass. I looked at the little girl, who was staring at me. I turned away and saw Jacob walking my way. I smiled as he sat down behind the thick plastic, in front of me. He wore an orange jumpsuit with a white T-shirt underneath. I was so glad to see him. We both picked up the receiver at the same time.

"I'm glad to see you finally came to see me. I was wondering when you were coming." His hair was growing out. Jacob had long hair. He needed to cut it. I could tell he'd been working out. He had always been tall and skinny. Now he was tall and muscular.

"Well, little bro, a lot has been going on." I put my hand up to the glass and he did the same.

Jacob sat up straight and squared his shoulders. "Yeah I know."

"What do you know?" He didn't know about Uncle Leon, or did he?

"Mama wrote me and told me about Uncle Leon a while ago."

She didn't tell me she wrote him a letter. "Oh." I wanted to be the one to break the news to him, but it was too late.

"Yeah that's sad. Old Uncle Leon... I can't believe he's gone."

"I know. It's been tough on everyone, especially me."

His eyes were sort of red and I noticed his skin was dry, probably from the water in there.

"So how's Mama and Sierra?"

"They're good. You know Sierra's going to college next semester." I was so proud of her.

"That's good. Look at my baby sister. So, what about Nevilla and Sharon?" Jacob wiped his forehead with the back of his hand. I looked behind him and the guard standing behind him, smiled at me. I grinned back, nonchalantly, and looked back at Jacob.

"Mama called me on my way here, talking about Nevilla walked to her house. She can't find Sharon and there was vomit in my damn sink this morning. So, after here, I gotta rush back to see what the hell is going on. Oh and by the way, Sharon's pregnant by Terry."

"Damn, I can't believe she's pregnant by that buster. What the fuck is wrong with her?"

I waved my hand at him. "You askin' me?"

"So how's she taking the news about Uncle Leon?" Jacob folded his arms on the table. I noticed he had a new tattoo on his arm. It was his initials. Jail house tat', those must hurt.

"Fine. To be honest, she really doesn't seem too upset about it. It's strange."

"Really?" I could tell Jacob was really thinking about my answer.

"While we are talking about Uncle Leon, I wanted to ask you something." I leaned forward on the metal stool. "In your last letter, you said something about Uncle Leon coming down here. What was that all about?"

"Hold on." Jacob pulled the receiver away and started to cough. Was he getting sick? I wondered about the food. I hated to see him in here. Here I am sounding like Mama. But he's a strong man.

"Yeah, Rahkel, Uncle Leon came down here. It shocked the hell out of me. You know they don't tell you who's visiting. They just tell you, you got a visitor. When I came out, I was expecting you, but it was him. Yeah it surprised me." Jacob sat up closer and leaned forward toward the window. He glanced back at the guard and lowered his voice. "You know what that fool wanted?"

"What?" I was eagerly anticipating his answer. "He wanted the name of the dentist who fixed my teeth four years ago. Remember when they were mostly all knocked out when I was in that motorcycle accident. Ain't that some wild shit? That was the only time he'd ever visited me, and that's what he came down here for." Jacob tilted his head, and made this strange face.

"A name of a dentist?" Now I was making a face. That made no sense to me. "Why the hell would he come all the way up here for that information?"

"Who the hell knows? The reason he gave me was because he was gonna start some new business with dental products. I don't know, it didn't really sound that legit."

"Well that does sound strange." I scratched my head trying to put the pieces together in my mind.

Jacob continued. "I gave him the name and then he left. On his way out, he did put twenty dollars on my books." Jacob grinned and looked back at the guard.

"Well what was the dentist's name?"

"Dr. Simon. Um…Charles Simon."

Over the speaker, a guard announced that visitation was almost over. At the end, Jacob and I stood at the same time. I waved at him and he smiled and walked away. I watched as the guard handcuffed him and led him away.

It was sad to see him leave. Jacob always had my back and Matthew was so fond of him. On one incident in particular, I remember Jacob coming to my house. I was with stupid ass and I'd just gotten my ass beat. My eye was black and blue. I couldn't stop my nose from bleeding and my arm was broken. My brother beat the hell out of my ex. He was only seventeen at the time. Jacob put him in the hospital for almost a week.

When I got to my car, I reached in my purse for my cell phone. There was one missed call. I sat in the parking lot and returned Mama's call.

"So what's going on Mama?"

There was a long silence.

"Well, Sharon told me she's pregnant. She was sick and needed to get some medicine at the store. She thought she'd get back before Nevilla woke up."

I wondered why Sharon would say that Nevilla was asleep. She was awake when I left. It seems like everyone's been acting strange since Uncle Leon died.

"So why didn't you tell me about Sharon being pregnant?" Mama asked.

"Mama, she just told me," I lied.

"Well, anyway, Sharon is over here now. I'm glad you gave me her cell number, 'cause the one I had was old." Mama always wanted to be in the know of everything that was going on. I can understand about this, but damn, if she doesn't know something, she'll get all upset.

"By the way Mama, do you have a key to Uncle Leon's house? It should be on one of those key rings Sharon gave you. I need to find something." I started up my car and took off.

"Yeah, baby, it's in the kitchen drawer. Have you decided what we are going to do with the house anyway?" I could hear the concern in Mama's voice.

"Probably eventually sell it. Since it's paid for, I don't have to think about that right now." Selling his house was the last thing on my mind.

"Well, whatever you and Sharon decide." Mama's concerned voice turned tired. Mama was only in her late fifties, but she was diagnosed with diabetes about a year ago and her cholesterol always seemed to be high. My mom was an overweight woman and had been on every diet there was to lose the weight. She'd lost weight recently, so I'm proud of her. All them neck bones, candied yams, fried catfish, *chitlins* and cheesecakes was too much for Mama. And she loves to cook. She'd cook every Wednesday and take it to the homeless shelter with her best friend, Sister Patterson.

"Okay, Mama, I'm on my way." I picked up my pack of cigarettes. *Damn, this is my last cigarette.* I got off at the next exit, headed to the gas station to buy me a new pack.

Chapter 13

Nevilla ran up to me and hugged me as soon as I walked into Mama's house.

"Mama's gonna have a baby. I'm going to have a little sister or a little brother." Her big brown eyes stared at me so innocently.

"So where is your mom now?" I looked in the kitchen and living room.

"She's sleeping."

"Oh." I caressed Nevilla's hair and sat her down in a chair as I braided it and placed a barrette at the end of each plait.

Nevilla got up, went off and sat down next to Mama. They both were watching old reunions of *What's Happening*.

Mama still had on her nightgown. She turned around and faced me. "So how's Jacob doing?" Mama asked, sipping' on a diet Coke.

"He's maintaining. Early next year, he's up for parole and hopefully he'll be out. He said Uncle Leon came to visit him some months ago." I went into the living room and sat on the couch. My feet were tired, so I took my shoes and socks off, and sat with my legs under me.

"Really? I'm surprised." Mama took another sip from her soda.

"Yeah me too." I didn't go into detail about why Uncle Leon visited Jacob.

"Well that's good. At least Leon got to see his nephew before he past. Thank God." Mama looked down at Nevilla and smiled at her. "By the way, can you go to the store for me later? I need to refill my prescription and I need to get me a few other things. The list is in the kitchen on the table."

"Alright, Mama. Where's Sierra?"

"She's at the mall with her friends."

I walked downstairs to the basement to check on Sharon. She had awaken and was slowly sitting up. She looked so pale.

Sharon's eyes were blood shot as she turned her head and looked up at me. I sat down, on the edge of the pull out sofa, next to her.

"So I see you got up the nerve to tell Mama you're pregnant?"

Sharon turned her face toward the television and reached for the remote to turn it on. "I didn't really tell her, she assumed, so I had to tell her. I decided to keep it." She propped up her pillows and laid back.

"So did you really go to the store, like you told Mama?"

"You know me too well." She giggled. "I actually went and got me some weed. I was only gone for a little bit. I can't believe Nevilla came over here."

I started to tell her off, but I didn't. I shook my head instead.

"You know tomorrow I'm going to the insurance place to cash out Daddy's $1,000,000 life insurance policy." She lifted her head and looked back at me. "You wanna come?"

"Um… no thanks." I didn't know he had a life insurance policy. I looked at her a little strange. And for $1,000,000. That's a lot of money.

"Well don't think I don't miss Daddy. I loved him. I'm just letting you know what I'm doing tomorrow." She returned her attention to the television. "I'm entitled to it."

Was she trying to convince me or herself?

"Well, I know you and your Dad don't get alone, but at least you have one, even though he's gay." She glanced at me to see my reaction.

"What do you mean, and why did you all of a sudden bring that up?"

"I'm just saying, I think you should call your dad. Y'all should work things out."

I didn't respond to her, as she channel-surfed.

I really thought about what she said. I hadn't talked to Daddy in almost two years. He sometimes called the house for Sierra and even wanted her to come down there to visit this past summer. He did mail me a Christmas card last year. It read: From Daddy and Phillip, Happy Holidays, We love you. He'd sent Sierra clothes, CD's and $1,000 to go towards her cosmetology schooling while she was in high school. Daddy didn't really have anything to do with Jacob since he was in prison. It was sad, but true.

Sharon's cell phone rang and it was Terry. I could hear her making plan's for them to go out of town. I'd thought about turning up the volume on the television on purpose, but I decided against being spiteful today. She glared

64

at me, as though she knew what I was thinking and snatched the remote from my hand. As soon as she got off the phone, she had a sarcastic smile on her face.

"So, does Terry ever ask about Jacob? Well let me think..." I looked up at the ceiling and then back at Sharon. "Well probably not since it's his fault he's in prison in the first place!" I emphasized almost each word as I said it. I knew I had started something, but I didn't care.

"Jacob is a man. He made his own decision. And yeah, Terry has asked about Jacob." Sharon got out the bed and put her hair up in a sloppy hair bun. She didn't say anything else.

"Sharon, Terry ain't nothin' but trouble. He's thirty-five and still sellin'. He ain't got no future and you ain't got no future if you stay with him."

Sharon rolled her eyes at me and headed upstairs. I could hear her huffing and puffing all the way to the top. She knew it was true. When he finds out about that insurance money, he's really going to try and be on her good side.

I heard her foot steps stop at the top landing. She turned around. "At least Terry's never beat my ass. Who's talking?" She continued to walk.

That pissed me off. I opened my mouth to say something, but I couldn't think of a come back. I guess she had me on that one.

I folded the sofa bed back into the couch. I was headed upstairs, until I saw Sharon standing in the kitchen making a sandwich. "Can you watch Nevilla please?" I should have said no, but I didn't.

"Yeah whatever." I passed her and grabbed a banana from the counter.

I decided to go back downstairs, just to straighten up a little bit, 'cause I knew Sharon wouldn't. I glanced around the room and took a bite from my banana. Nevilla's Barbie doll and other toys were scattered around. There was a pile of clothes in the corner, which I decided to at least sort and put a load in the washer. After about thirty minutes of cleaning up, Mama yelled downstairs and asked me what I was doing. I told her I was cleaning up and she thanked me. I reached for the remote and turned off the television. I got the vacuum and cleaned the floor.

After I was done, I looked around and was satisfied with what I'd done. I relaxed for a moment in the recliner. I started to examine the recliner and realized that Uncle Leon had given it to Mama and Daddy on their second anniversary. I couldn't believe Mama had kept it so long. I forgot she had it. It still had the same plastic over it. I pulled on a piece of plastic that was still barely hanging on. I tossed it across the way at the small trashcan right outside the bathroom. I flipped on the television again, and started flipping through the channels. I stopped when I came upon Saturday Night Live. I laughed when Eddie Murphy was impersonating Buckwheat.

I looked up at a painting that was off to the side, next to the piano by the window. I sat up and wondered if that was Uncle Leon's picture of the three black men playing instruments, with a little girl with pigtails sitting on the floor with a drum set. I got up to look at it. I wondered when Mama went to his house to get this. I brushed my hand across the face of the painting. It was dusty. I took it off the wall, carried it into the bathroom, grabbed a paper towel and dabbed it with water. After I wiped off the painting, and as I was putting it back on the wall, I felt something on the back of it. I flipped the painting over. There was a small silver key, affixed with tape.

"I wonder what this is for," I said out loud.

After I examined it, I stuck the key in my pants pocket and then placed the painting back on the wall.

As I turned around, Nevilla was standing there, staring at me with this blank look on her face, yet again. I stepped back and caught my breath, placing my hands over my heart.

"That's my Granddaddy's picture," she finally said. She continued to glare at me, with those big brown eyes. She wore flower jeans and a pink sweater-jacket.

I released a sigh. "Yes it is Nevilla. Auntie needs to make a quick run and then I'll come back and pick you up. You're going to spend the night with me. Okay?" I took her by the hand and led her upstairs.

"Yeah that's fine. Are you going to be long?" She sat on the couch.

"No, and maybe when I come back, we'll go to the store and get some movies and ice cream to bring back to my house." I smiled at her and patted her on the head.

"Sure Auntie."

Nevilla sat on the couch with Mama. I didn't see Sharon anywhere.

"Mama where's Sharon?" I glanced upstairs.

"Oh she just left. She said you were watching Nevilla." Mama was eating popcorn now and watching some movie that she was obviously really into.

Damn that girl is quick. "Well, Mama, if you don't mind, I have to make a really quick run, and I'll be back to pick up Nevilla."

"Okay." Mama didn't budge, nor did she remove her eyes from the television. She grabbed a handful of popcorn and stuffed it in her mouth.

Nevilla reached in the bowl and grabbed a few as well.

Chapter 14

Sitting in front of Uncle Leon's house, I looked at my watch. It was almost three-thirty. I turned off my car, and sat for a moment. I turned the radio on and Janet Jackson's *Pleasure Principle* was playing. Damn, I love me some Janet. I turned the volume up and sat, pondering whether I should go in. It felt sort of strange to be here. For a moment, a bad vibe shot through me, so I looked up at the clouds. I didn't really want to, but I was curious what I'd see. I saw a gray cloud in the sky, but that was about it. Maybe I was forcing it.

Twirling the key, that I'd gotten from Mama's kitchen drawer, between my fingers, I reminisced on the wonderful memories I shared in that house. Sharon grew up in that house, and I guess I did too. I was always over there. Uncle Leon lived there about thirty years. As I sat smiling at the house, in the passenger's side mirror, I noticed a homeless man approaching. I turned around slightly to get a better look. He had a shopping cart that was overflowing with junk. I wondered what he was doing over here. This was a decent neighborhood and it was not typical to see a homeless person. I watched him as he pushed his cart, his oversized coat was very dirty and his hair was stringy and long. With a beard that was thick and bushy, he dragged his left foot as he walked. He past me, then he stopped suddenly, turned around, and looked directly at me. When he walked my way, I didn't know if I should take off or lock my door. I locked the doors. He knocked on the passenger's window. I stared at him; he looked crazy. I assumed he wanted money. He knocked again, but he was crazy if he thought I was rolling down that window.

When he opened his mouth, he was missing at least five or six teeth. "Have you seen my friend Roger?" his muffled voice asked. I shook my head no. Then he began describing his friend to me. I shook my head again.

However, when he asked me if I knew where the man, who lived in the house, in front of me, was, I immediately rolled the window down slightly.

"How do you know Leon Wilson?"

He was stuttering. "He gave me and my friend food one day at the park and five dollars each. He gave me his business card and said to call him if we ever wanted to do some yard work around his house." The man reached in his pocket and pulled out one of Uncle Leon's business cards. He placed it up to the glass.

"He doesn't live there anymore," I finally responded.

There was sadness in his eyes and I suddenly felt very sorry for him. I reached in my purse and pulled out the only change I had on me, which was three dollars and a few pennies, and gave it to him. I always used my debit card. I told him if I see his friend I'll let him know. He said his name was Tim and would be at the homeless shelter downtown and thanked me for helping an old veteran. I nodded at him, watched as he turned around and slowly walked off, pushing his cart.

I reached inside my purse, pulled out my pack of cigarettes and lit one, took a long relaxing drag and then blew it out with ease. I thought it was odd that Uncle Leon would want two homeless men helping around his house, but then again, he was not always predictable. I was still wondering why I was sitting in front of his house. I convinced myself to go inside, after I smoked my cigarette.

Uncle Leon's house was nice: four bedrooms and three baths. Uncle Leon always gave Sharon everything she wanted. However, he'd threatened to cut her off a few times due to her being with Terry and some of the other men she'd dealt with in the past, but he never did.

After dusting away cigarette ashes that had fallen on my jeans, I opened the car door. I zipped up my leather jacket and grabbed my purse from the passenger's seat. Climbing out the car, I looked down the sidewalk and saw the homeless man several blocks down.

A little apprehensive, I inserted the key and opened the front door. There were piles among piles of paper stacked up on the couch. Noticing several sticky and memo notes lying around on the dinning room table, I picked one up. A lot them were Janetta's handwriting. Mixed in were several ATM receipts.

It felt eerie being here. I bit down on my bottom lip, fighting hard against the tears I refused to let fall. I missed him so much. Gathering my composure, I headed upstairs to the office, and tried to open the door, but it was locked. Moving down the hall, I reached his bedroom and jiggled the doorknob before entering. It was a mess, stuff everywhere. His closet was full of suits. I couldn't believe the police would leave his place like this, or maybe they didn't. I spent another fifteen minutes in the house, but didn't really find anything that stood out. I tried the key I found behind the painting on anything that had a lock, but nothing worked.

After leaving his house, I decided to go to the office. Maybe Janetta wanted to get lunch or go to the mall. She would never turn down food or shopping.

When I arrived at the office, a 'Closed' sign hung on the door. I must have missed her. I looked at my watch. Almost two hours have passed. I unlocked the door with my key and made a beeline to Franklin's office. His door was wide opened. I pulled opened one of his file cabinets and searched through the files. Then I opened the very bottom file drawer. As I searched through the drawer, a strange feeling took over me. I turned around slowly to see a tall man standing in the doorway. I was startled. He stood smiling. I caught my breath, after almost loosing my balance, and stood up.

"Can I help you?" I asked. He was a nice looking black man.

"Sorry, didn't mean to frighten you, Ms. Lady. The door was opened. I rent a town home from Mr. Wilson and I'm here to drop off my rent check." His teeth were so white; signs of good hygiene; I liked that about a man. He had on long shorts, tennis shoes and a Nike T-shirt.

"Are you new? Where's Janetta at? She's usually here when I come." He stepped aside and let me by. I went to Janetta's front desk to write him a receipt.

"No I'm not new. I'm Leon's niece and Janetta stepped out for a moment." I looked down and then back up at him. I reached my hand out for his payment. He gave me a money order for seven hundred and fifty dollars.

I looked at him for a moment with peculiar eyes. I guess you could say I was trying to scope him out. His hair was faded low and I admired how his sideburns connected to his nicely trimmed facial hairs.

I started to write out his receipt. "What's your name?" I asked without looking up.

"I'm Darrin Miller, 777 Grover Street."

After writing out his receipt, I looked up and he was smiling at me. The first thought that ran through my mind was that I hoped I didn't' look stupid. The second thought was questioning whether my hair was a mess or not. The third thought was confirming the fact that I hadn't had sex in almost two years. I displayed a quick smile at the bulge in the front of his pants, handed him his receipt, and placed the money order in Janetta's in box.

"What's your name?" he asked. He moved out of the way, as I walked around him and started cleaning up the table which had an empty coffee cup and a dirty napkin on it.

"Rahkel," Nervously, I walked down the hall, and I heard his footsteps as he followed me to the back of the office. I finished putting Franklin's files away, turned off his light and closed his door.

"Nice," he said, smiling. The way he said it, I didn't know if he meant my name or my butt. "So, Rahkel, are you married?" His voice was deep and it was actually turning me on.

I felt a little uncomfortable but in a good way. I hurried to the front area, before I turned around to face him. "No, I'm not. Are you?" I felt a smile creep across my lips, but then it faded. I looked into his dark eyes and then placed my hands on my hip.

He started to reach into his pocket. "Well here's my card. You should call me sometime. I'd love to take you out to dinner. You are a very beautiful woman."

Another smile appeared. I couldn't remember the last time someone called me beautiful, maybe pretty or cute, but not beautiful. I was flattered. I took the card and looked at it. Maybe he was looking for a booty call. If so, I wasn't interested.

"Darrin Miller, Private Investigator," I recited with a smile looking back and forth between the card and him. "What type of cases do you investigate?" I instantly thought about Uncle Leon.

"Missing children, crimes, cheating husbands…stuff like that." He smiled when he said the latter. "A lot of things actually." He smiled at me again. "And in my spare time, I'm also a personal trainer," he added. Yeah I could tell, as I took a quick glance of his bulging biceps. "Anytime you want to work out, I'm your guy," he said sincerely.

"Um, yeah…maybe." I felt nervous, because he kept staring at me. I pictured myself naked in front of him. I don't know why I had such a mental vision; it did nothing but made me feel worse. After he licked his lips at me, I turned toward the door.

"So where do you work out at?" he asked.

I was trying to think of some place, but I couldn't. "I work out when I can," I lied. Damn maybe he's trying to tell me something; that I need to work out.

"Well, here's my card to the fitness center down the way, a few blocks. You should stop by. I'll give you a two-month free membership to start you off." He handed me another business card.

That didn't sound like a bad idea. I needed to work out, so I wouldn't gain all my weight back. As I faced him, he immediately touched my shoulder. His eyes were looking down at my breast. How rude was that?

"Okay, well thanks," I looked at the card, "…Darrin. I have to get back to work." I walked to the front door and I opened it for him.

"Well, it was nice to meet you, Rahkel. Maybe next time, I could get your number." There was a pause. I looked at the ground. "Well, at least I hope I get the chance to see you again."

"Maybe." I watched him as he walked to his black pick-up truck. Damn he's fine. Again, I peered at his business card, before I watched him drive off. I wondered if I was too mean. I placed his card in the back pocket of my jeans and locked the door; both locks this time, and went around to Uncle Leon's office.

I was looking through Uncle Leon's deposit books. He'd made a few large deposits. I glanced behind his huge filing cabinet, and saw a safe. I had no idea Uncle Leon even had a safe in his office. The filing cabinet was too large to try and move. I stared at the file cabinet, and tried to open up one of the drawers, but it was locked.

Just when I was about to try to open another drawer, I heard the front door unlocking. I quickly peeked around the corner and saw Janetta. I took a sigh of relief.

I stood in the hallway looking at her.

She looked up at me. "Hey girl, how you doing?" Janetta asked. "I think it's gonna rain out there. What you doing here?" She had a large cup in her hand and a fast food bag. Janetta's hair were in braids. .

"Your hair looks nice. I just came up here to see if you wanted to go to lunch, but I guess you already have that handled."

"Oh. Thanks, I went to that new black hair salon downtown: Fabolouso. You should try it and stop always putting your hair back in a ponytail."

I walked up to her as she was settling in her chair. "Hey, Darrin Miller came by. What do you know about him?" I knew she had to know something.

"Oh, yeah, he must have come to drop off his rent. Girl ain't he fine?" Janetta sat at her desk, plopping her coat, purse and cup on top.

"Yeah, he's nice looking, I guess you can say." I watched Janetta open up her little small cabinet, where she kept all her snacks, and pulled out a big bag of Doritos chips.

"Want some?" She opened them up and stuffed about three or four chips in her mouth. She used a napkin to wipe the crumbs from off her mouth. She sipped on her soda and opened up her bag, pulling out a cheeseburger.

"No thank you." I picked up a magazine from the front counter, and browsed through it and then sat it back down.

"Darrin is thirty-seven and has a good job. You know I was thinking about hooking you two up," Janetta said, as she stuffed another three chips in her mouth and then took a sip from her cup then a bite from her cheeseburger.

"Yeah, well, he did give me his card." I watched her eat. She was making me hungry. I liked the sundress she was wearing.

"How's my girl, Sharon, doing?" She reached behind her and pulled out a few files.

"She's okay. Besides being pregnant, she's okay," I said, looking behind me out at my car.

"She's pregnant? Let me guess, Terry right?"

"You got it. I think she's six or seven weeks."

"So what else do you know about Darrin?" I wondered, changing the subject.

"He's single, if that's what you're asking me."

"And?" I wanted to know more. I placed my elbows on her desk and clasped my hands.

73

"Like I said, he's fine as hell and single and has two good jobs. What more do you need?" Janetta got up and started to fix her panty hose through her dress. "And he only dates black women. So there's an extra plus," she added. "And plus, you need a man to clear out all those cob webs down there." She pointed to my private area.

I gave her the don't-get-sassy look. She looked up toward the ceiling as to think about what else she was going to say. "He's works at a gym not far from here and is an investigator."

"Yeah, I know that part. He invited me to his gym to work out."

"Hell, take him up on his offer. I remember one time, he was in here. And I was up front. He was talking to Jenny, remember that temp that Leon had working in here during the summer? I was standing behind him, checking out his butt. Girl, he got a nice ass. Did you see it?"

"Sort of." I pictured him naked after she said that.

"Shit, that man has a nice body. I remember he'd just come in from working out. Jenny looked up and saw me staring at him. She smiled and tried to hold back her laugh. Girl, he turned around, and I couldn't hide it, you know me. I think he got embarrassed. But he just smiled at me."

"I'm surprised I never seen him before." I started pacing in front of Janetta's desk. "So has he ever tried to talk to Jenny?"

"Didn't I tell you he only dates Black woman and plus Jenny didn't talk to Black men. You know she was a young preppy white girl from Utah." We both laughed. "But it shocked me when Jenny agreed with me and said he was handsome. You know she be talking to them white nerdy guys. And they always have to be wearing glasses."

I sat in the chair beside her desk. "So what about you?" I leaned back my chair and crossed my legs.

"What about me?" Janetta looked at me, her eyebrows drawing inward.

"You think he's fine don't you?"

"Girl, please. I can tell his style. A dark built chocolate brother like to look at only skinny girls like you."

I gave her another look. I was not skinny.

Janetta pulled out a manicure set from her drawer and started to file her nails.

"I still have about fifteen more pounds to loose," I frowned.

Janetta rolled her eyes at me and turned her chair around as she was still filing her nails.

"Besides, I'll whip up something so severe on his dick; he wouldn't know how to take my ass." Janetta looked up at me with the biggest grin. I was trying to hold back my laugh, but I couldn't. She paused and stood up, placing both of her hands on the top of the desk. "Us big girls know how to ride it. Don't get it twisted girlfriend."

I laughed so hard, I knocked off the small clock sitting on the table. "Okay, Janetta," I said bending down to pick up the clock, laughing uncontrollably. "That's funny. I'm going to finish up some work in my uncle's office. How long you gonna be here today?"

"Probably another few minutes," she looked at her watch, "I got a booty call tonight, girl, with this fine African man. So you know I can't miss that." Janetta opened up her small refrigerator she had under her desk and pulled out a coke and a candy bar. "He's got an American black friend. Are you down or what?"

"Didn't you just eat?" I tried not to sound rude.

"Girl, I have to stay healthy. My men love me like this."

I smiled at her and shook my head. "No girl, I'll pass." I walked back to Uncle Leon's office and shut the door behind me. I pulled out my cell phone and looked at the time. I didn't want to be in here too long. I remembered that I'd promised to take Nevilla for ice cream.

Janetta yelled from the front. "The next time I ask you to go, you better or I'm gonna start thinking you're gay."

I ignored her comment and laughed to myself.

Chapter 15

Iturned to the other side because the sun was glaring in my face. I blew at the few strands of hair that were covering my eye, and combed my hair back with my hands. I stared at the clothes piling up in the hamper. It was so high that it overflowed, even though I'd already push the clothes down three or four times to make more room. I checked the clock and it was almost ten. I could hear Nevilla behind me, tossing and turning.

I was thinking about Sharon and Terry. I don't know what it was with her and men, but she always picked the thugs and she was so pretty. She could literally have anyone she wanted. Oh well, that's her life. The sun must have been shining in Nevilla's face too, with all the tossing and turning she was doing. I turned and looked at her. I smiled, she looked so innocent, and for a moment, I thought about Matthew.

I reached for my cell phone. I had two missed calls. One from Mama, and the other from a number I didn't recognize. I got out of bed and stretched my arms, yawning at the same time. I slipped my feet into my furry tiger slippers, grabbed my cell phone and cigarettes off the nightstand, and headed downstairs to the kitchen to put some coffee on.

While standing in the kitchen, I picked up Darrin's business card I'd laid on the table. With him being a private investigator, he actually could help me. I wondered what he would charge me? I shifted my weight to the other leg. I got my favorite mug, with a picture of Matthew and Nevilla on the front, out of the dishwasher and poured me a cup of coffee.

I went back upstairs, retrieved the box of receipts, with the CD and business card. The key I had taken from behind the painting, I threw in with the rest of the stuff and brought it back down to the kitchen.

I sat at the kitchen table still with Darrin's business card in my hand. I put it down beside the box and lit me a cigarette. From the kitchen, I turned on the television with the remote.

I decided to call Mama back. She informed me Sharon never came home last night, and wasn't answering her cell phone or house phone. I wasn't too worried because if I could bet on it, she was still laid up with Terry somewhere, probably at her house with her phone turned off as she does when she doesn't want to be bothered. I didn't tell Mama that though. I just told her I'd look into it.

I scrolled to the other missed call number on my cell phone. I didn't recognize it at all. Just when I was about to dial the number back, Nevilla came into the kitchen rubbing her eyes. Her hair was looking wild, still in a pony tail and she had her same pajamas on from the day before. I sat my cell phone on the kitchen counter, and took a sip from my coffee mug.

"Want some cereal, sweetheart?" I opened the refrigerator to make sure I had some milk. Two days until the expiration date, it's still good.

Nevilla pulled up a chair and sat down. She laid her head on the table. "Sure Auntie. I'm still tired." She yawned and wiped the tired tears from her eyes.

"Well you did go to sleep late watching those movies we rented." I switched from the news to the Cartoon Network. I had a big screen so it was easily viewable from where she sat in the kitchen. I sat the bowl of Cheerios in front of Nevilla. She immediately sat up and started to eat, with her eyes glued to the television.

I took my cup of coffee, cell phone and my unfinished cigarette upstairs, my long silk robe dragged on the floor behind me. I decided to take a nice long hot bath. Sometimes baths made me feel better. I made sure I poured my special Strawberry-Melon bubble bath under the running water.

Soon after, I sat up in the bed smoking on my forth cigarette for the morning. I put my hair back in a ponytail and laid my head against the headboard. I stared into the mirror on the wall in front of me. I inhaled the smoke and slowly exhaled it. I thought about Uncle Leon. Then my concentration switched to how boring I thought my life was.

I hadn't worn much makeup in a long time. I examined the pimple that was forming on my nose, and dabbed a bit of cream on it and rubbed it in.

Damn, now that I think about it, I haven't been on a real date in a long time. I took my robe off and got into the tub. I laid my head back against the cold tiled wall and absorbed all my thoughts. The hot water felt so good against my skin. It was relaxing and that's exactly what I needed. My thoughts switched from Uncle Leon to Darrin and then again to my pathetic life. After about thirty minutes, I decided to get out. As soon as I wrapped myself with the towel, I opened the door to my bedroom and Nevilla was standing there.

"Auntie someone just called for you. I answered it and there was a man on the other line."

"What? Go get me the phone please." I dried myself off and put my robe back on. In no time, Nevilla returned with the phone. I tried to dial *69, but the number was blocked. I sat on the bed and motioned with my hand for Nevilla to sit next to me.

"Okay, Nevilla, word for word, what did this man say?"

"Auntie, I picked up the phone and said hello, and the man on the other line said, 'Tell her to stay out of it.' And then he hung up. Can I go back downstairs now?"

"Yeah go ahead."

I didn't know what to think or how to feel. Who could that have been? I wondered if Nevilla was telling the truth.

As I finished my cigarette and placed the butt in the cigarette tray, my cell phone rung, startling me. I let it ring four times before I answered.

"Hello... Hello," I said. Someone was on the other end, but they weren't saying anything.

Finally, they spoke. "Meet me at Blue Dolphins Diner on Mason Boulevard, 10:00 sharp, tomorrow night. Come alone. I know your Uncle Leon. I promise I will not hurt you. But if I see you with anyone else, I will leave. I'll be in a white Cadillac," a man's voice ordered.

I'm sure I must have had the most confused look on my face. Before I could say another word, he hung up. I pulled the phone away from my ear and stared at it. I tried to replay the conversation in my head to see if I recognized the voice. Several thoughts were running through my mind. What was that about? I looked into the mirror across from me. Do I meet this man or not? Blue Dolphins Diner is a public place and its opened twenty-four hours. I thought more about meeting the stranger, and since the police station is only two blocks from the diner, everything should be fine.

I thought about calling Darrin, but I had second thoughts. I'm not calling a man I don't know. My thoughts turned to Detective Matters. I dialed the number from his card, and of course, I got his voicemail. Damn, this man never answers his phone. I hung up when I heard his voicemail. I called Janetta. I hope she doesn't have plans tomorrow night. Janetta didn't answer either, so I left her a message. I know she'll call me back soon.

Sitting in bed, I was so perplexed and confused. Who was this man, and why was he calling me? Was he the same man that called my house and spoke with Nevilla? I needed these questions answered, and answered soon.

Chapter 16

Janetta finally called me back even though it was the next day. I was downstairs, returning from dropping Nevilla off with Sharon. Yes, she really had been with me all that time. I looked at the time on my cell phone. It was getting close to four. I had about six hours left if I wanted to meet this man at the Blue Dolphin. Janetta was leaving the mall with one her male friends. She claimed that she didn't get my message until today. However, she would be home in a few and for me to come by.

Since Janetta lived about thirty minutes from me, I'd thought about picking up a bite to eat, but I was more than sure that Janetta would be hungry, so I decided to wait until I got to her house so we both could go grab something to eat.

It didn't take much to convince Janetta to follow me to the diner, and sit in the shadows, while I had my meeting. My girl didn't hesitate. There was no way she wasn't going to have my back.

To kill time, and to fill both of our stomachs, we decided to head to a nearby café for happy hour. After the waiter seated us on the back patio, we looked at a menu and agreed to share a large basket of wings and fries.

"So what do you think this man is going to tell you?" She asked as she licked a bone.

"Something valuable I hope." I put some fries on a plate and doused it with ketchup. Janetta was looking behind me smiling. I turned around to see what had her attention.

With a huge smile on her face, she got up and went over to the table behind us, and hugged some guy. He had three other friends with him. I turned around and pulled my baseball cap down, almost over my eyes. I placed a fry in my mouth. When Janetta returned to the table, she was holding onto some guy's arm.

"This is Patrick, meet Rahkel."

I wiped my hand with a napkin and extended it. He was cute actually, not that tall, but cute. He had a low fade and straight teeth. I loved a man with straight white teeth. Both Janetta and Patrick walked off to the bar. I watched as they kissed at the bar. They looked so cute together. He kept grabbing her ass and she let him. The table of girls behind them was pointing. Them bitches were just jealous. I ate two more wings. I looked behind me at his friends and one of them smiled at me. I quickly turned around, made a face and sipped on my Long Island. Then, I lit a cigarette and waited until Janetta got back to the table.

"Girl that man makes my toes curl. I've known Patrick for almost a year. He just got his divorce final a couple of weeks ago." She tilted her head and smiled at me. "He's got friends." She gestured with her eyes and picked up two chicken wings, exchanging bites between the two.

"Yeah I saw them. And, one of them has a curl. The other's front tooth is missing. And the third, well I'm not interested. They are all played out."

Janetta leaned to the side and looked over at the table behind us where Patrick's friends were seated. She looked back at me and we both laughed our asses off.

Before I realized it, I had only ten minutes to meet up with the man at the Blue Dolphins. We left the café and Janetta followed behind me in her car. Frequently, I looked in the rearview mirror to make sure she was still behind me.

I pulled up to the traffic light. A black Mercedes pulled up on the side of me. The windows were tinted, but I could still see a silhouette. The window rolled down slightly and a man looked at me. He waved at me. I didn't even know him. I tried to get a good look, but the light turned green. I sat there for a moment, watching as he drove off. Behind me, Janetta beeped her horn. Ignoring her, I grabbed my cell phone and punched in his license plate number. Then, I made a left turn onto Mason Boulevard.

A block from the Blue Dolphins Diner, I came upon police cars everywhere. I had to pull over because the street was blocked off. I pulled over and put my car in park. Looking around, there were people coming from out of the diner, rushing toward my car. The lights on the top of the police cruisers were spinning around. Everything seemed to go in slow motion. As me and Janetta walked closer, it was becoming evident that the yellow tape was surrounding a white Cadillac. Could it be the same car? I had a very bad feeling. I covered my mouth with my hand. There were bullet holes in the front windshield and on the driver's side. There was blood on the outside of the car's door. I looked around at the people standing. Some even terrified by what they saw. Janetta was holding onto my arm so tight, I thought I was going to get a bruise. I looked around again, trying to see if I saw anyone suspicious, but I didn't. I turned my attention back to the white Cadillac. They pulled the victim out of the passenger's side. I tried to get a better look. The man had on a gray cap, but it fell off as the police dragged the man out. His hair was white, but he was balding at the top. Before I could see anymore, they were zipping him up in a black body bag and toting him to the ambulance.

A woman quickly pulled up to the scene, darted from her car and ran up to the ambulance. She was in distress. I immediately went over to her.

"Do you know this man?" I touched her gently on the arm.

She was crying as she held her hand up to her chest and shaking her head. "Yes." She was trying to compose herself. "That's Dennis Lowry." She didn't look my way as she spoke; she kept her eyes on the ambulance as the doors closed.

"Who's Dennis Lowry?" I asked. She expected me to know.

She turned to me and looked me in my eyes. "He's a Dentist, like only the best Dentist in Illinois." She covered her face and wailed like a baby. Someone approached us pushed me out of the way to comfort her. I backed out of the way, and walked over to Janetta.

"What's going on girl?" Janetta asked me.

"That was the man I was supposed to meet, I think. I don't understand." We both looked at each other. A strange fear came over me. "His name was Dennis Lowry…"

Janetta stopped me. "What? Ain't that man a dentist from Illinois?"

I didn't even know who he was, how did Janetta know? "How do you know him?" I watched as the police was trying to clear the area. A fire truck and a tow truck pulled up.

"I've seen him on TV. I can't believe it. Are you sure you were supposed to meet this man?" Janetta pulled out a pack of gum and offered me a stick. I shook my head.

We both stood in silence, staring as the scene was unfolding before us.

"Let's go Janetta. This is freaking me out. Follow me to the office. I want to check something out." I wanted to look in Uncle Leon's office again. I think I might have found a way to get into Uncle Leon's file cabinets.

As we walked by the Blue Dolphins, I looked in the parking lot just to make sure I didn't see another white Cadillac.

"What the hell are you looking for? I feel like a detective now. You got me going to crime scenes, doing investigations and stuff. Damn, I could be on a booty call or something."

I looked at Janetta and pulled her arm. "Come on girl, just follow me, and stay behind me."

As I drove, I kept looking in my rear view mirror, making sure Janetta was directly behind me, and making sure nobody else was behind her. Or, at least, not too close. I looked again, and now there was a tan car behind Janetta. As we turned, the car turned. We came to a light and the car got into the next lane and turned off. I don't know if I was paranoid or what. I wiped the beads of sweat from my forehead. I pulled down the vanity mirror, grabbed a tissue from the glove compartment and wiped my face.

We finally pulled up in front of the office. I saw a light on in the upstairs storage room. I called Janetta on her cell phone, and suggested we park down a side street. Janetta was antsy, text messaging me constantly because she was tired of waiting. I needed her to hold on a little bit longer, because I wanted to see whom if anyone would come out. I already had my suspicion. As soon as I was about to call Janetta, low and behold Franklin's ass walked out. I knew it! What the heck was he doing here? It's almost eleven o'clock at night. He has to be up to no good. He walked a full block and then got into his car.

I watched as Franklin pulled up to the stop sign, near where we were parked. I slid down in my seat. He made a left turn and continued down the street. Why would he park down the street from the office? I thought about going in, but Janetta was nice enough to be out here with me and I knew there was no way I'd get her to go in. I'd thought about coming back, but I was afraid to go in alone, not knowing what I would encounter.

As soon as I got home, I took a nice hot shower and got in the bed. I tossed and turned all night long. I had a bad dream. It was dark and I saw

Uncle Leon coming in my room covered with blood. Nevilla and Sharon weren't far behind him, and they were pale as a ghosts. I woke up, afraid and covered in sweat.

Chapter 17

The next morning, I decided to have my hair done at the hair salon downtown Janetta told me to visit. It was time for a change, so I received the full treatment: washed, deep conditioned, pressed, trim and color. I was happy to see how much my hair had grown. However, after I left the salon, I pulled my hair back into a ponytail.

At the Blue Dolphins Diner, the police had everything practically cleared. Besides the small pieces of glass on the street, there was no evidence of a murder last night. I thought about the man, I now know as Dennis Lowry, as I sat in front of the restaurant. It occurred to me that Uncle Leon visited Jacob about a dentist. Something was strange, way too strange.

I didn't have a reason to be here, but after tossing and turning and unable to sleep that well last night, I thought I'd come to the diner. Maybe I thought I was going to see something or hear something.

I pulled out a cigarette and glanced around. A couple was walking out the diner hugging and kissing in front of me. Get a room. There wasn't that many people inside. Maybe I'll go inside and grab a little something to eat, before I head to the office.

Detective Matters left a message on my cell phone's voicemail. He said that Donald Hamilton was out of town on a business trip during the time of Uncle Leon's death and at least four witnesses can back up his alibi. He also went on to ask me if I knew a doctor by the last name Simon. I immediately thought about Charles Simon, the dentist who Jacob referred to Uncle Leon. I returned Detective Matters' call, but of course, I got his voice mail. I wondered how long we were going to play phone tag. I left a message informing him that I thought Simon was a dentist, and not a doctor. I thanked him for working on the case and for him to call if he found out any more information.

Then a crazy idea came into my head. I pulled out Darrin's business card. I probably sat in my car staring at his business card for at least a good five minutes, before I finally decided to call him.

"Hello," A deep voice said on the other end.

"Hi Darrin. This is Rahkel; remember me from Wilson & Carter Leasing? Were you busy?" I put my cigarette out in the ashtray. I was trying not to sound too nervous.

"Hello, Ms Lady, of course I remember you. I was hoping you'd call me sooner or later." He sounded so good on the phone. His baritone voice was deep and sophisticated.

"Did I catch you at a bad time?" I started to wonder if calling him was bad idea.

"No, Rahkel, you didn't. I just got done working out. I was actually about to leave here to go get some breakfast before I went to my office. You interested in meeting me?" I heard a door closed. Then I heard other men talking. I think he was in the locker room.

"Sure, why don't you meet me at the Blue Dolphins Diner? That's where I'm at now. I just pulled up." Damn, what am I saying? Why in the hell did I say I was here? I should have pretended I was busy or something. I reached in my purse, as I looked in the mirror, puckered my lips and applied lip-gloss. I took my hair out of the ponytail, and combed it down around my shoulders. Then I ran through it again with my fingers. Thank God, I just had my hair fixed.

"Sounds good, sweetheart. I'll be there. See you in like thirty minutes."

"Aright Darrin." *Sweetheart?* He's calling me sweetheart now. Okay I guess he can call me that.

Damn, what was I doing? Well, shit, who cares? I have nothing to loose. In addition to him being fine as hell, maybe he can help me find out some information on Franklin and help me find out who murdered Uncle Leon.

I looked down at what I was wearing. Well I'm too far to go back home: jeans, blue flip-flops and a white short sleeve baby T, with a blue tank top underneath. I had my jean jacket alongside side me. Plus, I had the nerve to apply eyeliner. I found it in my glove compartment along with some mascara. Damn, you'd think I was about go on a date. Well, I wanted to look decent, and it has been two years since I've been on anything remote resembling a date.

Shortly, I saw a white suburban with tinted windows pull up two parking spaces down from me. Of course, I looked for a black pick up truck, since that's what I remembered. I was trying not to be obvious and stare, but I couldn't see anyway. I hate when someone with tinted windows pulls up next to me, and I can't even see anything at all. So I nonchalantly kept glancing over, blowing my cigarette smoke out of the cracked window.

After only taking a few puffs, I put it out and started fiddling with my hands. I tried to stare again to see who got out on the other side. That's when I saw this tall, dark handsome man come around. Yes, it was indeed Darrin; hair nicely trimmed with—a slight wave to it—side burns connecting. His deep-set eyes were dreamy; lips not too thick, but evenly proportioned. Not that anything was wrong with thick lips. The short sleeve light yellow polo shirt he wore wrapped his athletic frame into a scrumptious package, and his slacks hung beautifully, hugging all of the right places, 'causing a lot of curiosity to make imagination run wild. Shit, what am I doing? But, damn, he looked good. However, he dressed quickly from coming from the gym. I grabbed my purse and got out the car.

Darrin had to be at least six-two, which was a good height. His wide smile exposed those pearly white teeth that attracted me in the first place. He leaned in to me and hugged me, catching me a little off guard. But, I liked it though. I don't remember the last time I was held like that. Okay, focus, focus, that's all I kept telling myself. A word of advice, never go two years without sex ever again.

"I'm glad you could meet me." I took the lead and walked toward the entrance.

"It's my pleasure, I'm glad you called."

I was wondering if he was staring at my butt. Although I had jeans on, they were my hip hugging jeans so maybe he was. I was already wondering how I could approach the subject of him helping me with Uncle Leon's murder. Go with the flow, and don't rush the conversation was the best way to handle it.

After the waitress seated us, he took me by the hand. "Nice nails. I can tell you are the type of woman who takes care of herself. You can tell a lot by a woman's hand."

Okay, what the hell, how is he going to start off a conversation like this? I didn't even get my nails done. I just kept them cleaned and filed, but if he thought I had nice nails, then I'll take the credit.

"Oh, thanks," I smiled, as I slowly pulled my hand away. "So have you ever been here before?"

"Oh Yeah, I've been to Blue Dolphins several times. This is a good late night spot."

"So tell me about your investigation job. Do you have to work today?" I sipped on the cup of coffee the waitress brought me. I liked my coffee black, with just one packet of sweet and low.

"I don't have a specified time. It's case by case. But now I'm working on a kidnapping case, so I may be there late today just to get as much as I can done."

"Oh, that's nice." That sounded dumb. How is it nice that he's working on a kidnapping case? I took another sip of coffee.

The waitress took our orders. He ordered orange juice, steak and eggs. I ordered pancakes and eggs. I pulled out my pack of cigarettes.

"You know those are killers right?"

Oh boy here we go. He was one of those. "Yeah been tryin' to quit for years, but it's gotten worse ever since my son died." I threw the sympathy card on the table. I always say that, every time someone says something about my smoking. I lit it, inhaled, and blew the smoke out the corner of my mouth. I moved the ashtray off to the very edge away from him. I looked at him and smiled.

"Sorry to hear that. When did he die?" Darrin placed both of his arms on the table, folded them and leaned in closer.

"About three years ago." I pulled the ashtray a little closer to me, and tapped my ashes into it.

I noticed throughout breakfast, he kept staring at me. It really made me feel uncomfortable. I almost said out loud, "What the hell are you staring at?" but I didn't. I stared back and kept smiling.

I pulled out another cigarette when we were done eating. He made it so obvious that he did not like me smoking, but I didn't really care. I had to smoke.

"I'm just curious," he began. "How do you keep your teeth so white since you smoke?"

I grinned and put my cigarette out. I'll just smoke later. I can't believe he just asked me that. I actually consistently use a teeth-bleaching kit I'd bought from a late-night infomercial awhile back but I didn't tell him that. "Well I brush my teeth with banking soda," I said, speaking the first thing that came to mind, remembering mama use to make us do that when we were little.

"Oh, just wondering."

Really, his reaction made me want to stop smoking. I decided to change the subject. "So how much do you charge for investigations?" I was trying my best to lead up to what I really wanted to know.

"Well it depends on the investigation, but I charge hourly anywhere from $50 to $300 an hour. Sometimes more." He sipped on his last swallows of orange juice and flagged down the waitress to bring him another glass.

"Oh." That was a little expensive, but it was probably worth it.

"Well, how much would you charge me?" I smiled at him, as he took my non-smoking hand and gently kissed it. It was almost like an appreciation for me putting out the cigarette.

"Well what are you trying to investigate?" He appeared very intrigued by my question.

"Well, my uncle." I figured he knew or heard.

He sat back in his seat, with the most disturbed look on his face. "What do you mean? Who's your uncle?"

"My Uncle Leon was murdered a couple of months ago." I couldn't believe he hadn't heard about it.

"Leon Wilson was murdered? Oh man, wait till I tell Calvin." His hands were moving this way and that way, before he pulled out his cell phone.

"Yes, didn't you know?" I paused. "Who's Calvin?" His reaction sort of startled me.

"Calvin works with me." He went on about how sorry he was and offered his condolences. He started dialing a number on his cell phone. I stared at him. I wondered what all of that was about. Just for that, I picked up the remainder of my cigarette and lit it again.

After he got off the phone, I asked him again about helping me. He let me know that he had no problem with helping and that he'd do anything he could. Yeah, that's what Detective Matters was supposed to be doing. Hopefully, he'll find out more information then he had. He asked me a few questions about what happened. I ended up telling him everything I knew, even about the metal box I had and last night with Dennis Lowry's murder. He said he knew about that, because he heard it on the news this morning. I also went on to tell him about my suspicions of Franklin and gave him the license plate number from the Mercedes. He finally asked me for my phone number and I gladly gave it to him.

I don't know why I trusted this man. Maybe it was because he was so fine, maybe because he paid for my breakfast, but just maybe because he seemed sincere and showed he cared. I also told him that Detective Matters was working on the case. Darrin knew who he was immediately and didn't seem like he liked that too much. He asked me not to tell him that I knew him. I thought that was a little strange but didn't think much else about it. I'd eventually ask him about it. But all Darrin said was that sometimes investigators and police didn't get along. Darrin seemed to have connections all over the place, so I was confident in him. He told me he'd meet me later on that night. I wondered if he really meant it. I knew he was working on a kidnapping case and that men say stuff that they really don't mean sometimes.

We parted our ways and I decided to go to the office. I was definitely happy about calling Darrin. I wanted to tell Janetta. I hope she wouldn't blow it up too big. Her only question would probably be, "*When do you plan on giving up the ass to him?*"

Chapter 18

When I arrived at the office, I saw Franklin's 1990 Blue Chevy Impala parked in front. I wondered what he was up to now. Inside, Janetta was with a customer. I waved at her and sat in the waiting area on the couch. I picked up a copy of Jet magazine and browsed through it. Feeling a little antsy, I got up and went toward the back to the bathroom. I passed Franklin's door and it was cracked. I tried to peek inside, but I couldn't see anything, so I put my ear up to the door. His phone rung.

Not sure who it was, but whoever was on the other line, Franklin stated, "He's dead, man." I assumed he was talking about Uncle Leon. Then I heard Franklin say, "I have a good alibi." Then I heard him say something about a dentist. Damn, what is going on with dentists? I was trying to listen more, but that's when Franklin got up and shut the door. I planted my back against the wall because I didn't know if he was going to see me or not. I put my ear up to the door again, but I really couldn't hear much. Then Franklin got loud, and said, "Well, I haven't got my money, and I want it, or I'm going to the police." Right after that, I felt a tap on my shoulder. I must have jumped at least a foot. It was Janetta.

"Girl, what are you doing?"

"I'm eaves-dropping, what does it look like?" I took her by the arm and led her to the front desk. "I think Franklin had something to do with Uncle Leon's murder or maybe even that Dennis Lowry from last night."

"What? Girl you crazy." She sat behind her desk. "Why would you think something like that? And by the way, you're hair really looks nice. About time you did something with that bush."

"Thank you, I guess. But anyway, I just heard Franklin telling somebody that if he doesn't get his money, he's going to the police. And he also said something about having a good alibi." I folded my arms and switched my weight on one foot. "Now you tell me, doesn't that sound suspicious?"

Janetta opened up a file and started typing. "I don't know girl. I don't think Franklin had anything to do with it. He's too big; he stutters and can hardly see. Plus him and Leon go way back."

Something didn't seem right to me and regardless who believed me, I had every intention of looking into it. I decided to change the subject. "Guess who I met for breakfast this morning?" I rested my elbows on the counter in front of Janetta's desk. She stopped typing and looked up at me. She was awaiting my answer.

"Darrin, girl." I was all smiles as I said his name. I was feeling like a little girl with a schoolgirl crush.

Janetta was getting excited for me. "What? Are you serious? Don't be lying. I can't believe you called that man. I'm glad, 'cause you just can't let anything fine like that just pass you by."

"Yeah, he even said he'd help me in investigating Uncle Leon's murder."

"Well that's good, but what about that detective who's working on the case, have you heard anything from him?"

"Not too much, it seems like we've been playing phone tag if anything. He did leave me a message though, and said that Donald Hamilton was out of town, during Uncle Leon's murder, and has been cleared as a suspect. So at least I don't have to worry about him anymore."

"Oh, well that's good. 'Cause you worried me to death about that man. But girl, I am so happy for you. You are finally stepping out of your box." Janetta continued typing away on the keyboard.

"Hey, I'm about to leave. If Franklin asks if I came around, just say no. I'll call you later."

Crossing the street, I thought about my meeting with Darrin later. Then I couldn't remember if I was supposed to call him or if he was going to call me. I also need to show him the contents in that box.

As I was crossing the street, I saw something red out the corner of my eye. I froze up for a second. It was a car about six or so feet away. My mind was going a mile a minute. Finally, I leaped to the side, falling and rolling towards the sidewalk. The contents in my purse flew everywhere. I got up immediately, and got a look at the back of the car. I can't believe it. A few more feet closer and that car would have made me into a pancake. It sped off fast, leaving a dust trail. I looked at the license plate, but all I could make out was C2D. The car was swerving so much and then turned at the corner. I dusted off my clothes, as well as the dirt in my hair. When I looked up, Janetta was running out of the building.

"Girl, are you alright? I seen that red car almost hit you." She was swiping dust off me as well. She turned me around, as if she was looking for injuries.

"Yeah, somebody just tried to kill me. Can you believe that shit?" My adrenaline was pumping. I was in shock; I couldn't believe what had just happened. We both looked at each other and then down the street. Tire marks were left behind, along with a cloud of dust. Looking back toward the building, Franklin was standing at the front door. He stared at us, and then went back inside. Janetta and I looked at each other in amazement.

"Did you happen to see who was inside?" Janetta asked me. We walked over to my car.

"No, I didn't." I was breathing so hard, then I realized my purse and everything inside it was still in the street. So I went back and picked up everything. Janetta helped me. However, I kept my eye on the road, in case the car decided to finish off the job.

After calming my nerves, Janetta asked if I was all right to drive home. I told her I was and to watch out for Franklin. She looked at me with unbelieving eyes and then went back inside, after telling me to call her when I got home.

I got in my car and wrote down the partial license plate number I remembered on a piece of paper: C2D. I drove home, constantly looking in the rearview mirror until I pulled into my driveway.

There was a message on the answering machine. The light frantically blinked at me. I pressed the button to listen.

"Just stay out of it. Just stay out of it," the voice said. I played it again, and then again. I didn't recognize the voice. I think it was computerized. But it was definitely a male's voice. I stood staring at the phone. I looked in each room to make sure no one was in my house. I also went down to the basement. I called Janetta and asked her where was Franklin. She stated he was in the back room with his door closed.

I called Sharon who was over at Mama's house. I asked her and Nevilla to come by to keep me company. I didn't tell her what happened. I didn't want to worry her.

I sat down at my kitchen table. My head dazed from the earlier events. Damn what is going on? A picture of Matthew and Uncle Leon sat on the end table in the living room. I peered at the photograph before I covered my hands over my face and rubbed my eyes. I lifted one of my hands off my face and kept one covering my forehead. I looked out the window and saw an image of Uncle Leon's face. I rubbed my eyes again, and the image went away.

Chapter 19

After dinner, Sharon decided to call it a night. "Well, let me get Nevilla to bed." Sharon lifted a sleepy Nevilla and cradled her in her arms. "Thanks for coming by. I really appreciate it, Sharon."

"Not a problem. I'll talk to you later."

After opening the door for them, I kissed Nevilla on the forehead and embraced Sharon around her shoulders. "Drive safe."

As I watched Sharon nestle Nevilla in the backseat, I realized I hadn't heard from Darrin. Disappointment washed through me. I guess I got my hopes up too high. I could have called him, but I decided not to.

After brewing a cup of tea, I retired in living room and turned on the television. Seeing the newspaper on the couch next me is when it dawned on me that I hadn't read my daily horoscope. Sitting my cup of tea on the end table, I opened the paper and turned to the horoscope section. *You may not know some of your loved ones as much as you think.* Taken by surprise, I sat the paper to the side, slouched down on the couch and laid my head back, as I thought about my horoscope.

Craving a bag of popcorn, I pulled myself up from the couch and went into the kitchen. As I waited for the popcorn to finish popping in the microwave, I felt a little chilly, so I turned up the heat to seventy-seven. Before going back into the kitchen, I looked out the front window. I could see into Mrs. Jenkins' living room. She had company over, a man at that. "Go ahead, Mrs. Jenkins," I chuckled to myself. They were seated in the living room watching television, and he had his arm around her. "How cute," I mumbled.

After popcorn and a movie, I dozed off. When I woke up, it was almost eleven. After deciding to call it a night and halfway up the stairs, the phone rung. It was Darrin. I was surprised he was calling me so late. He apologized, saying he was tied up with his kidnapping investigation, and lost track of the time. He also said he had some information that I'd be really interested in. He asked if it was too late for him to come over. I said no, although it was, but I really wanted to know what information he had. He'd ask if he could bring me anything. I told him no and quickly hung up the phone. Excited, yet nervous at the same time, I looked down at what I was wearing. I still had on the same outfit from breakfast with him earlier. I thought about changing, but what for. I did take off my T-shirt which left me wearing a blue tank top. I looked down at my breast. I didn't want to show too much cleavage. I also looked at my pouch for a stomach. Damn, I have to start doing sit-ups.

Sitting on the couch, I pulled out a cigarette. I better get my smoke on before he gets here. I had the metal box, and all of its contents, on the coffee table.

I got up when I heard my doorbell. Damn that was quick. "Who is it?" I asked, knowing it would be Darrin. I straighten up myself and ran my fingers through my hair.

"It's Franklin," the voice on the other end said.

What in the hell? I looked through the peephole. I couldn't believe it. Franklin was at my door, looking as if he had ran a marathon, with beads of sweat dancing on his forehead. I didn't know whether to answer the door or not. Was he here to kill me?

"Franklin, what are you doing here? It's late," I yelled through the door.

"I have to talk to you, Rahkel." He sounded out of breath, and I was concerned

"Franklin, let's talk tomorrow at the office, I'm expecting company any minute. I'll meet you at the office early in the morning." He didn't respond. "Franklin?" I looked through the peephole again. He was gone. What is going on? I rushed to the back door, to make sure he wasn't back there. He wasn't. Within fifteen minutes, I heard another knock.

"Darrin?" I yelled through the door.

"Yeah, it's me."

Opening the door, I looked past Darrin to make sure I didn't see Franklin or any one else. I even stepped out on the porch.

"What's wrong?" Darrin asked.

96

"Franklin just came by, something about he wanted to talk to me, not sure what about but I didn't open the door. Then he left. Something really strange is going on."

I closed the door behind him and locked all three locks on the door and I motioned for Darrin to sit on the couch as I walked into the kitchen.

"I'm about to make some coffee, do you want any?"

"Sure. You have a nice house, Rahkel. It has a nice woman's touch. That's what my place needs."

"Thanks, I've lived here for about ten years. The sellers were going through a very nasty divorce, so I got a really good deal on it."

I sat his coffee on a coaster and occupied the space next to him. I lit a cigarette. He looked over at me, as to say, *Could you put that out?* But I just smiled at him. I told him I have a ventilation fan, so I got up and turned it on. He seemed to be okay with that, as if he really had a choice. After all, it's my damn house.

"So what do you have for me?" I sat on the couch next to him with my legs furled under me. He reached for his leather-meeting bag, pulled out a few papers, and placed them on the table. He then pulled out his laptop and sat it on the table as well. He had his cell phone charging up in the socket next to my fish tank.

"Well first off, the license plate number you gave me for the Mercedes belongs to your uncle."

I almost choked on my coffee. I put the coffee mug down on the table and straightened my posture, with my cigarette still in hand.

"*What?* How could that be? My uncle never owned a Mercedes. He owned a Lexus, but not a Mercedes." I thought about it for a moment. "Well who was the person inside? It definitely wasn't my uncle."

"Well it gets more interesting. The person inside was probably a doctor by the name of Charles Simon. He was working for your uncle. Not sure what for, but I was able to pull your uncle's cell phone records and he made numerous calls to him a couple of months before his death and there were incoming and outgoing calls between the two just prior to his death." Darrin pulled more papers from his black bag. "And I got in contact with the dealership that sold that Mercedes and they said both Leon and Charles were present at the dealership when Leon bought the car. I talked with the dealership man, and he commented that your Uncle was buying it for Dr. Simon as a business gift. Whatever that meant." Darrin started typing something into his laptop.

After that startling news, I put my cigarette out and sipped on my coffee. Completely dumbfounded, I looked down at the floor and scratched my head. I was confused. I then showed Darrin the CD and the receipts. He agreed to take the CD with him. He said he might know of a computer guy named Stan who could retrieve the information off the CD.

"The coffee was great, but would you by any chance have a beer?"

"I think so."

In the kitchen, I grabbed the only beer I had from the refrigerator and poured myself a glass of Sutter Home. My intentions were to relax my nerves. I was really confused right now, frustrated, and upset all at the same time. I watched Darrin from the side. His arms bulged from his shirt; he was busy looking up some information on his laptop. I took a sip of wine. I tried to think about something else, like him. Wow, he looked so damn good. I thought of what Janetta said about his butt. I was hoping he'd get up to use the bathroom or something, so I could take a look for myself. I think he felt me staring at him, because he turned around slowly and smiled.

"You're very beautiful, Rahkel."

I smiled, nervously. "Thanks, Darrin. You're not so bad yourself."

That did it. He could've had me that night, if he'd said the word. Get a hold of yourself, Rahkel. How could I be thinking about sex when someone's trying to kill me?

We both were relaxed as I told him about my family. He told me about his as well, including his older sister, Jaime, who has leukemia who is being cared for in a nursing home.

"I'd like for you to meet Jaime one day."

"I would like that."

Before I knew it, it was almost one in the morning. He stood and took me by the hand, pulling me up off the couch.

"Well, it's getting late." He smiled, leaned in and kissed me on the lips. It was unexpected but certainly welcomed. "I'll continue to look into this for you. If you need anything at all, or if you're in trouble, give me a call."

"Thanks, I will. I appreciate you coming by and sharing the information with me. I swear my head is swimming right now. However, I will be honest with you, Darrin, I'm afraid. Someone is trying to kill me and I don't know who."

"Try not to worry too much. You have a good night."

Before closing the door, I watched him walk away. Janetta was right; he does have a nice ass.

I climbed into bed thinking of Darrin.

Chapter 20

With Darrin's kiss still sewn to my lips, stitched into my skin, I woke up early the next morning and went to the nursing home to pick up my paycheck and put in a few hours. Afterward, I drove to the office, while trying to call Franklin on his cell phone, but he didn't answer, so I left him a message. Then, I called the office, but there was no answer.

I expected to see Janetta seated behind her desk, filing her nails, but the CLOSED sign hung on the door. Maybe she was running late, so I unlocked the door and went in. Looking from the digital read out of the time on my cell phone, the office should have been opened an hour ago.

Walking to the back, I peeked inside Franklin's office. I grabbed the accounts payable receipts and went into Uncle Leon's office. Since I was there, I figured I'd get a little work in. Opening the file drawer, I retrieved the deposit books. When I closed the drawer and turned around, I came face to face with Franklin. Startled, I bumped into the file cabinet and dropped a file on the floor. Franklin didn't look good. He looked like he'd been up all night and he smelled like liquor.

"What's going on? What's wrong with you?" I asked. He was scaring the shit out of me.

"It's a long story, but I need you to meet me tonight? I'm taking a chance of meeting you here, but I knew you would be here. I have something to give you?" He walked closer to me. I held my hand out for him not to come any closer. "Rahkel, I'm not going to hurt you, I want to help you. You have no idea what's going on."

"What? What do you mean? Whatever you got to give me, why can't you just give it to me now?" Franklin was acting strange, and I didn't like it one bit.

"Because someone is probably watching." He looked over my shoulder as Janetta was unlocking the door. "Meet me at Blue Dolphins Diner tonight at eight." He backed up, and darted for the back door before Janetta could see him.

Damn why does everyone want to meet there? The last person who planned to meet me there was dead. I ran out the door after Franklin to tell him to meet me somewhere else, but he was gone.

Shaking my head, I went back inside and locked the backdoor.

"Girl, you wouldn't believe the hangover I had last night." Janetta had her hair wrapped up in a scarf with no makeup on, but her eyebrows were nicely arched. She pulled out two McDonalds breakfast sandwiches, sat down and started *grubbin'*.

"Franklin just left." I said. "He looked a mess. What the hell is going on around here?"

"Where's he been? I have been taking so many messages for him. That man ain't never nowhere to be found. I was surprised he was in here that one day."

"I don't know, but I'm supposed to meet him tonight. He says he has something to give me."

"Well don't ask me to go, 'cause I'm going to be resting tonight. I hope you don't mind me leaving early. I called the temp, Emily, and she's going to come in here later and finish up the rest of my shift." Janetta looked so tired.

A customer came in the front door. I left Janetta up front to attend to him, and returned to Uncle Leon's office and sat down in his chair. He had pictures of Nevilla, Sharon and one of me in his office. I finished up the bookkeeping and the payroll, and cut everyone's checks. I had a feeling that's why Janetta even came in today, since it was payday.

After I was done, I called Darrin, he didn't answer. His voice mailed picked up so I left a message. I even tried to call Detective Matters. But, of course, he didn't pick up, so I left him a message as well. I let my head fall into the pile of papers on the desk and released a long sigh. "Oh God, why me?"

Later that evening I met with Franklin. At first, I was hesitant, but I wanted to know what he wanted to give me. Detective Matters never called me back and neither did Darrin, but I figured Darrin was busy, but I was sure, or I guess you could say hopeful, that he would call me back before the night was over.

Arriving at Blue Dolphins Diner at 7:30, it was actually pretty packed. I was surprised, but then again it was bingo night in one of the large rooms adjacent to the diner. I looked around before I got out of my car. I didn't see anything that looked suspicious. I also looked inside to see if I saw any men seated alone. Just a couple, but they looked harmless. I couldn't believe I was doing this, again. However, I knew Franklin, so I wasn't that concerned. I left my purse under the seat in my car and brought in my pack of cigarettes, my cell phone, a ten dollar bill which I stuck in the pocket of my sweater, and my keys.

As I walked up to the entrance, a car pulled up with a man inside, alone. Maybe he was nobody or maybe he was somebody. While the waitress led me to a table, I looked over my shoulder at him. I made sure she sat me next to a window. I pulled my hat down a little and glanced outside. The man sat in his car. Maybe he was waiting for someone. He had long blonde hair and mustache, that biker look.

I ordered a cup of coffee, and a glass of water. I looked at the clock on my cell phone. It was exactly 7:45. Pulling out a cigarette, I pulled the ashtray close to me, as I looked back at the car in the parking lot. It was gone. When I turned back around, as I was about to light my cigarette, I saw Franklin walking towards me. He was much cleaner than before. He'd even changed. I stared at him. He smiled at me.

He took off his jacket and placed it across the seat. He had a hard time fitting in the booth. He moved the table closer to me and sat down.

He let out a loud, long sigh and glanced outside. He then stopped the waitress, as she was passing by, and ordered eggs, bacon, steak, pancakes, with a side order of grits. "Do you mind paying?"

I frowned up my face. "I guess so." I lit my cigarette and looked over at the couple next to us. They were talking loud. "So, what's up? Lets make this quick." I didn't want to sound rude, but I couldn't believe he had the nerve to ask me to pay for his food. Besides, everything about Franklin was now questionable. I was planning on getting to the bottom of all this mess. Franklin appeared agitated and asked me for a cigarette. I know he doesn't smoke, but I handed him one anyway. He kept looking outside. His legs were even shaking like he was on crack or something.

Franklin leaned toward me after looking outside again. He spoke in a low whisper. "Look, there are a lot of things you didn't know about your uncle. First off, I'm on the run 'cause I'm scared for my life right now. When we're finished here, I'll give you something. It's in my pocket. I'm leaving the country, so this is probably the last time you'll ever see me." There was something about Franklin's eyes. He balled up his fist. There was a long silence. He sat back in his seat. "Now, first of all, where's the box of receipts and CD that Leon gave to Janetta?"

I was wondering how he knew about the box. I wondered if Janetta said anything. No, she wouldn't do that. I played dumb.

"What do you mean?"

Franklin banged his fist on the table. "Damn it, Rahkel, just tell me where it is?"

I put my hands out toward Franklin, trying to quiet him. I looked around, the loud couple next to us stopped in mid-sentence and stared at us, then continued there conversation when I gave them a dirty look. Franklin realized how loud he was and glanced outside again, then back to me. "Okay, sorry. Well, at least tell me you mailed the box to the address that Leon gave you?"

I didn't know whether to answer that question or not. Finally, I said, "No I didn't."

Franklin balled his fist and hit the table again. "God, damn Rahkel, why not?"

This time, people at a few tables in front of us stopped there conversations, turned around and glared at us. I smiled at them and grabbed hold of Franklin's wrist.

"Look, after Uncle Leon died, I forgot," I said, wondering why it was so important that I mail it.

"Okay, well I need the metal box from you? I need it now." Franklin stood up as the woman was placing his large plate of food on the table.

I looked at him with evil eyes. "No I can't. I'm not giving it to you. Why the hell should I trust you?"

"Because if you don't, you might regret it." Franklin's eyes were stern.

I looked up at the waitress. She glanced at both of us. I'm sure she was wondering what was going on. She quickly sat the plate down and walked away.

In a quiet and polite way I leaned toward Franklin, with both elbows on the table and looked up at him. "Did you kill my uncle?" I wanted to ask him that question for sometime now. And, there was no better time than the present.

Franklin stared at me, and shook his head. "Rahkel, your uncle...."

All of a sudden, the glass shattered across our table. The noise was so loud. I closed my eyes and I could feel pieces of glass hit against my face. I opened my eyes slightly and Franklin was hit in the side of his head. A bullet must have pierced through the side. I'll never forget the sight. Brain matter exploded from the side of his head. There was so much blood. His eyes were still opened. He was still staring at me, as he fell sideways to the floor. I screamed and hit the floor. There were several screams throughout the diner. People were running and scattering very quickly. I crawled under the table with my eyes tightly closed and arms shielding me.

Out of nowhere, a man asked if Franklin was all right, and checking for a pulse. He shook his head at me, got up and ran. I didn't know what to do. I stared at Franklin's dead body lying lifeless, full of blood, on the floor. I was horrified. I then remembered Franklin saying he wanted to give me something, and that it was in his pocket. I didn't know if he was talking about his pants pocket or jacket. So I quickly checked both pockets of his pants, nothing. I crawled to his side, reached in his coat jacket, pulled out a small bag and took off running. Police were already pulling up to the diner when I was running out. I wasn't even thinking. I knew I should stay. The police probably would want to question me, but I didn't even think about that, until I was halfway home. I thought about turning around, but I didn't. I didn't want to go back to Blue Dolphins Diner, not ever. I looked down at my clothes and there was blood all over my T-shirt. I floored the gas and sped off home.

As I drove the rest of the way home, I opened up the bag. There was a key inside. I had no idea what it was for, but I had three keys and had no clue as to what they opened. However, if I'm not mistaken this key looked very similar to the one I'd found behind the painting. I stuck the key back in the paper bag and placed the small bag inside my purse, constantly looking in my rearview mirror. I was shaking all over. My heart raced and beat so fast, I thought it would jump out of my chest at any minute.

As I pulled into my driveway, the ringing of my cell phone scared me half to death. It was Darrin. He'd just heard there were shots fired at the Blue Dolphins Diner. I told him to meet me at my house as soon as possible.

Chapter 21

It's been several weeks since Franklin was murdered, and the police still didn't have a clue. Everywhere I go, I constantly looked over my shoulder; wondering if or when would I be next. Keeping Sharon, Nevilla or Darrin close by, or going over to Mama's, kept me sane. Darrin had taken me to the gym a few times to relieve my stress, which was a good thing. I've noticed my stomach getting a little flatter.

Detective Matters called me back the morning after Franklin's murder. He was coming up with the same notion I had about Franklin killing Uncle Leon, but now that he's dead, neither me nor Detective Matters knows what the hell was going on. Not too long ago, I met Matters and the police at Uncle Leon's office. They drilled me with a bunch of questions they had previously asked me: Why was I meeting Franklin, why didn't I stay after he was shot, what type of relationship me and Franklin had and on and on? If I didn't know any better, I would've thought they were labeling me as a suspect. I was mostly truthful with them, except I still haven't told them about the key in the brown paper bag. I wanted to find out what that key was for.

Detective Matters got a search warrant and was looking into Wilson & Carters accounts to see if they had enemies of some sort, bad business deals and the like. This whole thing has taken a heavy toll on me. Darrin said he'd help me run the business; that was if they didn't shut it down and Janetta agreed to stay as well. I hired the temps, Emily and Jessica, permanently and Rob agreed to take on more hours and more days when needed.

Janetta said she was going to call her cousin, Gary, who may be interested in moving down here to work at the business. Sharon even said she'd fill in sometimes when needed, if Janetta needs to take some time off.

Considering all the madness that was going on, I must admit, I didn't think I'd meet someone like Darrin. Still seeing each other it's been three months, and we still haven't had sex yet. It's been close though. But then again, there's been so much going on. Every other day or so he's been coming by or calling me to see how I've been doing.

Since it was Saturday, and I was bored, I agreed to watch Nevilla. She always cheered me up. Plus Darrin hasn't called.

I agreed to let Nevilla's two little friends, Sasha and Libby, have a sleep over. Wrong idea. I made them go downstairs. They were starting to get on my nerves. I called Janetta to see what she was up to. She was going on a date, of course. She's been going out with some guy for about three weeks now. That's a long time for Janetta. Maybe they were getting serious. I told her I was bored and me and the girls were coming over to help her get ready for her date.

"So which color, girl, blue or black? I gotta look fine for Michael. He's taking me out to dinner at a nice restaurant with waterfalls and stuff." Janetta held up two outfits while I sat on her bed. The girls were downstairs watching television.

"I like that blue strapless dress you have." I felt happy for her.

"Nah, the blue dress makes my hips look too big. I'll wear the black one." She picked up a large bag of chips and started crunching on them. She offered me some and I took a few.

"Why are you eating? I thought y'all were going out to eat?" I said with my mouth full of chips.

"Well a snack ain't never hurt nobody," she said, grabbing a few more out of the bag.

After thirty minutes at Janetta's house, I could tell the girls were ready to go. "Okay, girlfriend, well you and Michael have fun. Tell me all about it tomorrow."

"You know I will, girl." Janetta started laughing.

Me and the girls left and stopped by the grocery store on our way home. When we got home, I went upstairs, put on my pajamas and sat on my bed. I could hear the girls downstairs laughing and having a ball. I'd got them a few movies from the video store earlier. They had all the snacks and movies they could want. I turned on the television in my room. I looked over at my nightstand and saw Darrin's business card. I suddenly thought about him. I should call him. I don't always want to wait until he calls me. I thought about how wonderful he was. I was eager for the moment when we would finally make love.

I gave in. I picked up the phone and dialed his number. The phone rang about six times and then it went to his voicemail. I listened to his entire message, because it reminded me how sexy his voice was. I visualized his pearly whites as he spoke. *"Hello you reached Darrin Miller. Leave a message and I'll call you back at my earliest convenience."* I left a short message. I didn't even expect him to answer. It was Saturday night and the weekend before Halloween. He was probably out having a good time, where I needed to be.

I decided to go downstairs and pop a bag of popcorn. The *TV Guide* indicated that there was a good movie about to come on. Downstairs, the girls had there blankets spread out on the floor and eating the pizza I bought from the store.

"Hi Auntie Rahkel," Nevilla said.

"Hi Rahkel," the other two girls said.

"Hi girls, I'm just going to pop me some popcorn and I'll be out your way." They were watching some Halloween kiddy movie. Back upstairs, I checked my cell phone; I had a missed call. I didn't even hear my phone. I looked at the number and it was Darrin. After a few seconds, the phone started to ring again.

"Hello?" I answered.

"Hey, baby, how are you? Is something wrong?" I loved when he called me baby. It made me feel special.

"No Darrin. Just wanted to hear your voice. My niece and her friends are over having a slumber party. So what are you about to do?" I wondered.

"Well there's this party me and Calvin are on our way to."

"Oh okay."

"But tomorrow, I'm meeting with someone about that PO Box address you gave me and the CD. I'm pretty sure I'll have some answers for you on that tomorrow. But I still don't have anything on that partial license plate number you gave me." I could hear music in the background.

"Okay, well just call me tomorrow if you find out anything or even if you don't, give me a call." I was definitely smiling when I said that.

"Yes, I will do that." He said in a sexy deep voice. "Do you have plans tomorrow night?"

"Nothing. I mean no." I was anticipating what he was going to ask me.

"Well, I hope you like Italian food, because I'm taking you to El Tonio's tomorrow at 7:30, so be ready."

"Yes. That sounds good to me. I'll be looking forward to it." I cut the conversation short, because it seemed like he was in a hurry. Plus I'd already received the answer I wanted. "Well, just call me tomorrow, Darrin. I'll let you get back to your party. Have some fun for me."

"Alright, baby, but I'll be thinking about you."

"Okay, bye." I waited until he hung up the phone.

Once the call ended, I tossed the phone on the bed and jumped up and down like a schoolgirl. I was smiling so hard. Then I stopped for a moment. It seemed weird for me to be happy especially because of Uncle Leon and Franklin. And then I felt guilty, mostly about blaming Franklin for Uncle Leon's death.

For the first time in several years, I really liked someone, and was excited about dating again. Then my emotions started to shift again. I felt sort of scared, thinking of who could have killed Franklin and Uncle Leon, and if I was next. I tried not to think about that too much, but it kept entering my mind.

I sat down on the bed, and after smoking a cigarette, ate my popcorn and watched one of the best movies I'd seen in a long time.

Chapter 22

I met Janetta for an early lunch at the mall to tell her about my dinner plans with Darrin. Since Sierra had plans for that night, she tagged along; she wanted to pick up an outfit.

Wanting to buy something to wear on my date with Darrin as well, I wasn't up on what's hot, but I knew Janetta or Sierra would help me out. Besides, Sierra was a fashionista, so with those two, I knew I couldn't go wrong.

"Guess what?" I said, walking to the table where Janetta and Sierra were seated in the food court. I'd just come out of the jewelry store. I had Sierra to order me something from the Chinese restaurant. I sat two bags beside me. "I found a really cute bracelet." I pulled it out the bag.

"Did you find any cute men while you were in there?" Janetta asked, pulling out a large egg roll from her bag.

Sierra laughed. "Yeah Rahkel, didn't you see all those fine men that went in there?" Sierra is almost as bad as Janetta, that's why they always got along. Sierra is pretty, but she doesn't date all that much, but she does have plenty of male friends. She's supposed to be starting school in a few weeks in Illinois. Daddy gave her ten thousand dollars toward her schooling and she's going to get the rest in loans.

"I have a man now, and his name happens to be Darrin," I heard myself say, not realizing how stupid it sounded until after I said it.

Janetta and Sierra looked at each other and then at me. Then we all fell out with laughter. I grabbed the bag of food Sierra had gotten me and pulled out the box of pork-fried rice.

"Well, he may not be *my* man, but we're going on a date tonight to El Tonio's. You know that is like the hottest Italian restaurant in town." I was happy.

"Y'all are going to El Tonio's? You go my sister girl, that restaurant is very nice." Sierra gave me a high five.

Taking a sip of diet coke, a babies' cry caught my attention, so I glanced around. My eyes landed on a man staring directly at me. Or at least it seemed like he was. He was standing outside the bathroom area. I turned back around. I looked up at Janetta and Sierra. "Look toward the bathroom you guys; do you see a man with a blue sweater and baseball cap on over there? Is he still looking this way?"

Janetta and Sierra both looked on both sides of me.

"What man? I don't see anyone," Sierra said.

"I don't either. Was he cute or something?" Janetta stuffed a spoon full of fried rice in her mouth.

When I turned around, he was gone. "Okay well whatever." I looked behind me one more time just to make sure. That was strange.

"So girl, what about Darrin? Are you excited about tonight?" Sierra asked.

"Yes very." I thought about telling Sierra and Janetta about what's been going on with Franklin's and Uncle Leon's cases. Even though Janetta knew some of the stuff already, Sierra didn't know too much of anything. I didn't want to spoil the moment so I decided not to bring it up.

Taking a bite of food, I turned my attention toward Janetta. "So enough about me, how did your date go with Michael?"

"Oh just wonderful, girlfriend. Michael is so sweet. You know he rubbed my feet last night. That man certainly has the touch. And boy can he put it on me. I think last night topped some of the best sex. I had the most amazing orgasm. And yes girlfriend he can eat it just as well."

Sierra and I laughed, although I was nearly embarrassed by her statement.

"Yeah I know how that is," Sierra said.

Janetta and I looked at each other, before we all broke into laughter.

As soon as I got home from the mall, Darrin called.

"Hi, Ms. Lady, are you ready for tonight?"

"Yes I sure am. So how should I dress?" That was a crazy question since I already had picked up a new outfit at the mall.

"As long as it's sexy, I don't care. And regardless of what you wear, I'm sure you'll look beautiful." It looked like someone was trying to win him some points. Well, it was working.

I decided to have him pick me up, because it was going to take a while for me to get dressed. Janetta came over to do my makeup and Sierra spiral curled my hair. I didn't realize I could look this good.

After all was said and done, I took one last look in the mirror. I was very happy with the image looking back at me. I hadn't gotten dressed up in a very long time, and I was feeling good about myself. I grabbed the small black purse that I'd also bought at the mall and waited downstairs by the front door.

While I rummaged through the kitchen drawer, looking for scissors to cut a piece of thread from the bottom of my skirt, I noticed a picture of me, Uncle Leon and Nevilla in the drawer. I pulled it out. I hadn't seen this picture in a long time. I held it up, and it made me realize how much I missed Uncle Leon. I saw a white Suburban pull into the driveway. I put the picture back, and headed outside, locking the front door behind me.

When I was walking down the steps, Darrin climbed out of the SUV and leaned against the door on the passenger's side.

"Damn you look sexy as hell." He walked up to me and turned me around. "Damn girl." He gave me a hug and then we kissed passionately.

"You look handsome yourself."

Darrin had on tan slacks with a button down black dress shirt. Whatever cologne he wore made me want to jump him right then and there.

Darrin opened the passenger door for me. "I sure am a lucky man to be taking out such a beautiful lady."

I looked at Darrin and smiled. I loved when he called me beautiful. He really was making me feel good with the compliments. Was it too good to be true?

When we pulled up to the restaurant, the valet opened my door, as Darrin rushed around to give him the key and receive the valet ticket. Damn I wish it could be like this forever. I was totally in the moment and didn't want it to ever end. Tonight will probably be the night; we both had waited long enough. I know I sure had

It was my first time at El Tonio's, and I'd heard a lot about it.

"Miller," Darrin informed the woman behind the host stand.

She smiled and immediately seated us. There were men playing violins off to the side as we walked down the aisle.

From the corner of my eye, I watched Darrin. It seemed like he had everything planned. I love when men plan things; it makes it so much easier.

As we were seated, a bottle of wine was chilling in a silver bucket of ice. It was my favorite: Sutter Home.

"You remembered what I drink." I picked up the bottle and looked at it.

"Yes, I pay attention to detail."

I smiled at him and put it back in the bucket of ice.

Nervous, my palms were clammy and I kept fidgeting. I thought about pulling out a compact mirror to look at myself. I wondered if any of my makeup had smeared. I excused myself and went to the restroom. As soon as I walked in, they had mirrors everywhere. I looked over to the corner and there were small baskets lined up, some had tampons, others had small packets of lotion, condoms and mints. I tend to always judge a restaurant by there bathrooms. And, this one tipped the scale. I took a condom and put it in my purse. I'm sure he had one, but just in case. Soft velour benches sat in front of the mirrors. I sat down and examined my makeup. Pulling the compact from my purse, I touched up my make up. Then, I stood in front of the mirror, and twirled around. My skirt was so short it made my ass look bigger. But that's alright. I adjusted my strapless top and pulled it up a little. Damn, I hope I didn't look too slutty. Typically, I would have never worn such an outfit.

When I returned to the table, Darrin had poured me a glass of wine.

He smiled at me when I sat down. "Is everything alright?"

"Yes, just had to freshen up a bit. Darrin this is really a nice restaurant." I scooted closer to him, since we were seated at a round booth. I nudged him on the arm.

"Only the best for the best," he said, as he wrapped his arm around me, pulling me closer in to him.

A waiter came by and sat two glasses of water on the table. We glanced at each other. I was curious to know what he was thinking.

At the table across from us, flames from the skillet of steak fajitas was something to see, as the chef prepared stir-fry on the side, tossing it up from the pan, as if flipping pancakes. It was kind of exciting. This definitely was not the Blue Dolphins Diner.

As the phone rung, I silently fussed at myself for not putting it on vibrate. It was Mama. She knows I'm out on a date. I sent the call to voicemail. Knowing Mama, she probably wanted to know what was going on before it even started. I know what she's thinking, *"Did he pull the chair out for you?"* *"What type of shoes did he have on?"* *"Is he being a gentleman?"*

After we placed our orders, I excused myself to the bathroom again. What in the hell was wrong with me? I didn't know why I was feeling so nervous. I took several deep breaths before leaving the restroom.

As I passed by the payphone, a man was on it. His back was turned to me, but I heard him hang up the telephone after I'd passed him. Then I could feel him so close behind me. I stopped abruptly. He bumped into me as he passed by. I looked at him, but he had his head down. He didn't look up at all, and the idiot didn't even say excuse me. I yelled after him, but he kept walking, and fast I might add.

I watched as he turned the corner heading toward the front of the restaurant. He had on dark sunglasses and a large hat.

When I returned to the table, I told Darrin what happened. He told me not to worry about it. But something wasn't sitting right with me. I did however take his advice and didn't worry about it, at least for tonight. I wanted to enjoy the rest of the evening with Darrin.

After dinner, we went to the movies. We saw a twisted romantic drama about a man and a woman who fell in love in a psychic ward. It was interesting.

Darrin invited me back to his place. I told him that would be fine, but I wanted to go by my place to get a few things.

When we pulled up to the house, I gave him a quick peck on the cheek. "I'll be right back." When I reached the porch, I looked back at him, and smiled.

All evening we hadn't really talked much about the case. I was wondering however if he'd found out any new information since the police wasn't having much luck.

As soon as I opened the door, I noticed the kitchen light was off. I never turned that light off when I leave the house. I looked up the stairs and the ceiling light gently swung. Panic shot throughout me, as I looked down at the floor and saw something smeared, but I couldn't tell what. I bent down, wiped my finger across the floor and stared at the red residue on the tips of my fingers. It couldn't be. Backing up, my eyes roamed from the kitchen to the living room to the window by the stairs. I slowly reached behind me to turn the doorknob, while holding tightly onto my purse.

As I turned around to walk out the door, I screamed.

Darrin stood in the doorway. "What's wrong?" He paused. "I wanted to see if I could use your bathroom."

"I think someone broke into my house." Shoving him in his chest and moving him out the way, I walked backward looking into the living room.

He looked down at the floor. "What is on your floor?" He bent down, examining it with his eyes.

"I don't know, but it's red. Let's go." Closing the door, we walked back to his truck.

Staring at each other in disbelief, I tried to gather my thoughts. I pulled the cell phone from my purse. The battery was running low, and as soon as I tried to dial, the phone turned off.

"Let me use your phone, my cell phone is dead."

He immediately reached in his pocket and pulled it out. I'm sure at this moment I was looking terrified.

"Are your doors locked?" I asked him.

He pressed the knobs and locked them quickly. "I should go in and check your house."

"No, I want the police to check. Two people are already dead. We don't need to be next."

As tears welled in my eyes, I tried not to fall apart, but I was. I kept glancing up at the house making sure I didn't see anyone. I looked across the street at Mrs. Jenkins house; her porch and bedroom lights were on. I thought I heard something, so I looked behind me, on the side and on the ground from inside the truck.

Darrin placed his hand on my shoulder. "Alright, calm down, Rahkel, everything's gonna be alright."

"Yeah, I hope so."

He put his arm around me, and held me for a moment while I still had his cell phone in my hand.

Dialing 911, I kept a watch on the house. I took a few quick deep breaths and pulled away from him when they answered.

"I need the police. Someone's broken into my house."

"Where do you live?" The female operator on the other end asked.

"555 Langley Avenue. It's a white and blue house."

"What is your name?" Her voice was very stale.

"Rahkel Williams. Can you hurry up and send them?" I had both hands on the cell phone. Then I moved it to the other ear.

I was shaking, and I knew I was borderline hypertension. I glanced over at Darrin, he was looking passed me at my house.

"I'll be right back, okay?" he said, as he was opening his car door.

I pulled the phone from my ear. "No! Where the hell are you going? You sit here with me and wait until the police get here." He wasn't about to leave me in the car alone. I held tight to his shirt. Just when I realized what I was doing, I let go. Realizing how afraid I was, he closed his door and locked it.

"Hello, Ma'am? Hello?" The operator called out.

"Yes!" I shouted.

"Are you there at the residence now?"

"Yes I am here?" I was starting to get annoyed.

"Ma'am, we'll send police right over." As soon as I hung up, I released a sigh of relief.

Darrin reached over and took me by the hand.

I laid my head back against the seat. "I can't believe this. Do you think someone's trying to kill me?"

"No. Don't think like that, baby."

I sighed again. This was like a bad dream turned nightmare. I combed my fingers through my hair, wanting to scream. "So did you find out any information about my uncle?" I asked, trying to get some light of all of this.

"Well a friend of mine has your CD. He hasn't gotten back to me on if he was able to retrieve any information on it, but I'll give him a call

Monday." I looked toward the house again. I looked behind me to see if there were any police coming. I heard the sirens, but it soon faded away.

"I was going to tell you later, but as far as the PO Box address you gave me, it belonged to a dentist by the name of Dennis Lowry."

"What?" I yelled. Sitting erect in the seat, I faced him. I could feel a frightened feeling come over my entire body. I think I startled Darrin, because his eyes grew big. "I can't believe this." I looked down and then back up toward the house. Lowering my head, I covered my eyes in distress.

"What's wrong?" Darrin leaned closer to me.

"Remember that was the same man that I was going to meet at the Blue Dolphins Diner. He's now dead." I was so confused and scarred out of my mind. What in the hell is going on?

"Oh yeah that's right. Okay, you have to trust me, Rahkel; we're going to find some answers real soon and get this whole situation cleared up."

I'm sure Darrin was trying to make me feel better, but the fact of the matter was that someone had broken into my house, and was obviously trying to kill me.

Soon after, I could hear and see the red sirens flashing against the dashboard. Climbing out of the truck, I walked toward them. So did Darrin.

I looked at the time on Darrin's cell phone which I was still holding. Anger rose in me; it took the police twenty minutes to get here. I could've been dead by now.

One of them asked me for my name and took down information. The other police officer went on the other side and started asking Darrin questions.

Finally, the two officers, with Darrin and me in tow, walked toward the house. It was so strange, because even though I had all these people with me, I was still frightened to go inside my house. Maybe I was afraid of what I'd find or not find.

Darrin, a police officer and me walked upstairs. The other examined the red residue on the floor.

I stopped halfway up the stairs and turned around. "What is that, by the way?"

The police officer rubbed a piece of tissue paper against the floor and smelled it. "I think it's ketchup mixed with something." He smelled it again. "We have to take samples just to make sure."

Upstairs, everything looked fine so far. In my room, I quickly grabbed a small suitcase and filled it with clothes. I did not intend to stay here tonight, that was for damn sure. Darrin watched me and asked if I needed any help. I told him no. I have no idea how I'm going to be able to come back here. I'd be scared out of my mind being here alone.

Darrin looked under the bed and opened the closet door. He picked up the picture of Matthew from the nightstand. "This must be your son."

"Yes it is." I was stuffing everything I could in the suitcase. I figured tomorrow, I'd go to Mama's.

"You can stay with me as long as you'd like," Darrin said. He took my hands in his and kissed me gently on the lips. Then he zipped up the suitcase.

"Thank you, but I'll probably stay at my Mama's house." If I was to stay at his house, while he was at work, I'd have to be alone, and I definitely didn't want that.

"You should install an alarm. That's what you need to do, so you won't have this problem again. I have a friend who works at Brinks Security. I can talk to him for you. He could probably hook you up." Darrin suggested.

Actually, that wasn't a bad idea. The other police officer came up stairs. "It looks like whoever broke in, came through your back door. The knob wasn't damaged though. But it was left slightly unopened. You might want to call a locksmith tonight to get the locks changed." He was writing something on a notepad.

"Well I didn't leave the door open when I left," I said out loud. This was getting worse. Does someone really have a key to my house? I looked over at Darrin. He was already on the phone making the call to a locksmith.

"You can come down tonight or tomorrow to make out your police report, but I have all the information I need for right now. I dusted for finger prints on your door knob, so we'll let you know."

"I'll be down tomorrow, if that's okay."

"Sure Ma'am." I noticed the police officer looking down at my chest. How rude. I cleared my throat and pulled up my top.

118

After having the door knobs changed, I was exhausted. Darrin insisted that he pay for it, and I didn't put up an argument.

"I can bring you back tomorrow to get your car," Darrin said.

"I really don't want to come back here, so I'll follow you to your place."

While driving, I kept looking in the rear view mirror. Depending on what the police have to say tomorrow when I talk to them, I really didn't know what I was going to do. I was frustrated and frightened.

Darrin pulled into the parking lot of a liquor store. A nervous wreck, I sat idle as he darted inside. Desperately needing a drink, I smiled when he came out of the store, holding up a bag. I figured he was getting me something, probably a bottle of wine.

We pulled up into a townhome community. Darrin lived in a gated secured area. This was what I needed, security. He punched in a code and the gates slowly opened, I followed quickly behind him. We pulled up to a two-level red brick townhome, which looked different at night.

Hopping out of his truck, Darrin jogged up to my car and helped me with my bags. He was really going all out to make me feel comfortable, and I appreciated it more than he'll ever realize.

Inside, he carried the bags upstairs, before pouring me a glass of wine. After we sat and talked for a few, he went upstairs, and returned with massage oil. He took off my strapped high heel shoes and rubbed my feet. This soon led to him taking off my shirt, massaging my back. I was very tense, but when he finished, I was very relaxed, all the while he was telling me not to worry about my house and that everything would turn out just fine.

After three glasses of wine, I was beginning to forget about the break in. Wearing nothing but a black strapless bra and lace G-string, Darrin picked me up over his shoulder and carried me into this bedroom. Laying me down on the massively large bed, he took his time and kissed me from head to toe, while taking off my bra and masterfully pulling down my G-string.

Crawling up beside me, he stroked his fingers through my hair, as we gazed into each other's eyes, sending chills throughout me. Sliding his hands gently over my breasts, he kissed them softly. I was in heaven. I haven't been touched like this in a long time. Damn, this felt so wonderful. Spending a full hour on foreplay, concentrating on nothing but pleasing me, he knew exactly what he was doing, and I wasn't complaining.

Bodies intertwined, with magical ease, he eased his masculinity inside me. Wanting to scream, all that escaped was an explosive moan, as his massive hands grabbed me around my waist, as he gently stoked the burning fire between my thighs. Tightly, my hands wrapped around his muscular biceps, as he pushed deeper and harder inside of me. In an explosive euphoric state, my mouth wide opened, I wrapped my thighs around his waist and prayed it would never end, as a single tear dropped. For the first time, in a long time, I felt safe. Can it please be like this every time?

As Darrin spooned me, I couldn't stop thinking about how amazing the sex was. I'd finally had my first orgasm and it was out of this world. Now I know what Janetta meant when she talked about orgasms. If I was dreaming, I didn't want to wake up. His body was so strong, but he was gentle when he needed to be.

He held me in his arms until I fell asleep, but I woke up a few times throughout the night. I looked at the clock on the nightstand; it showed three thirteen. Darrin was fast asleep, as he softly snored in my face. Turning my back to him, I pulled the covers just under my chin.

Unable to sleep, I looked out of the bedside window, gazing out at the moon, thinking about my house, about Uncle Leon, and about my life. Was I going to be next? Who was looking to hurt or kill me? Why?

Before closing my eyes, an image of my house and me, Sharon and Nevilla, appeared in the night sky. I blinked a couple of times and the images went away. Reaching for Darrin, I grabbed his hand, pulled his arm over across my waist and clenched onto it as hard as I could. He moved slightly. I took a deep breath. How could something horrible and, at the same time something great, be happening to me?

Chapter 23

The next morning, Darrin offered to take off from work at the gym to go down to the police station with me, but I told him he didn't have to. I wanted to take my suitcase of clothes with me, but he insisted that I leave them at his place. I figured I'd come back later on today to get them. On one hand, I didn't want things to go too fast between Darrin and me. However, on the other hand I liked him a lot; and after last night, damn that man's got me hooked.

His sister, Jaime, called while he was getting dressed for work. I learned later that a week ago, she was transferred from the nursing home to the hospital for chemotherapy. I felt bad, especially since he hadn't mentioned anything about it to me. He said he was going to visit her after work, but he was still going to call his friend to see about having an alarm system installed in my house. Darrin is so considerate. But even with an alarm system, I was still concerned about returning home. It was going to take some time.

When I left Darrin's house, I realized I hadn't called mama back and nobody knew anything about the break in last night. I figured I'd drive by my house and then to mama's house before I went down to the police station. I didn't want to worry her about it, but I did need to tell her.

Nine missed calls and four messages, two from Sharon, one from Detective Matters and the rest from Mama. I listened to the message from Detective Matters. He heard about the break in and wanted me to ask for him when I went down to the police station to give my report. And, he wanted to know how I knew Darrin Miller. What did that mean or have to do with anything, and how did he know I knew him? That's strange.

Remembering Darrin asking me not to tell Detective Matters that I knew him, I hadn't decided what I was going to say to Matters. I was baffled. I guessed that I would find out everything soon.

When I got to Mama's, both Sharon's and Sierra's cars were parked out front. As I was walking to the door, Nevilla peered out the living room window at me. When I was about to unlock the front door, Nevilla opened it for me.

"Auntie, where have you been? Grandma and Mommy have been looking for you."

I looked around and didn't see anyone. "Where is everyone, Nevilla?"

"They're down stairs." Nevilla grabbed my hand and led me to the basement.

Mama sat up from the couch as soon as she saw me. "Why didn't you return any of my calls? I was calling you all night. I know you were out with that new guy you met but you could at least return my calls." Mama seemed upset; I didn't think it was that big of a deal.

"Mama, my place was broken into last night, and plus my phone was dead. It was a hectic night last night."

Mama and Sharon both looked shocked, as I sat down on the couch next to Sharon.

"Oh my God, Rahkel! Who would have broken in? Did you call the police?" Mama placed her hands on her chest.

"Of course I did, Mama."

"Well do they know who did it?" Sharon asked.

"No, but after here, I'm going down to the police station."

"Well, I'll go with you," Mama said.

"No, that's alright, Mama. I'll tell you all about it when I get back. I don't need you worrying." I got up from the couch and headed for the stairs. "And Darrin's gonna help me get an alarm installed later."

"What exactly do you know about this Darrin, Rahkel?"

Stopping at the edge of the bottom step, it was just like Mama to ask something like that. "What do you mean by that? He had nothing to do with it, Mama. We were out to dinner last night when it happened." What was Mama insinuating?

"Well, I'm just worried about you, Rahkel. There has been a lot of bad things happening since you met him, and I want to make sure you're alright."

"I'll be fine, Mama. I'll call you two later." I started to walk up the stairs.

"Rahkel," Mama walked over to the bottom of the stairs, "look, just be careful, okay? Oh yeah, and someone by the name of Simon called, or maybe that was his last name," she pondered. "Anyhow, his number is on the kitchen table. Maybe it has something to do with Leon's business." Mama turned around and walked back to the couch.

Simon? What in the hell? Who was Simon and how did he get my number? Could it be the dentist, Dr. Simon? I rushed upstairs and grabbed the piece of paper on the table.

Driving to the station, I was now more eager to talk to Detective Matters; maybe he had something new to tell me. I also wanted to ask him about his message he left me about Darrin. Trying not to think of the worst, I kept an eye on every car that tailed me.

Chapter 24

After filling out paperwork and talking to the two police officers that were at my house last night, I waited in a cold gray room. The clerk at the front desk said that Detective Matters was with someone and that it would be another thirty minutes before he was free. I felt like leaving and rescheduling, but waited it out. I really wanted to talk to him and find out what new information, if anything at all, he had to tell me.

After getting a Diet Coke from the pop machine, I sat down and wondered if it was a good idea to tell Matters that Darrin and I had been working on the case. I figured if the police did their part and I did my part, sooner or later the truth about this whole mess would come out about Uncle Leon, Dennis Lowry and Franklin.

I called Mama and told her I was at the police station. She said her, Sierra, and Nevilla were going to the movies. Sharon was with Terry, they were shopping for the baby. But, most likely, he was spending all of her money and not buying a thing for the baby. With not a pot to piss in nor a window to throw it out of, there was nothing stable about Terry, not even a job. What she sees in him, I'll never know, but what I do know is that if Uncle Leon was alive, he would be quite angry in his daughter's choice of men.

Taking my last swallow of Diet Coke, looking to be in his mid-sixties, Detective Matters walked in. "I apologize, Ms. Williams. It's been busy around here." He reached out and shook my hand. "Please follow me. We have some things to discuss."

Following him down the hall, we passed his desk which had a sign on it that read: Edgar T. Matters, Head Detective. Inside the room adjacent to this office, someone with short blonde hair, rolling a cigarette, sat at a long steel table. He was about to light it, until we walked in. He looked young, at least twenty-five.

Detective Matters closed the door behind us and pulled out a chair for me to sit down. "Rahkel, this is Detective Hudson. He recently started working on the case. Detective Hudson is new with our department and new to the field, but he's done excellent work for us."

Hudson stood up to shake my hand, and then both of them sat down simultaneously.

There was a mirror behind Detective Hudson facing me, reminding me of the movies. I bet someone was watching us on the other side. I sat my purse on the floor beside my chair and stretched my arms across the table while clamping my hands together. There was a window off to the side and I glanced out it, immediately seeing a picture of a hammer in the sky. I turned away scratching behind my ears. Resting my chin in the palm of my hands, I looked out the corner of my eye.

"Are you okay?" Detective Hudson asked me. He sipped his coffee, his lips thin and his small blue eyes stared at me, but in a kind way. I eyed his cigarette that was lying in the ashtray. I needed a smoke right now. Detective Matters looked out the window, pushing his reading glasses back on his nose, then back at me with a raised brow. He opened a folder he had laid out in front of him.

"Yes, go on." I placed my hands back on the table.

"Okay, let's get started. We believe Leon Wilson and Franklin Carter were killed by the same person. We also found evidence that a dentist by the name of Dennis Lowry was tied to both Wilson and Carter, as well. We know you were going to meet with Dennis Lowry the night he was murdered, and I want to know for what?" Detective Matters leaned in closer to me. "Rahkel we want to help solve your Uncle's murder. So we need you to start being honest with us." I sat quietly for a moment. I had already gone over this went them. However, I felt a little bad that I wasn't totally being honest with them. I now felt that I was a suspect again. Staring at Detective Matters, I didn't like how his bushy peppered colored eyebrows caved it when he talked.

Thinking about Darrin, I knew the next line of questioning would probably be about him. I had no choice, but I'd also be cautious as well.

I responded by giving them the exact answers I had given to them the last time they asked me. And as far as Dennis Lowry, I told them the truth. He'd told me he knew my Uncle and he wanted me to meet with him. I knew no more than that.

Then Detective Matters asked me the inevitable. He took off his glasses and looked into my eyes with the most serious look. "Why didn't you tell us you were going to meet Dennis Lowry the night of his murder?"

I didn't know what to say. I wondered how he even knew. They were police, I supposed they knew everything, so it seemed. I guess I should have told them, but I didn't think about it or thought it was that relevant. I felt stupid. I was innocent, but now, I felt guilty as hell.

I tried to get my words right. "Well yes, I was going to meet with Dennis Lowry. I wasn't trying to keep it a secret. I didn't even know the man. He called me and asked me to meet him at the diner. He told me not to bring anyone with me. I was afraid. He said he knew my Uncle. Before I even got there he was dead and police were everywhere." I stopped at that and waited intensely at what they were going to say next.

"Well the bottom line is that you should have told us. When murder is involved, in this case three murders, we need the truth." He looked over at the other detective and he nodded his head.

I felt like a child being scolded.

Detective Matters continued. "We do know that your uncle was going to pay this man approximately one million dollars. We just don't know why."

Detective Hudson pulled out a sheet of paper. "Do you know anything about this?" Detective Hudson slid the paper across the table. It looked like some sort of contract. It had Uncle Leon's signature at the bottom.

I looked at it carefully. "No, I don't." I slid the paper back to Detective Hudson.

They both rolled their eyes and swapped stares. I don't think they believed me.

"Okay, so let's talk about Darrin Miller. We know you've been seeing him. Do you know much about him?" Detective Matters asked.

Having somebody know your business when you've never told them, really is the most uncomfortable and deceiving thing ever. They know we've been seeing each other. How is that? Are they spying on me, or something? They had to be.

"Okay, so what? Is it against the law for me to date or something?" I didn't mean to sound smart, but where were they going with all this?

"Did you know that Darrin Matters was tried for murdering his ex-girlfriend but all charges were dropped because the police didn't obtain a search warrant when they entered his apartment?" Detective Matters pounded his hand on the desk.

I jumped.

He pushed a piece of paper out of his way. It almost slid off the table. "There was a misunderstanding between two police officers. Darrin served six months in prison and then all charges were dropped. I bet he didn't tell you that."

I sat looking at Detective Matters. I was thinking this was some type of joke or something. I sat back in my chair. I was looking back and forth between Detective Matters and Hudson hoping one of them would say this wasn't true but they didn't. Staring at me intently, they silently waited for my response. But, what on earth was I to say to such a claim about Darrin? That any man who gave me the most amazing pleasure last night could not have done what they claim. I took a deep breath and didn't say anything.

"Did you also know that Leon was going to evict Darrin out of his townhouse five days before he died?" Detective Hudson stated in addition while scratching his head.

"We plan on bringing Darrin in for questioning." Detective Hudson said.

"I don't believe this…. Darrin has helped me a lot. I just don't believe this. You've got the wrong man." I stood and pushed my chair under the table. "Detective Matters even you said that it was a possibility that my Uncle may have had some bad business deals. Maybe somebody was trying to get back at him. Who knows?" I paced the floor with my arms folded. I was finding it hard to believe any of what I'd heard, but questioning it at the same time. This wasn't happening. I refused to believe it.

"Who could this person be?" I said in a low voice. I was actually talking to myself in distress.

"Somebody like Darrin?" Detective Matters answered, reaching for his thin-rimmed glasses, placing them back on his face.

"Have a sit Ms. Williams," Detective Matters said. His voice was stern.

I sat down feeling frustrated and out of control. I placed my hands on each side of my head. I could feel a terrible headache coming on.

"We may need you to take a polygraph test," Detective Matters said.

I don't believe my ears. "A what? But, why?" I was the one who just got my house broken into. The way I was being treated, I almost wondered if I needed a lawyer.

I looked at Detective Matters and then back out the window. There was no picture outside and worse yet, it looked cloudy. It was probably going to rain.

The ringing of my cell phone broke my trance. I looked down into my purse. It was Darrin. I sighed and then looked up towards Detectives Matters and Hudson. They looked at me as though I was supposed to tell them who it was calling me.

Chapter 25

It was time for my life to get back to normal. Over the past few days, I'd been staying at Mama's, too afraid to stay at my place. After what Detective Matters laid on me, I couldn't get Darrin out of my mind. Badly, I wanted to call him, to ask him if what Matters said was true, but a part of me didn't' really want to know, for fear that Matters was right.

Darrin had been ringing my phone off the hook, and texting me like crazy. Honestly, I didn't know what to say to him, or whom to believe or what to think. I figured I'd have to break down and call him sooner or later, preferably later. Could it be that I don't want the truth to smear the memories of that wonderful night of lustful bliss? I just don't know. I'll give him a call when I get to the nursing home.

Janetta and her cousin, Gary who flew in some days ago, were able to handle the office, the two temps were there, and even Sharon and Sierra offered there help as well. Sierra will start college soon, and I will miss her, I figured I'll stop by the office when I get off.

Arriving at the nursing home, Pete the janitor greeted me. I received hugs and condolences for Uncle Leon and Franklin, all around. The murders were top stories on the news so I couldn't avoid it if I wanted to. He tipped his cap to me and smiled. I heard he was only in his early forties, but his wrinkles around his mouth and forehead made him appear older. I admired his spirit. He's dating one of the nurses, there're always sneaking off somewhere. Either an empty room, closet, car, wherever. Once I caught them under a bed. I couldn't believe it, but I was too embarrassed to say anything. There are strange things that can happen at a nursing home, well at least at this one.

I finished preparing the residents' morning snacks and drinks and started my rounds. I passed by Ms. Langler's room. She had both her head and legs propped up with pillows; she'd lost a lot of weight. As I filled her water pitcher, she paid no attention, and kept her eyes glued to the television.

My next stop was Mr. Wood's room, and I couldn't believe my eyes, dumbfounded. Mrs. Anderson was lying on top of him and they were naked. A disgusting sight, two wrinkled old folks doing the nasty, I thought I was going to be sick. They paid me no mind, as they humped each other, slowly like two old turtles. With room service tray in hand, I backed out of the room and pressed my back against the wall. Using my two-way radio, I called for the emergency crew.

Peeking around the corner into the room, "You two stop that. That's disgusting," I said, and they still weren't paying me any attention.

Eventually Mr. Wood turned to me and smiled. He'd even taken his false teeth out. I was too through. I quickly entered the room, sat a juice and cup of fruit on each of there trays and left, as three emergency crewmembers were running my way. I pointed into there room.

After that ungodly sight, I needed to take a short smoke break. Heading out the back door, I saw Miguel. He hadn't been working here that long. He wanted to work construction, but they never called him back after the job interview. With a wife and five kids to feed, I don't how he does it. I wondered if he got that second job, he was telling me about. With a chill in the air, I sat on the bench with my jacket wrapped tight around me. Miguel sat next to me, with a half-finished cigarette in hand.

"So how's it going?" he asked.

"Oh, its going I guess. Mr. Wood and Ms. Anderson were in there fucking. The aids had to come and pull them apart."

"Again? Them two are always at it. Isn't Mr. Wood like 100? I bet he was a pimp back in day." We both laughed, and then Miguel pulled out a small bottle of tequila and took a sip.

Miguel offered me a sip. At first, I hesitated but figured what the hell. Taking it, I took a sip. It can't possibly make me feel worse then I already felt..

"Damn, that is some strong stuff."

"Oh yeah, Ma' it gets the blood going. This is imported from Mexico. You don't get Tequila out here like this," Miguel said, taking the bottle from me to take another sip, looking around to make sure no one was watching.

"You know some not so good things have been going on with me. My house got broken into a few days ago. I've been seeing this one guy who I like a lot and then I find out by the police that he killed his last girlfriend. And I feel like I'm always looking over my shoulder all the damn time." I pulled out my pack of cigarettes and offered one to Miguel. He gladly took one.

"Damn, girl. Your house got broken into? Did them bastards steal anything?" Miguel rubbed his hand over his baldhead. He was sort of short, but he was a cutie and a hard worker. His wife should be very proud of him. "I did hear about your Uncle and his friend. It was all over the news. That's crazy girl." Miguel shoved his bottle inside his jacket.

"I know. Nobody stole anything and the police are getting on my nerves. I've been staying at my mom's for the last few days. And the worst about all this is that I think the police may suspect me." I looked out into the distance at the traffic.

"So what's up with this new guy you were talking about? Did you tell him what the police said about him?"

"Not yet, but I'm going to today."

"Yeah talk to him first." Miguel got off the bench and zipped up his jacket. "Damn it's getting cold out here." He finished his cigarette and flicked it onto the concrete. "Hey I got that second job I was telling you about. And it pays way more then this. I'll be a security guard. Shit, as soon as they have a full-time opening, I'll probably leave from this place."

"That's good, Miguel. I'm happy for you." I shoved my hands inside my jacket pockets.

"Rahkel I'm about to go in. See you later. And take care of yourself." Miguel said, as he waved at me.

I looked down at my watch. It was practically time for me to go in as well.

Sidetracked at lunch, I wasn't able to call Darrin. After my shift was over, Lindsey, the receptionist, told me I had a visitor looking for me. She said they were waiting outside for me. With furrowed brow, I tried to think who could be looking for me. I was scared. Was this the killer? Looking out the window, I scanned the surroundings before leaving the building. I asked the guard to walk out to the parking lot with me. It was still daylight.

Walking to my car, I spotted Darrin, looking concerned and upset. I gave the guard a nod, indicating I was okay and he went back inside.

"We need to talk." He reached for my hand, but I held back.

"Darrin how did you know where I worked?"

"You told me." I didn't recall telling him any such thing.

"I'm sorry I haven't called you. I was going to today though, at least to get my stuff." We stood in the middle of the parking, beside my car. He asked for a hug, at first I hesitated but I gave him one. I really did miss him. And I know I should have called, but I was confused.

"I know why you haven't called me." He looked so good. I wondered where he was coming from. He had on a suit.

"What do you know?"

"Well Detective Matters called me. He had me come down to the station and asked me a few questions. I knew right then and there that he must have told you something." Darrin looked at me with sincere eyes.

I gazed at him, my inner being craving every inch of him, but I pushed the thoughts out of my mind, refusing to be sidetracked.

"First of all, me and Matters haven't gotten along in a while. We worked on a case together a long time ago, and I got most of the credit for solving it. I received an honorary award for it. Jealously on his part, I guess is what happened between us, who knows. I just know Detective Matters has had it out for me ever since. But, anyways, besides that, look Rahkel, I'm not perfect and I have done some bad things in my life. But I promise you, I did not kill my ex-girlfriend. Her husband killed her because he found out about her affair. I bet Matters didn't tell you she was married. I didn't even know myself. But of course it was the perfect opportunity for the husband to put the blame on me."

I was shocked. "So where is the husband now? And wasn't he questioned?" I pulled out a cigarette.

"He's in Mexico now, I think, and yeah, he was questioned but he had the perfect alibi. That asshole set me up. And six months of my life was wasted behind the whole bullshit!" Darrin leaned against my car. Anger seething from him, I could tell he wanted to pound the shit out of my car, but he resisted and rested his hands on the roof of the car and let out a long aggravated sigh. "He framed me Rahkel and he got away with it. The only

132

thing that really saved my life was that illegal search warrant. If it wasn't for that and a damn good lawyer, I probably would still be in jail. But it took them bastards a fucking six months to realize that." Facing me, Darrin stared at me and shook his head.

"Was the girl Mexican?" I don't know why that mattered, but I wanted to know.

"No, she was black." Darrin shook his head again. "Now how was I supposed to tell you a story like that and let all my baggage out? I would have eventually told you." He embraced my hand in his. "Now do you understand?"

I nodded my head. I was thinking about what Darrin had just told me and then my thoughts moved over to what Detective Matters had told me. Either Darrin was a good liar or Detective Matters really didn't like Darrin. I was a little perplexed, but in the end, I really wanted to believe Darrin.

"I've missed you." He gave me another hug. "Where have you been staying at? I've been to your house and you haven't been there."

"Oh, at my mom's. I haven't been able to go back to my house. Well I went back with my family to get some clothes, but that's about it."

"Come on, Rahkel. Follow me back to my place. I'd love it if you could spend the night. We can talk some more and I'll fix you dinner." I flicked my cigarette butt across the pavement. "Baby, I also set up an appointment to have an alarm system installed for you tomorrow. I hope that's okay."

"Sure that'll be great. I've missed you too." I gave him a kiss and then pulled my hood over my head. I wasn't looking the best, with tennis shoes, blue scrubs, no make-up, and my hair in a ponytail, but he didn't seem to care. When I got in my car, I sat in complete thought for a moment. I think I believed Darrin, and plus he's never caused me harm, and he seemed like a good man. I called Mama, and told her I wouldn't be home tonight and to kiss Nevilla for me. I followed Darrin to his place. I really did miss Darrin, and I was looking forward to us making love again. That thought alone put a very big grin on my face. I decided to give him the benefit of the doubt for now.

Chapter 26

The next day, Darrin called his friend at Brinks Security and had the alarm system installed. I figured now I'd feel safe, at least I hoped. I stood in my kitchen watching Darrin and the Brinks' rep in my living room. Darrin was telling him where to install the alarm. I was smoking a cigarette and sipping on freshly brewed coffee. I looked at Darrin; he was in sweats and a T-shirt. I think this was the first time I'd seen him so casual, but shit even casual this man was so fine; his hair still neatly faded, with every wave in tact and his face nicely shaved. He would look up every once in awhile and smile at me with his pearly whites. I had on flip-flops with a T-shirt and Capri pants. Darrin had seen me casual on several occasions.

While Darrin spearheaded the installation, I thought about what he told me the day before. I trusted him, I really did. I think it was starting to sink in that I was falling for this man and hard. After pouring me a second cup of coffee, it dawned on me that he hadn't gotten back with me on that CD. I wondered if he found out anything. It also occurred to me that I hadn't mentioned that Detective Matters told me about the disagreement he supposedly had with Uncle Leon. While the man was installing an alarm pad in my bedroom, I pulled Darrin to the side.

"Whatever happened with your friend and the CD I gave you?"

"Oh yeah, actually he's out of town. But I'll get with him as soon as he gets back, which should be in about a week. Don't worry baby, my friend is good. Whatever information is on that CD he should be able to retrieve." He gave me a gentle kiss on the lips and patted me on the behind.

I smiled at him. "Well what about the license plate number?"

"I have some possible leads. I'll bring my laptop over to your house later, or we can go back to my house, and I'll show you what I came up with."

That sounded good to me. I prepared myself to ask him about Uncle Leon. There was no good time or good way to say it. So I just said it.

"Um, Darrin what happened between you and my uncle? Detective Matters mentioned something about a disagreement between you and him five days before he died." I looked into his eyes to see if I noticed anything shady.

"Rahkel," he began. He leaned against the wall, looking up to the ceiling. "Your Uncle tried to black mail me basically. Someone called my partner Calvin to investigate on your uncle's business. Calvin didn't get too far with his investigation." Darrin turned toward me. "Look, your uncle found out somehow about the investigation and threatened me and wanted to kick me out of my place. We did get into a disagreement at the office. I think one of the workers witnessed it. It was a short white girl." He looked at me as to help him identify the short white girl.

"It was probably Jessica." I stood with my arms crossed. I looked in my bedroom and the man seemed to be almost done installing the alarm.

"Yea, well…that's about it Rahkel."

"Why didn't you tell me any of this before? And, who called Calvin to tell him to investigate into my uncle's business? This could be the person who killed him." I couldn't believe he didn't tell me. I was pissed off.

"Look Rahkel. It was business and it didn't have anything to do with your uncle being killed or else I would have told you. A man named Donald Hamilton initiated the investigation because Leon owed him money. In my opinion, it was irrelevant. So I didn't bother you with it." Darrin looked irritated with my line of questioning, but I didn't care.

"Whatever, Darrin, the bottom line is that you should have told me. My uncle was murdered and I originally thought that Donald Hamilton was a suspect."

Soon I dropped the subject. When the man said he wanted Darrin to look at something, he left me standing in the hallway and went into my bedroom. They came out and he passed me without saying a word as they walked downstairs.

Later that night, Darrin came by my house. I had Janetta over until he got there. I was so glad to be back and it felt good to have Darrin here with me even though he'd pissed me off earlier. I couldn't stay mad at Darrin too long, I was beginning to learn. He made that hard to do. While Darrin was looking through his laptop, I went upstairs in my room to unpack my suitcase he'd brought over that I left at his house. I looked around, nothing out of the ordinary. I opened my son's room and it looked normal as well. I exhaled. I looked in my lingerie drawer to see what I could find that was sexy. I pulled out a red short silk lingerie gown and slipped it on.

I went downstairs and into the kitchen. Darrin took a double look and smiled at me. He turned on the television and flipped to the sports station. He closed his laptop and came over to me.

"You look good, baby," he said, turning me to face him.

"Thank you," I smiled, as his lips grazed mine before his tongue slid between my lips.

Grabbing hold of my ass and squeezing it, his tongue traveled down my neck to my chest. Chills shot through me, igniting a fire between my thighs. Damn this man knew how to work me over. As I pressed my hips against him, he abruptly stopped and went back into the living room. Where was he going? I wanted to have sex right there in the kitchen.

I poured a glass of wine and got a beer for Darrin. When I was looking through my purse to get my lighter, I noticed the piece of paper I'd gotten from Mama's house. Damn, with so much going on, I never called back this Simon person. I assumed it had to be Dr. Simon. I took the piece of paper into the living room and showed it to Darrin. He suggested I wait until tomorrow to call him. I agreed and sat the piece of paper on the living room table. Darrin and I enjoyed a nice evening. I was happy he was back in my life.

Nodding on the couch, Darrin was busy on his laptop. I got up and made me a cup of coffee. Darrin called me from the living room.

"Rahkel, I want you to take a look at two possible leads that I came up with off that partial license plate number you gave me."

I poured water in the coffee maker, went back in the living room and sat down. I turned his laptop around and looked at what he had on the screen: Gregory Foster.

"Who is that? I don't know anyone by the name of Gregory Foster."

"I'm not sure myself. But Leonard Wilson also comes up." Darrin switched to a different screen on his laptop. I looked closely.

"Well that can't be right, unless someone's stealing my uncle's identity." I thought about that for a minute.

"Yea, that's very well possible. Now I'm curious to see what's on that CD you gave me. I'm gonna make sure I get an answer for you soon as I can."

It was starting to get late. After we had sex on the couch, we had a few drinks and then Darrin was knocked out. Staring at him from head to toe, I was mesmerized by the deliciousness of his naked beautiful manly body. After I activated the alarm system, I. retrieved two blankets from the hall closet; I draped one over him and cuddled up with the other one. I channel surfed, coming upon reruns. I looked over at Darrin again; he was sleeping like a baby and snoring as well. I put the remote next to me and laid my head back on the couch. Hours later, I was awakened by my cell phone. I looked up at the clock and it was almost two in the morning. I looked at my cell phone to see who was calling.

"Uncle Leon?" I mouthed.

With raised brows, fear shot through me. Why was Uncle Leon's cell phone calling me? I looked over at Darrin. I didn't know if I should wake him or not. I wondered if I was dreaming or maybe I had too much to drink. I blinked my eyes several times. It was still ringing, so I decided to answer it, but the person on the other end hung up. I tried calling the number back, but there was no answer.

Chapter 27

The next morning, after cooking breakfast for Darrin, he left and went to work. I never told him about the phone call. I was still in disbelief, not sure, if it was because I'd been drinking or if it was a dream. I wanted to pretend it didn't happen. I figured that maybe I'd tell him later. I called into work, went up to my room and took a nap.

After my nap, I decided to go to the grocery store. By the time I'd finished grocery shopping and ran a few errands, it was late afternoon. Sitting in the car outside of the grocery store, I thought about the phone call from last night. I decided to call the number again. This time it was disconnected. Was I going crazy or what?

Deep in thought, I almost missed Janetta's call, asking if I could come by the office later to help with a few things. Actually, I had plans to stop by the office. I wanted to see how Janetta was doing, and how everyone else at the office was handling their job. I decided I wouldn't tell her about the phone call.

When I arrived at the office, Sierra and Jessica were at the front desk.

"Where's Janetta?" I asked looking around the office.

"She had to run a few errands. She took Emily and Sharon with her. They should be back any minute." As I was walking to the back, Sierra stopped me. "Hold on there's a call coming in. Wilson and Carter, how may I help you?" Sierra sounded so professional. I'd found out school was about to start for her in about a week. She'd be starting at Langston University.

Well that's strange, Janetta told me to come down here and help. Oh well. I glanced outside, and the sun was setting. Daylight savings was right around the corner. I looked towards Jessica. She was busy filing paperwork in the cabinets. I wanted to ask her about the argument between Darrin and Uncle Leon, but decided against it.

Until Sierra finished her call, I moseyed toward the back office, peeking in the back office and saw Janetta's cousin, Gary, typing up rental contracts. I'd only met him a couple of times. In his late thirties, he wore thick black framed glasses with the most fucked up looking dreadlocks I'd ever seen. Dreadlocks aren't for everyone, especially dreads that look like that. He was a smart businessman thought. Janetta said he was a nerd in school and made straight A's. It looks to me like Gary was still a nerd.

"Hey Gary, how's everything going?"

He didn't answer. It was probably due to the CD player on the desk, earplugs in his ears.

When I approached him and tapped him on the shoulder, he jumped and so did I.

He pulled the earplugs out of his ears. "Hi, Ms. Williams."

"Hi, Gary. You can call me Rahkel. So how is everything going?"

"Oh everything is going lovely. I got a lot done today." He held up a big pile of neatly organized paperwork. "I have all of these contracts processed."

"Well that's really good, Gary. You know I really appreciate your help."

"No problem. Hey, do you know where I can go to get my dreads did? They're starting to look a little dry."

"Um no I don't, but there is a black nail and hair salon not far from here. Janetta goes there sometimes to get her hair and nails done, maybe you could ask her." I flashed a fake smile walked back to the front desk, where I saw Janetta and Sharon coming into the office. It was raining now and they both had umbrellas in there hands.

"Hey girl, what's up? It's a mess out there." Janetta pulled a scarf from her head.

"Where's Emily?" I asked.

"Girl, you know Emily, baby daddy problems. She said she might come in later. She told me to tell you she's sorry."

"Oh, I guess. So, did you get your hair did?" Janetta looked a little different.

"Yes girl and my nails and toes. I figured I'd try a new place. They hooked it up. It looks good, don't it?" She turned around, giving me a better look.

"Well your cousin back there was asking me if I knew anyone who did dreadlocks. I figured I'd leave that one up to you."

We all started laughing. I looked at Sharon's hands. She'd gotten her nails done as well. She usually doesn't get her nails done. Leave it up to Janetta. Whomever went with her was sure to come back either with a new outfit, there hair did and maybe there nails and toes too. Sharon went in the back with Gary. Sierra and Jessica got up from Janetta's desk. Sharon was definitely beginning to show, but she was all belly.

"Jessica, how's it going girl?" Janetta asked her.

"Oh, okay. After I finish these files is it okay if I leave, Rahkel?" Jessica asked, turning around, as she looked my way.

"Sure," I said. Jessica was sort of quiet. She didn't talk too much, but she was nice and a hard worker for a temp.

Sierra grabbed her purse and jacket. "Well, I'm about to go y'all." She pulled her hat over her head. "I gotta go to the store for Mama."

"Okay, Sis, see you later," I said, giving her a hug.

"Bye, girl." Janetta sat down and pulled a pop and chips from the side desk drawer.

"So what you up to?" Janetta opened her pop and poured it into a cup with ice.

"Not too much. What did you need help with?"

"The billing, there's too much of it."

"Okay."

In Uncle Leon's office, working on the bills, I heard the front door open. I stopped what I was doing and listened. I heard Janetta saying hello to someone. I went into Franklin's office, where Sharon and Gary were working, and snuck a peek down the hall to see who it was. I saw a man out the corner of my eye. No sooner than I stepped foot in Franklin's office, Janetta called out my name. Damn!

The man standing at the desk wore a long dark blue trench coat, his shoulders drooped low and at first, I really couldn't tell his age. Walking closer, I needed to get a good look at him. Did I know him? As soon as I got within a few feet of him, he smiled, almost as if he knew me. He had to be in his mid-fifties at least, I could tell by the wrinkles above his eyebrows and around his mouth, not to mention the gray that had made a permanent home around the edges of his forehead.

"Hi Rahkel, it's finally nice to meet you. I'm Doctor Charles Simon." He extended his hand.

I hesitated a little. I was surprised to see him, and eagerly wanted to know why he was paying me a visit. I had questions for him too, like why exactly did my uncle give him a Mercedes as a gift and how did he get my mama's phone number.

"I want to start off by saying that I am deeply sorry about the death of your uncle. He was indeed an outstanding man."

I finally extended my hand. "Well yes he was. So I see you tracked me down." I can't believe I'd said that. I looked over at Janetta, the back of her head was facing us, but I know Janetta, and she was definitely all ears. "I received your message and have been meaning to call you, but didn't get around to it. So what brings you to me?"

He turned around and looked at Janetta then quickly back toward me. "Is there somewhere we can talk in private?" He leaned closer to me. I could smell his cologne. It was a mixture of Old Spice and Lysol spray. He didn't have any facial hair. That was weird.

"Sure, follow me." I led him to Uncle Leon's office. The door was shut, I didn't think I shut it, but I opened it and motioned for Dr. Simon to go in first. I looked back towards Janetta who was also turned around looking at me. We both had confused looks on our faces. I shrugged my shoulders at her and went inside with Dr. Simon.

As I was closing the door, he reached in his coat pocket and pulled out a large folder that was folded in half.

"Rahkel, I'm glad I have a chance to talk with you. I'm sure you're wondering why I've been trying to get in touch with you." Dr. Simon unfolded an envelope and laid it flat on top of the desk, and neatly smoothed it out with his hands.

"Well yes, that is what I was thinking." What else did he want me to say? I figured I'd let him do all the talking. I wanted to hear everything he had to say first. However, if the situation allowed, I might bring up the fact that I

141

saw him that one night driving a black Mercedes that was registered in my uncle's name. I closed the blinds to the side window.

"Okay, first all, I knew your uncle very well. We did a lot of business together. I've been looking for you, because you might be in danger."

"What type of danger do you mean?" I sat straight up in the chair.

"Well, your Uncle owed a lot of people money and even I have gotten some phone threats myself."

"So what type of business were you and my uncle in?"

"Well, first off I'm a dentist. A self-employed dentist with my own office that is, and your uncle and I would exchange business leads.. In addition, he owned one-third of my business. We signed a contract and I haven't received my share yet. So I'm here because I own part of this leasing business now that he's no longer with us."

"*What!*" I didn't even let him respond. "There must be some type of mistake. The only two people that were invested in this building was my uncle and Franklin. And their both dead." I paced the room, while keeping an eye on Dr. Simon. Who in the hell did he think he was coming in here thinking he has a right to my uncle's business?

"I know that having to deal with your uncle's death has been hard. So I wanted to bring you the paperwork. I'll leave it with you and your attorney if you have one. Please look over it. It'll confirm what I've told you. In this envelope, there is some very important information that you will find very vital. But I prefer it come from this paperwork and not by me telling you." Dr. Simon leaned forward with this look that said he knew more than what he was saying. "Believe me when I say that."

As he was about to leave, he pulled out what I think was a cigarette out his pocket, and suddenly the lights went out and it was pitch dark.

Janetta screamed and there was commotion across the hall room where Gary and Sharon were. I couldn't see at all in front of me, not even movement. I touched the file cabinets and made my way to the door. I called out to Dr. Simon, but he didn't answer. I finally made my way to the light switch, which of course was not working. I opened the door and, with my arms stretched out in front of me, I went to the office across the hall.

"Are you guys okay?"

"Yeah, we're fine. What happened?" asked Gary.

"I don't know."

As I walked back into the hallway, I tripped over something on the floor and fell to the floor..

"Damn, what is that?" I said, lying in the middle of the hallway. I felt a hand on me, helping me up.

"Here let me help you." Gary's nerdy voice was even more annoying without having to see his face. He pulled me to my feet.

"Come up here you guys," Sharon said. She'd made her way up front. An emergency light suddenly came on. As Gary and me were walking closer to Janetta and Sharon, I could see the horrid look on Janetta's face.

"Why is he laying on the floor?" Janetta asked as she pointed behind us. Dr. Simon wasn't moving at all.

Using the emergency lights to see, we checked on Dr. Simon. I stepped over him to get to the switch box, which was in the back, and Janetta knelt down beside him.

As soon as Sharon yelled, "Oh my God," I had the lights back on. I think I stopped breathing for a few seconds when I looked down at Dr. Simon. Blood and everything else oozed out the side of his head. It was an awful sight seeing his head half way blown off.. I was speechless and in shock considering I never heard a gun shot.

"Let's not stand here, lets get out of here and call the police." Janetta ran back up to the front desk. I was in total shock; I didn't know what to think, or what to do. I stepped over the dark red puddle of blood and Dr. Simon's body and went into Uncle Leon's office to call the police. The paperwork that Dr. Simon had left on the desk was gone. This really freaked me out.

"Get out of the office, now!" I yelled, throwing the phone down and jetting out of the office, stumbling over Dr. Simon and out the front door, with everyone in tow. .We paired up, Sharon was with me and Gary was with Janetta. We sat in our cars, scared shitless and when I looked in the rearview mirror, Janetta was on her phone. I hoped the police would be here soon. Sharon was crying and that made me almost lose it. I had to maintain, I couldn't break. I kept looking around, completely paranoid trying to see if I saw anyone, but I didn't. I pulled a can of maze I had from the glove compartment.

Five long minutes later, the police finally arrived. We all climbed out of our cars as soon as we heard the sirens coming up the street. I looked down at Janetta and they got out as well.

"Rahkel what the hell is going on? People are getting murdered," Sharon asked as she hugged me. I was speechless and scared. I was certain that I'd be next. I watched as all the police cars, ambulance and fire truck pulled up. I wish I knew the answer. I could feel my heart pounding. The last police car to pull up was Detective Matters. We made eye contact. I stood as he walked toward me. Burying my face in my hand, I slid a hand over my head, feeling completely helpless. I heard my phone ringing, I looked down at it, and it was Darrin.

Chapter 28

Darrin came down to the office, bringing his partner Calvin with him. It was obvious Darrin and Detective Matters were avoiding each other. Especially the way Darrin kept turning his back toward Matters whenever he'd look our way and vice versa. I watched as the police examined the small hole in the window. The blinds also had a small hole in them. It dawned on me that that bullet might very well had been meant for me. The thought sent chills down my spine. The police wouldn't let any of us back in. I watched everything from outside. At this point, I'm really considering closing the business, selling the building and maybe even selling the business itself.

Janetta's been working for my uncle in this building for the last four years. She would have to find a new job. I felt sort of bad about that. Hell, I don't know what to do. Maybe I could give her four or five months worth of salary from the sell of the building, which would tie her over until she found a new job. However, that was the least of my worries. I was a little more concerned for my life.

Detective Matters pulled me aside while Darrin and Calvin were talking to Sharon and Janetta. He again warned me about Darrin, and was surprised I was still with him. I informed Detective Matters that Darrin and me talked about the whole thing, and that I was a big girl, and if he'd please leave the situation alone about me and Darrin. He asked if I could come down to the station tomorrow, I agreed. He also wanted Janetta to come too; he said he'd talk to her. I looked over at Darrin and he was looking directly at us. I pulled out a cigarette and walked over to Darrin. As I was getting closer, I saw a gun on Darrin's hip, when he lifted up his leather jacket. It stunned me, because I never knew he even carried a gun. Maybe all PI's carry guns. I started to wonder how many times he'd had that thing with him when we were together.

145

I looked over a few feet from where Darrin was standing and saw Calvin and Janetta talking. Sharon was standing there too, but she had her back turned to them and was talking on her cell phone.

"What was Matter's talking to you about?" Darrin asked.

"He wants me to come down to the police station tomorrow." I drew in the smoke from my cigarette and zipped up my jacket.

"Do you want me to come with you?" I can't even believe Darrin asked that. Maybe he was being nice. He wouldn't be able to stand being in the same room as Detective Matters.

"No Darrin, that's alright. He wants to talk to Janetta too, so she'll be coming down with me." I looked behind Darrin and watched as Detective Matters walked up to Janetta and started talking to her. I have to talk to Janetta later and let her know not to tell Detective Matters about the box.

Not long after, Janetta announced she was about to leave. I went over to Janetta and Sharon and hugged them both, and told them I'd call them tomorrow. Janetta took Sharon home and Gary rode with them. Detective Matters already let it be known that the office was going to be closed until further investigation. I had a feeling of that anyway.

Darrin introduced me to Calvin. He was nice. He had an accent of some sort. I was sure it was Jamaican, since he said, "Hey Mon," every other word. His hair was short and curly, and he had a stocky build.

Before I left the scene, I gave the extra set of office keys to Detective Matters. I wondered if I should have done that. Oh well. I didn't have anything to hide, and even if I did, he'd get a search warrant anyway.

Darrin walked me back over to my car. "Follow us, baby. I'm gonna drop off Calvin and then we'll go back to your place." Darrin gave me a comforting kiss. I got into my car and followed behind them.

After pulling up to an apartment complex, Calvin got out, turned toward me and waved.

Darrin got out and came up to my window. "Did you want to stop on our way to get anything?" He was so irresistible. Even at a time like this, I felt secure.

"No, we can just go straight to my place." I smiled at him and he gave me another kiss.

146

Searchable Whereabouts

On the ride home, it started to bother me how worried Detective Matter's was that I was still seeing Darrin. Not that I'm all that, but was he envious or what? Was he really concerned? Or was there something else? Tomorrow, I don't know how I was going to ask, but I wanted to know if Detective Matters was married. I wanted to find out something about him for a change.

On the drive to my house, the silence was deafening, nothing but thoughts clouding my mind, and making me a little crazy, to be honest. None of this was making sense to me. People were dying left and right around me. What did Uncle Leon do? What did he see? What did he not do?

The situation I was involved in was so unreal. My best inclination was to avoid it, as if none of this was even happening. But to be truthful, I was so scared.

I think tomorrow after I go down to the police station, I'm going back to Uncle Leon's house, I'll take Darrin with me. I want to see if I can find any clues that I might have missed.. Last time, I'm not sure if I searched hard enough. Maybe this second time I'll find something, anything.

I pulled up to my driveway and sat there for a moment. I'd forgotten Darrin was even following me. I rested my head in the palm of my hand. He came up to the side of my window and knocked on it. It startled me. As we were walking up to the door, I let Darrin in first and I turned around looking out into the dark sky. The moon hiding behind the clouds made the sky look foggy. I shook my head hoping and praying that I would find an answer to all of this. Before shutting my front door, I looked up and down my street, just to make sure I didn't see anything or anyone. It was really becoming apparent to me that my life depended on me finding out the truth to all of this very soon. I convinced myself that I had to stay strong. Thoughts of Matthew and Uncle Leon entered my mind.

Chapter 29

I remember waking up at three in the morning with a funny feeling. Rubbing my eyes, which were still very tired, I looked to the side of me. I had to look again, and focus my eyes, to see that Darrin wasn't there. I didn't have any clothes on, so I grabbed my silk blue robe Darrin bought me. I tied it around my waist and went over to my alarm pad, which was disarmed. I always knew that Darrin had the code, that never bothered me; he helped installed it.

I opened my bedroom door very slowly and peeked out. I heard Darrin talking on the phone downstairs. I couldn't really hear what he was saying, so I opened the door more and tiptoed quietly out to my stairwell. I was lucky my floors didn't squeaked, well at least so far. I leaned over the railing, he couldn't see me. I listened quietly.

"I'm not sure," Darrin said. I wish I could see what he was doing. "Well, call me tomorrow. I'll see if I can get her to come." There was a long pause. "She's already scared for her life, so she might suspect something." I think my heart stopped for a moment, but I continued to listen. What the hell was he talking about?

"Dr. Simon died last night. I'm not sure if the bullet was really meant for him." I let out a small gasp. I pulled myself back; I hoped he didn't hear me. "Hold on for a minute."

I quickly backed into the bedroom, closed the door gently, took off my robe and slid under the covers.

I'm not sure how many minutes passed. It seemed like forever. Finally, the door opened. I had the covers up to my neck. My back was turned to the door. I pretended to be asleep. He pressed buttons on the alarm pad. I assumed he was arming the system.

I heard his footsteps as he walked closer to me, on the opposite side. I could feel his eyes peering at me. It took him a while before he came around to the over side. I immediately started to think about the gun I saw last night and the fact that he'd never told me about it. He finally came around to the other side and climbed into bed. I could feel him looking at me; then he leaned over me. He pulled my hair from my face and kissed me on the cheek. I moved a little as though I was sleeping restlessly and turned to the other side, facing the bedroom door.

I didn't sleep well. I had no idea what was going on. Part of his conversation kept running through my head: *"She might suspect something." "She's already scared for her life." "I'm not sure if the bullet was meant for him."* I tossed and turned all night. Light seeped through the blinds. I looked over at the alarm clock and it read five o'clock. I looked back at Darrin, his eyes were closed. As I proceeded to get up, he grabbed me by the arm.

I looked back at him. He'd caught me off guard.

"Where are you going?" Darrin was wide-awake.

"Darrin, I'm going to the bathroom. Where else would I be going?" I snatched my arm away from his grip, and reached for my robe that was lying on the floor and started to put it on. His arm came under mine and he reached for my robe and threw it on his side of the bed.

"Well if you're just going to the bathroom, you won't need this." I didn't even look back at him. I got up and went into the bathroom in my room, shutting the door behind me. I looked in the mirror. My nipples were hard. I was cold. I started shaking and I tried to control it, but I couldn't. I kept telling myself to calm down. Something didn't seem right. I sat on the toilet and looked up at the second door in the bathroom, which led to the hallway. I looked back at the other door and then at the second door. When I was done peeing, I got up and ran the water in the sink. I took a deep breath and opened the door to the hallway. To my surprise, Darrin was standing right there in his boxer shorts.

"Where are you going?" he asked calmly.

I took a deep breath. "Look, this is my house, I can go wherever I damn well please." I pushed him aside, went into the bedroom where I grabbed my robe and slipped it on. I glanced back at him.

"Baby I'm just joking. You're acting all scared and paranoid. Did you have a bad dream or something?" He let out a sarcastic laugh.

"No, I didn't." I'm sure the expression on my face looked serious. "So what time are you leaving?" I'd thought about the words that slipped from my lips.

"Are you trying to get me out of here or something?" He came over and gave me a hug from behind, grabbing on my breasts.

"No, I just need to get dressed and get out of here so I can go downtown to talk to Detective Matters." I pulled away from him and started walking to the bathroom, but he stopped me.

"Are you sure you don't want me to go down with you?" He turned me around and put his hand under my face.

"Yes, I'm sure." I went into the bathroom and turned on the shower. I left the door cracked.

"I need you to meet me later, like around five or so," Darrin said. I stopped in my tracks while I took off my robe thinking about the conversation from last night.

"What for?"

"It's about your uncle. Just meet me. I'll explain it to you later. I'm going to use your other bathroom downstairs. Okay?" I didn't answer him. I wanted to ask him about his phone call last night, but I figured I'd ask him later after he left, and it would be over the phone, not face to face. Was this his chance to kill me? So many thoughts, I couldn't take it.

Later after Darrin left, I stood in the kitchen and smoked a cigarette, waiting for my coffee to brew. I looked out the curtain and saw Mrs. Jenkins across the street. I didn't even realize it had snowed.

Of course, she had her sprinklers on, and was standing in her driveway with snow up to her shin and only her housecoat on, with rollers and a hair net. What a sight to see. A minute or so later, the neighbor from next door came over to her house and turned her sprinklers off. Then he told her something; probably to get back in the house.

I poured me a cup of coffee, took a sip and glanced back out the window. Mrs. Jenkins was outside again, this time with a hat, gloves and coat on. She was standing on her porch as the same neighbor next door was shoveling her driveway. She looked up and saw me looking out the window. The next thing

I know, she started walking toward my house, with her purple Moon boots on. I put both my cigarette and coffee down, closed the curtain, and went to open the front door, before she had the chance to knock. I was wondering why she was coming over. I thought maybe she needed to borrow something from my kitchen.

I felt a cold breeze come in as soon as I opened the door. "Hi Mrs. Jenkins. What's wrong?"

"Rahkel," she started. She was hunched over a little. Her face was full of wrinkles. "It's Thursday."

"Okay Mrs. Jenkins. It's Thursday, so what can I do for you?" I didn't have a clue what she was talking about. She moved me aside and walked inside. I rolled my eyes and looked at her, with my hands on my hips.

"What? You don't celebrate Thanksgiving anymore?"

"Damn, I forgot." I hit my forehead slightly with the palm of my hand. With everything that was going on, I was side tracked. I forgot to bake her something.

"Okay, Mrs. Jenkins. Hold on one minute." I looked in the fridge, trying to find something to give her. I looked in the pantry and every snack I had was opened. I opened the fridge and grabbed an unopened expensive bottle of Sutter Home that Darrin bought me. "Damn it. I really don't want to give this away." I whispered to myself. I pulled it out. I decided to grab a bag of bread I had as well on my counter.

I came back into the living room and handed both the wine and bread to Mrs. Jenkins. She looked at both, and examined what I'd given her. She put her glasses on, which were hanging on a necklace around her neck. Damn, how long was she going to stand in the middle of my floor and examine my wine?

She smiled and walked over to my cabinet. After opening two cabinets, she grabbed one of my wine glasses. I had to bite my lips to stop me from saying something.

She didn't even say a word, she just walked right past me and opened my door and walked back across the street to her house. "You're welcome Mrs. Jenkins," I yelled at her.

She turned on her sprinklers on her way back into the house. I wanted to run out and warn her neighbor, who was almost done shoveling the snow from her driveway but it was too late, he was soaked. I shook my head and turned back around, walking upstairs to take a shower and change my clothes.

After I was done, I came back downstairs to the kitchen and poured me another cup of coffee. I turned around looking down at my socks with pink soles. I had on a pink jogging suit with a white top underneath.

I looked toward the couch where Darrin was sitting last night. I imagined him talking on the phone. What I remember him saying was running through my mind again and again. I picked up my cell phone to see what time it was. I had about ten minutes until I had to leave for the police station. Janetta left me a message to pick her up on the way. She must have left it while I was in the shower.

I looked closer at the couch and saw something sticking up from in between the couch. I sat my coffee down. It was Darrin's business card. I pulled it out and turned it over. I saw names. Each name was marked off except the last name. The names read: L. Wilson, F. Carter, D. Lowry, and C. Simon. The last name was: R. Williams. That's me! My eyes grew big. I couldn't help but think that all those people were dead and there names were crossed out, except for mine. A chill ran through my body. I looked at the alarm pad and ran over to it to make sure it was armed. Then I put the chain on my door. I had an idea; maybe I should change the code to the security alarm. I went to the kitchen and opened the drawers searching for the Security manual. I found it and went back to the alarm pad. I went through all the instructions listed and even entered my code. Then it asked me for a master code. I entered the only code that I knew- 6288, which stood for the first four numbers of my son's name, but it didn't work. It read: Master Code Denied. I referred back to the manual. The book says that the master code was different than the regular code, but of course, I didn't know it. But I'm positive Darrin does. I can't believe he hasn't told me my own master code.

"Damn it!" I slammed the book on the floor and put my head against the wall. My phone rang. I went over to it and it was Janetta. I'm sure she's wondering where I was. I turned on the alarm and headed for the door to pick her up.

Chapter 30

After spending almost an hour at the police station, I asked Janetta to go with me to Uncle Leon's house. Inside the car, my phone vibrated, alerting me to my missed calls: two from Darrin. I figured he could wait. I told Janetta about Darrin's phone call last night and about the business card with the names on the back. She admitted it did sound sort of suspicious, but that I shouldn't think the worst. Even though I heard that from Janetta, I was still skeptical.

Driving to Uncle Leon's, my phone was ringing.

"Aren't you gonna answer that?" Janetta said looking at me.

"No girl. It's Darrin. I don't want to talk to him now," I said making a left turn.

"You are so silly. You worry too much. You know that?" Janetta shook her head at me and tied her sheer scarf around her neck.

"Whatever. Just don't forget people are getting murdered around here. And what about this?" I stated, trying to introduce what I was about to say next. "I can't even change my alarm code. It keeps asking me for a master code. You know Darrin helped me get it installed, right? Now why wouldn't he tell me that I had a master code, huh?" I glanced over at her and then focused my attention back to the road. We were only a few blocks from Uncle Leon's house. I was sure she would agree with me now.

"Rahkel, if you are so concerned that Darrin is trying to kill you, or whatever is going through that head of yours, then why didn't you bring any of this up to Detective Matters while we were at the police station? *Duh...Duh.*" I didn't have anything to say to that.

There are too many things going on, that I don't really know what to believe. Maybe I'm paranoid, but maybe not. I dropped the subject about Darrin.

When we pulled up to Uncle Leon's house, I turned off the car and sat for a moment, looking around.

"What are you looking for?" Janetta asked as she looked around.

"Just anything out of the ordinary. Damn, Janetta, you act like you didn't just witness that doctor being shot with his brain guts oozing out his head. We all did. I'm sorry my nerves are shaken up and yours isn't." I was getting annoyed with Janetta.

"Okay, I'm not trying to think about it. I guess. Believe me; I was scared that night as well." Janetta touched me on the shoulder. "Sorry girl." I looked at her and grinned slightly, and then we both got out the car.

Inside, everything looked pretty much the way Uncle Leon left it, except for the spider webs that had formed around the windows. I'd already placed sheets around most of his furniture.

"So why are we here again?"

"I'm looking for clues, and not only that, I'm thinking about putting this house up for sale." The latter thought just entered my mind. I saw a box in the closet that I didn't remember seeing before. I pulled it out and started rummaging through it.

"Okay, well do you want me to go upstairs?" Janetta opened the refrigerator. "*Ooohwee*...There's still food in here, *gross*." She stepped back and pinched her nose.

"Oh, yeah, before you go upstairs can you get a trash bag from under the sink and put everything in there please? I thought Mama cleaned out the fridge, but I guess not." I continued looking through the box.

It was full of junk and papers, including unopened mail. I opened one of the pieces of mail which was from the Indianapolis Vehicle Registration department. The front of the envelope was dated in January and was addressed to my uncle. Opening the envelope, immediately I saw the license plate number: C2D1T3. The first three digits sounded familiar. I repeated it out loud: "C2D." Where do I remember that from? And then it hit me.

"*Oh my God!* Janetta come and look at this." I got up from off the floor and met Janetta in the living room. "Look, remember that car that nearly killed me, the first three digits were 'C2D' like this one." I gave her the paper and she looked closely at the registration.

"Well, I'm sure there's other vehicle license plate numbers that start with 'C2D', but that is a little strange?" Janetta gave the paper back to me and scratched her head.

"But you have to admit, that sure is a coincident." I was almost positive it was the same car.

"So what are you getting at?" Janetta walked back into the kitchen.

"Maybe somebody forged my uncles identity to get this, or maybe he really did buy a car and somebody stole it. There are many possibilities."

I took the envelope, placed the registration back inside and stuck it in my purse. As I continued searching through the box, there was a knock on the door.

"Who's that?" Janetta came from the kitchen.

"I don't know, should we answer it?" I put my head down and ran to the kitchen where Janetta was. Whoever it was, they knocked again.

"Rahkel it's me, open the door." A voice on the other end called out. I looked at Janetta. In unison we said, "That's Darrin."

Looking through the peephole, it was indeed Darrin. For a moment, I contemplated not opening the door. . Then finally, from behind me, Janetta said, "Open up the door, girl!"

As I opened the door halfway, Darrin practically pushed his way in. "Why the hell haven't you answered my phone calls?" He looked angry. It frightened me a little. Was it really that serious?

I looked over at Janetta, she had a look like, *I ain't in it.*

"What is the big deal? I came over to my uncle's house to look for something. And how did you know I was here?"

Darrin waved at Janetta and then he looked at me. "Can we go outside for a minute? I need to talk to you."

"Let's just go in the back room." I turned and was leading him down the hallway, when I felt a pull on the back of my jacket.

"No, let's go outside, I said." Darrin gave me this look that said he was serious, so I surrendered and followed him to the door. When we got outside, I faced him. "What is your problem?"

"Lower your voice. I don't think it's safe for you to be here." Darrin looked around and pulled me closer to him.

155

"Safe from who? If anything, I should be concerned if I can trust you." I waited for his reply but he stared through me instead. So I continued. "I overheard you talking on the phone last night and I found a business card with my uncle's name on it crossed out as well as everyone who's been murdered so far. What's that about? Huh?" I pulled away from him and stepped back. "And why was my name on the card? My name was the only person on there that wasn't crossed out." I stood with my hands on my hips.

"Look, Rahkel, I finally got in touch with Stan and he says he found what was on the CD. That's what my conversation was about last night and that's why I wanted you to meet me, so we could go and pick up the CD but now it may be too late. We were supposed to be there like an hour ago." Darrin glanced down at his watch. "You overheard wrong. And the name thing, I was just writing, putting pieces together. I write to try to make sense of things. You'll see all kinds of notes on my desk at home. Believe me, Rahkel, it was harmless." He gave me the eye and shook his head.

I pulled away when Darrin tried to touch me. I know I was being stubborn, but I didn't care. "Well, what about my alarm pad? I tried to change my alarm code, and it says I need a master code. You never bothered to give me that."

"Rahkel I never thought about it. I'll give it to you; no big deal. It's your son's birthday backwards." Darrin removed his black cap, dusted off the snow particles and put it back on. He pulled me closer and kissed me on the forehead.

"So what's on the CD anyway?" I asked, changing the subject. I was standing with my back against the porch railing facing him. I pulled out a cigarette. Darrin was about to answer then he paused. His eyes were stern and focused ahead, as he looked directly out into the street. Before I could turn around to see what he was looking at, he yelled at me.

"*Get down!*" Darrin grabbed me and pushed me down to the ground. My pack of cigarettes flew out my hand and cigarettes were everywhere. There was a large bush in front of me, when I hit the floor of the porch, so I couldn't see what was going on in front of me. I balled my body up and covered my head with my arms. All I heard were gunshots. I looked out the corner of my eye, and saw Darrin standing up beside me, pointing a gun straight ahead. He shot two times and then ran down the steps. I immediately crawled back to the front door, reached my hand up to the door and opened it. When I crawled in, I saw Janetta on the kitchen floor huddled in a corner. I crawled over to her.

"What the hell is going on out there? I heard shots." Janetta's was really shaken up. I could see the panic in her face.

"I don't know. Someone shot at us, and then Darrin shot back." I held onto Janetta's hands.

Right when I motioned her to follow me to the back door, we heard the door open. A fear like no other chilled my entire body. I hoped that was Darrin, but then again, I didn't know. There was silence, except for the footsteps that were getter closer. I looked around to see what I could grab. Then I thought about the mace on my key chain, I recently bought. Damn it my purse was in the living room on the floor. I remembered there was an extinguisher under the sink, so I carefully opened the cabinet and grabbed it. We both waited eagerly to see who it was. The seconds seemed like minutes as we waited. Then Darrin appeared right in front of us. He was covered in snow, and holding a gun.

"Everything's clear. Whoever it was got away, but I managed to shoot the back of there window out. I even got the first two numbers of there plates." He put the gun in a holster inside his jacket. He reached his hand out to me first and then to Janetta and pulled us off the floor.

"Why does C2 sound familiar?" he asked out loud, looking up at the ceiling.

For a moment, I looked between Darrin and Janetta, and then I hugged Darrin so tight, and cried like a baby. I couldn't even get the words out of my mouth to answer his question.

Chapter 31

The next few weeks were hard. I didn't want to be anywhere or go anywhere alone. Between Sharon, Nevilla, Janetta, Darrin and Mama, I had somebody with me at all times. I even had Janetta's cousin Gary go with me to the grocery store.

I spoke with Detective Matters. He had a police car patrol my house randomly almost every night. I was going out of my mind. I had been so stressed out, that I'm losing weight. My size eight jeans are loose on me now. You would think that was a good thing.

The rare occasions that I do have to be at home alone, I'd sit upstairs in my room with my door locked, and alarm engaged with the panic button in hand . I convinced Darrin to put two additional locks on my bedroom and bathroom doors. I didn't like living this way not one bit, but what else was I suppose to do? One day I broke down in front of Darrin. I couldn't take this. He held me. I don't think he knew what to say either. How long will I have to live like this? I think the police are getting closer; at least that's what Detective Matters said.

I finally decided to have a yard sale which I held at Uncle Leon's house. Maybe this was my way of trying to move forward. Darrin and Richard were even there. Mama wanted to keep some of Uncle Leon's stuff, but other than that, I sold a lot. I held the sale for two days. After it was over, I put up a *For Sale* sign on the house. What didn't sell was donated to a thrift store. With the money, I paid off some of Uncle Leon's bills from the business. Kareena and Shawntel even flew back down for the garage sale, with her greedy ass. She left with an old antique watch of Uncle Leon's, that she'd probably give to her husband.

For all of our safety, I convinced Detective Matters to have two police cars across the way, just to watch out during the garage sale. Darrin wasn't too happy about that, but I didn't care. His life wasn't on the line.

I finally decided to tell Janetta that I was thinking of selling the business. I really didn't know how she was going to react. I knew she wouldn't make that kind of money as a receptionist anywhere. But, surprisingly, she wasn't upset at all. I was so relieved. She said that she was thinking of telling me to sell it anyway, because it didn't seem safe working there anymore. Not only that, she admitted she'd been looking for another job. So that worked out well and made me feel a lot better.

Within a few days after the yard sale, Uncle Leon's building was sold, as well as his investment properties. I sold the house that Kareena wanted in Florida too, and boy was she pissed.

Darrin paid off his townhome, so he could keep it. I was feeling very generous and gave all the employees at the leasing office six months severance in addition to their last paycheck. Needless to say, they were very happy with me. I was moving, whatever it took. I was keeping hope alive and believing they'd catch whoever this was before it was too late.

Chapter 32

I decided to leave the nursing home early, I wasn't feeling well and my head was pounding. It had to be stress, so I took two extra strength Tylenols and headed home to lie down.

Half way home, I received a phone call from someone by the name of Adam, wanting to look at Uncle Leon's house. I was very excited because it had only been on the market for a week, and already I had an interested buyer. I tried calling Darrin, but he and Richard were in the city of Gary helping out another PI on an investigation.

Adam sounded pretty interested, so I wanted to show him the house today, if possible. If I could sell the house sooner than later, it would take more stress out of my life.

I called Janetta. She and Gary were at the mall but told me she'd meet me at Uncle Leon's house in about an hour. When I called Adam, he indicated that he and his wife, and two small children, would meet me. Actually, I was a little relieved and delighted that I'd be selling this house to a family. I told him to meet me in about thirty minutes. I figured by the time Janetta and Gary arrived, I would have started the tour of the house.

I arrived at Uncle Leon's about a quarter to six. I looked around and didn't see anyone. There were teenagers up the street playing ball in the street. As I unlocked the door, I looked up and down the street. I almost went back to my car, but I looked down at the time on my cell phone, and Adam would be here soon, and Janetta shortly thereafter. So, I decided to go in.

The house smelled of fresh flowers. There was a little dust on the panel near the entrance, which I wiped away with a damp Kleenex. The hardwood floors were clean and shinny; even if we did work our butts off getting them that way. I headed for the stairs and made sure I didn't see any dust and that everything was perfect. I think the only thing in the house I had to be replaced was the dishwasher, other than that, I would say Uncle Leon took very good care of his house. I walked upstairs and opened the doors to each of the four bedrooms. Each room was painted a sea green color, except for Sharon's childhood room. It was painted pink and yellow.

I smiled as I looked into Sharon's old room, the many sleepovers and memories as children we'd had in this room. I even remember the first time Sharon told me she'd lost her virginity; she never told me who he was. I think she was only twelve or thirteen.

I turned around to go back down stairs. When I got to the bottom, a man was standing right in front of me. I backed up and let out a small scream. I placed my hand over my heart.

The man was an older white male, who was a little pale in the face. He smiled with a fairly big grin. His teeth had a yellow tint to them. And he had a fading peppered colored beard.

"Sorry Ma'am. I'm Adam. Adam Rowdosky. The front door was opened. I hope you don't mind. Nice to meet you." He extend his mitten-covered hand.

I was relieved and met him halfway. "Well hello. Sorry I was so startled. Let's start out at the lower level and work our way up." I reared him first toward the stairs.

His hat was covering his head, so I truly couldn't tell exactly how old he was, but in the face, he sure looked pretty old, especially since I remember him stating he had two small children.

"So where's your wife and kids?" I looked out the front door. I saw an old gray Chevy pickup truck parked in front.

"Oh I'd dropped them off at that corner store on the next block. My son became ill and threw up on himself, and my wife went to buy something for him. This weather has really gotten to him. He's only three you know. My daughter also went with them, she's five. My wife may have to look at the house another time if that's okay."

"Sure, no problem."

He smiled at me. "Wanna see a picture of my family?" Without waiting for a response, he pulled out his wallet and showed me a nice picture of him, his wife—who was Asian, I think—and two very cute little kids.

"That's a beautiful family you have," I said while walking him into the kitchen.

He began asking me about the neighborhood. I told him it was pretty much a quiet neighborhood and that there was a park nearby, nice and big with plenty of swings for his kids.

I then went on to ask him where he and his family were from. He said they'd moved from Colorado and came here to be closer to his sister who lives in South Bend.

We moved from the kitchen to the den and then the living room. He admired the fireplace. I told him my uncle had built that himself.

I noticed he had a limp. I asked him what happened. He said he was injured in 1965 in the Vietnam war, and that's where he'd met his wife. Her mother, father and younger brother were killed and he brought her back to the United States with him. This reminded me of stories Uncle Leon used to tell us about him being in that war. I only remembered a few though. I asked him if he knew a Leonard Durman Wilson that served in the war. He indicated he didn't.

We walked back upstairs. He seemed very interested. I was getting excited. Finally, when we returned downstairs, I told him there was a fully furnished basement, and that's when Janetta and Gary entered the house through the front door.

"Sorry girl, there was an accident on the highway." Janetta dusted the snow off her coat and stomped the snow from her boots on the front entrance rug. Gary walked in behind her. He'd cut his hair and he didn't have his glasses on. I couldn't believe it. I had to take a double take. He actually looked sort of cute.

"Nice look," I said waving both of them towards us.

"Girl you know I couldn't have my cousin going on looking like that. We had to cut that shit and get him some contacts," Janetta said walking closer to us, when she noticed Adam. "Excuse my language."

I introduced Janetta and Gary to Adam.

"Well here's the basement, Mr. Rowdosky. I'm sure you'll find it's quite spacious, especially since you have little ones."

We all started to walk down the stairs, when I heard someone's cell phone ringing. We all looked down into our purse and pocket.

Mr. Rowdosky answered his phone. He apologized and announced that he had to leave to go back and pick up his family. He said he'd call me real soon to take another look at the house. He indicated he had another house to look at today, but so far, he liked what he saw. I looked out the window and watched as he started up his pick up truck and took off.

"So what did you think about him?" I asked, looking at Gary and Janetta.

"He was nice," Janetta said.

"Yeah he was nice," I said. However, something was a little strange about him, but I couldn't put my finger on it. "Oh well, who's up for going to happy hour, my treat?"

Walking back to the door, Gary asked, "Where are we going?"

"The Black Haven," Janetta said as she looked at me and smiled. "I'm gonna call Michael to meet me. You should call Darrin."

"I did earlier, but he's in Gary with Richard."

"How is Richard doing?" Janetta asked. She had the biggest smile on her face.

"What do you mean?" I asked her as I locked Uncle Leon's front door. I faced her. "Oh no you didn't," I said, emphasizing every word.

"Oh yes I did," Janetta said. "And it was…." She motioned her fingers indicating how small his penis was and frowned up her face. I held my mouth so I wouldn't laugh so loud and hard. I looked back at Gary and he was looking like he did not want to be involved in our conversation.

As we all started to walk down the stairs, I saw two of those teenaged boys from earlier throwing eggs at my car. I yelled at them, and they immediately took off running. I guess it was just a reflex move, but I took off running after them, particularly the little one. I saw Gary come out of nowhere, running ahead of me, grabbing the little one by the hood of his coat. As soon as he did, he slipped and fell to the ground.

Gary picked him up and turned him around, facing me. "Didn't your mama ever teach you manners boy? What the hell you throwing eggs at my car? We're gonna take you to your mama's right now," I yelled, pointing my fingers in the little boy's face.

Janetta came up behind us. "Damn, y'all got me all out of breath trying to keep up with you."

We all took a few steps toward the house he pointed to that was his.

"Wait! Sorry Ma'am, but that man that just left paid us to do it. I promise you. I'm sorry, don't tell my mom. I'll clean it right now." The boy looked frantic. I looked up and didn't see any of the other boys. They ran too fast for us. I replayed what this boy had just told me. I assumed he was lying just to get out of it.

"What? You talking about that old man in the gray pick up truck that left?" I asked.

"Yes, see," he nodded. The boy lifted up the side of his coat and pulled out a crumbled up twenty dollar bill from his pocket. "He paid me and my friends twenty dollars each."

I didn't understand. That really didn't make sense.

"I think he's lying. Let's go talk to his mama," Janetta said, as I stood with a confused look on my face wondering what I should do.

"No I'm not," the boy insisted.

I looked back at my car and one of the other boy's came out of nowhere and threw another egg at my car. We were already several feet away. I yelled at him to stop and then began walking, almost running toward my car. "Hold him." I yelled back at Gary and Janetta. The boy opened my car door on the driver's side. He had a carton of eggs in his hands which he was about to dump inside my car. I ran faster towards him. But at that very moment, there was the biggest, loudest sound I'd heard in my life.

The car exploded throwing the boy like a rag doll several feet away. I'll never forget that sight. I felt the impact and covered my face as I fell backwards to the ground. I wasn't sure if I fell or if I was thrown. I heard screams and smelt smoke. I saw blood dripping from my head into the freshly white snow. As tears flooded my eyes, I could hear everything that was going on around me. I was trying to crawl back to where Janetta, Gary and the other boy were. It seemed like it took me forever, as I crawled wet dirty snow. Several thoughts were running through my dazed mind. Nothing seemed real anymore. I panicked, feeling my heart pounding fast and my breathing was off beat. I could hear people's voices and astonishments as they ran out of there houses. I stopped crawling because I no longer had the energy. I opened my eyes and my vision was blurred. I did however manage to lift myself up against a parked car, but I fell back to the ground. I didn't see Janetta and Gary anymore. I began feeling light headed. I sat on the ground, leaning against the car, looking around to see if I saw them, but I still didn't. My vision was getting very blurry and things were spinning. People were running past me yelling. There yells and screams turned into muffled sounds. I soon heard sirens from a distant. I tried my best to focus my eyes, but things and people were still blurred. I looked to the side of me and saw a clear picture of Nevilla walking toward me. I shook my head, not knowing if it was my imagination or if it was really her. But she continued to walk towards me. My head pounded with severe pain. I moved my lips, but nothing came out. My eyes were closing, but I tried hard to keep them open. I reached my hand out to her as she was getting closer to me. I could almost touch her. She stood in front of me and stared directly into my eyes. I was seeing double. I fell sideways to the ground and then she kneeled down to me. She began whispering a song in my ear, a song I remember Uncle Leon singing to me when I was little. '*Lay down my little precious, sleep tight, tonight is your night. Don't fight. Good night. For tomorrow will be another day. I have to turn off the light. Your Uncle Leon loves you.*' I felt my eyes closing. Nevilla sang the song over and over again, and then I fell unconscious.

Chapter 33

I remember being surrounded by lights, and hearing Mama's voice. Like a little girl, that voice always comforted me. It seemed like every time I was hurt, she was there. That's when I realized I was in the hospital.

"How are you, baby?" Mama was wiping my forehead with a wet warm washcloth. I opened my eyes slowly and looked at her. She was trying to keep calm and composed, but it really wasn't working. I saw fear in Mama's eyes, reflecting my own feelings. I pulled myself up slowly. A sharp pain shot through my back, which hurt like hell. I let out a small groan. Janetta and Gary were off to the side at the bottom of my bed. Janetta came up to me and took my hand.

"That boy didn't make it, Rahkel." She was trying to hold back her tears, but she couldn't, and released my arm and went over to the corner by the window. Gary smiled at me, but it was more of a sympathetic grin, and then he put his head down and followed after Janetta.

I took a couple of deep breaths trying to relax my body, as I leaned back. Then I sat up with alertness. I ignored the pain that tore through my back.

"Where's Nevilla?" I asked looking around, pressing my hand firmly against my lower back, trying to suppress the pain. Everyone looked at me.

"Sharon and Nevilla are at my house, baby," Mama said squeezing my hand.

"No! I saw Nevilla walking right up to me when I was laying on the ground at the accident."

Everyone was quiet. Mama and Janetta exchanged looks.

"No Rahkel, Nevilla was at school today and now she's with Sharon at my house." Mama started to fix my pillow. "Look, you've been through a lot, lay back and get some rest. The doctor is going to prescribe something for your back, because you have a big bruise back there. You also have a cut on your head. The doctor said he may release you later on today or tomorrow. I'm gonna go talk to him now and tell him you're up." Mama left the room.

"Why are you saying that Nevilla was there?" Janetta asked walking over to me. She'd been crying; smeared mascara with red and puffy eyes. "So you didn't see her?" I asked leaning back slowly. I stared into Janetta's eyes hoping she would say yes. But instead, she shook her head no. I looked up toward the ceiling, resting my hands on my stomach. "Never mind, just forget it." I closed my eyes for a couple of seconds. I wished this was a bad dream.

Janetta started to pour me some water. "You should sip some of this," she said, handing me a small plastic cup. I took it and gulped it down with one swallow. I tried to turn to my side, but my back seemed to hurt even worse, so I laid there thinking about the recent chain of events. I told Janetta and Gary that I wanted to be alone. Janetta hugged me and they both left the room. Not long after, I fell asleep, but when I woke up, I turned my head to the side and looked out the window. And I saw an image of Nevilla's face with Uncle Leon behind her, resting his hand on her shoulder. She was singing that damn song again. I immediately turned my head the other way and saw Darrin in the doorway. I smiled, because I was so happy to see him. Then right behind him was Nevilla. He was holding onto her hand. My smile faded a little; although I really was happy to see her, but I had questions and was scared thinking no one would have the answers.

I didn't really get to talk to her. I didn't want to say too much in front of Darrin. Not long after, Mama came in the room and said her and Nevilla were about to leave. Nevilla blew me a kiss as she walked out and I blew one back to her wondering if all of this was one big paradox.

Chapter 34

The next day I decided to go over Mama's house. Darrin loaned me his other truck, an '89 Ford pickup. He said I could use it as long as I needed to. I had insurance on my Caprice and had plans on filing a claim sometime later on in the week. Janetta said Detective Matters was at the scene shortly after I'd passed out in the street and had my car towed to the police station after the fire truck hosed down my car. She said the entire street was covered with police cars and fire trucks. On my way to Mama's house, I called Detective Matters and left him a message, giving him the name and number to Adam Rowdosky and told him what the teenagers had told me. I hoped he'd call me back soon.

I wanted to see how Mama was doing, and plus she made me promise I would come by. The doctor prescribed Vicodin for my back. The cut on my head was healing slowly. When I got up this morning, my back ached so bad, so I took a pill.

My mind couldn't help but wonder what kind of day this would be. Darrin said he would come over later and cook me dinner, so I was excited about that. I was feeling so tired and stressed out, and honestly scared out of my mind. The feelings were overwhelming. I didn't really know what to think, what to believe or even who to believe. Nothing made sense. Mentally, I was already preparing my funeral.

Mama was cooking breakfast. I saw two glasses on the table. I figured it was for me. I went over to Mama and gave her a hug.

"How are you feeling, baby?" Mama had her apron on. I noticed she was struggling a little with the arthritis in her leg. Mama had two surgeries on her leg within the last year. I was starting to worry her leg was beginning to bother her again. But of course, she hadn't mentioned anything.

"I'm good, Mama. The question is how is your leg? You have been taking your insulin shots haven't you?" I stood beside Mama and dipped my finger on the edge of the glazed apple mix she was making to put on top of the pancakes. Mama slapped my hand like she used to do when I was a little girl.

"My leg is fine. I go to see the doctor next Friday. He's going to give me a different prescription for my arthritis and do an X-ray on my leg. And yes I have been taking my insulin shots." Mama took another glass from the cabinet and sat it on the table.

"Who's the other glass for?" I asked.

"Nevilla's here. Something about Teacher's Day. Sharon dropped her off about an hour ago," Mama said, without looking up. She continued whipping egg batter and then poured it into the skillet.

When I turned around, Nevilla was standing there. She smiled and then ran up to me. "Hi Auntie, you're out of the hospital. How are you?"

"I'm good, Nevilla." I patted her on her back, and brushed my fingers through her long black curls. I stooped down to Nevilla's level and could feel a stretch down my spine. "So you happy to be out of school today, my little princess?" I gave her a peck on the cheek and slowly stood back up.

"Yes, I'm glad to be home with Grandma. We're having apple pancakes and eggs." She pulled out a chair from the kitchen and sat down.

I smiled at her, went into the living room and sat down on the couch in front of the television. I reached for a pillow from the corner of the couch and propped it behind my back. Looking from the television to the kitchen, I was thinking of how I could get Nevilla alone. Taking her to the movies would be one way, she would love that.I wanted a cigarette bad, but I was so comfortable on the couch I didn't feel like getting up to go outside, so I asked Nevilla to bring me a glass of orange juice instead. I looked into the kitchen, as Nevilla was helping Mama put a plate of bacon on the table, and then she retrieved the paper plates from under the cabinet. I turned around toward the television and sipped on my orange juice. I took a couple of deep breaths thinking about everything that's been happening since Uncle Leon's death. I was confused, anxious and scared all at the same time. I couldn't get those thoughts out of my mind. I didn't know what was going to happen next and I wasn't sure if I wanted to know.

After breakfast, Mama went downstairs to wash clothes. I insisted to help her, but she claimed the stairs were good exercise for her. So I helped her take the laundry basket downstairs anyway. Big mistake. Pain shot through my back, something fierce. Mama asked if it was my back, but I told her no and sucked it up. I guess Mama and me were just alike; trying to act like we weren't in pain when we were.

"You know, Rahkel, Jacob called me collect yesterday. We talked for a few. Have you went and saw him lately?"

"Well just the last time I told you about Mama. But I'll probably go see him soon. Not sure when."

"I remember Jacob and Uncle Leon got along really well. I know Jacob will miss Leon," Mama said out of nowhere.

"Yeah we all will, Mama." I touched her hand gently, before throwing a load of clothes into the washer for her. She stood and looked out the window. I'm sure she was doing this to avoid crying. She turned around and gave me a hug. There were no words exchanged.

When I attempted to put one foot in front of the other, to climb the stairs, I was really in pain. With one hand affixed tightly to the railing, and the another hand behind pressed against my back, I slowly walked up the stairs to the living room, where I fell back onto the couch. Propping a pillow behind me, I popped another Vicodin. I looked at Nevilla sitting at the kitchen table, putting together a picture puzzle. I called out to her, and she came and sat down next to me.

I took Nevilla by the hand, came right out, and asked, "Nevilla were you there? At Uncle Leon's house yesterday when I got hurt?" I looked into her eyes. I didn't know what she was thinking. She showed no emotions.

"Auntie, I don't know what you're talking about. Are you still seeing pictures in the sky?" She pulled her hand away, returned to the kitchen table where she worked on her puzzle.

I was dumb founded. I walked into the kitchen. "What do you mean pictures?" I've never told anyone about the images I've seen in the sky.

"Well Auntie, I see how you look up at the sky sometimes." Nevilla never took her eyes off her puzzle.

Turning, I slowly walked backward into the living room, keeping my eyes glued to Nevilla, as she sat at the kitchen table, kicking her leg back and forth, with the other leg folded beneath her. She was so cute, but yet there was something that terrified me about her and I'm not sure exactly what, but I think I was the only one who noticed it. Wanting to say something, I couldn't. I was completely speechless.

Uncle Leon and Nevilla were close. Since Nevilla's father had never been in her life, Uncle Leon was the only father she knew. Nevilla has handled Uncle Leon's death better than I had originally expected. Or maybe her acting weird was how she's handling it. I stopped thinking about it and looked back in the kitchen. She was still busy with her puzzle.

Managing to pull myself off the couch, "I'll be on the front porch," I called out to Nevilla. The Vicodin had kicked in and I needed a damn cigarette.

"Alright, Auntie."

Pulling my hat down over my ears, I wrapped my red matching scarf around my neck. Thanks to the cold and snow, this would be a short smoke. Across the street, Mama's neighbors were coming outside—a single dad, his two sons and little daughter—to shovel snow out of their long driveway. The father waved at me, and I waved back.

An idea came into my mind like a flick of a light switch. I wasn't sure if it would work, but it was definitely worth a try. I couldn't tell anyone, especially Mama. I flicked my cigarette butt in the snow and went back inside the house.

Sitting on the couch, I sifted through my purse. I was looking for a business card that a friend of mine have given me a long time ago. While still rummaging, my phone rung. I could tell form the caller ID that it was Detective Matters. My worse nightmare yet. Detective Matters said they found the homemade bomb that was placed underneath my car on the drivers side. I was terrified by the news. He also went on to say he'd called Rowdosky and had him come down to have him fingerprinted, but his prints didn't match the fingerprints that were on the bomb. The two boy's fingerprints didn't match either. All of this was really getting crazy. Nothing made sense. Someone was having too much fun playing games, at my expense. I was speechless. "Rahkel are you there? Hello? Hello?"

I held the phone glued to my ear. I looked in the kitchen where Nevilla sat. She looked up at me and knew something wasn't right.

Chapter 35

My back was feeling a lot better today. I stood in the mirror with just my panties on with my back to the mirror, looking at the bruise on my back. It really looked awful; like I'd been smacked with something large. It was blue and purple.

I thought back to the day of the accident. I don't even remember injuring my back. I'm not sure if I'll ever find out what happened that day. The appearance of Nevilla walking towards me and singing was so real. But no one knows anything or believes me. The last thing I wanted people to think was that I was going crazy.

Later in the day, I figured I'd pay Darrin a surprise visit at his office, even though yesterday I mentioned that I might stop by. On the way to Darrin's office, I stopped off at Subway to grab lunch. Walking through the revolving doors of the five-story building, I strolled across the lobby toward the elevator and waited, for what seemed like forever. When the elevator doors opened, a young couple was hugged up and kissing. They might as well have been having sex right in front of me.

"Sorry about that," the girl said. She glanced at me and they both started laughing.

"No problem," I said getting on the elevator.

Getting off on the fifth floor, I entered Alliance Private Investigators. I passed the receptionist, slightly acknowledging her, and went toward the back. Darrin's partner, Calvin, stopped me as I walked past his office. He called out my name. I poked my head into his office.

"So how's your friend Janetta?" He was sipping on a steamed cup of coffee.

"Oh she's fine. I just talked to her the other day." I was thinking about Janetta and how she'd already given me the scoop. She eventually told me they went to lunch, and afterwards went back to his place. She'd also said they'd did it so quick it was just plain ridiculous. She looked up at him and he had the nerve to look at her with the utmost of confidence and asked her how it was. She said she left him there and went back to work. Later that night she called her friend Patrick to make up for the lack of pleasure.

"I'm sure she told you how good of a time we had," Calvin said.

I wanted to laugh in his face, but I didn't. "Sure." What a prune. "Have a good one." I continued down the hall.

I entered Darrin's office and hesitated, because he was on the phone. He smiled and motioned for me to come in. Sitting the Subway bag on his desk, I took a seat in the chair positioned in front of his desk. Twiddling my thumbs, I looked around the office. It was nice, nothing special, but nice.

While I waited for his call to end, I focused on the wall calendar of fancy sport cars and the painting of snow top mountains, on the wall behind him. After his call, he came around to the front of the desk and gave me a big hug and a kiss. He picked up the bag of Subway and extended his hand to me.

"Let's go downstairs in the cafeteria. Did you bring you something?"

"Yeah, it's in the bag." Damn, was he that hungry, that he didn't think I was gonna eat?

We past the front desk. "See you later, Darrin."

The receptionist was a young little thing, maybe nineteen, not that I was old or anything. The way she smiled at him, without acknowledging me sort of irked me. For her to be sitting at the front desk, she sure did have a lot of cleavage showing. She might as well have been at the dance club. I'm sure Calvin has tapped that ass a few times. I smiled at her when we left but she flung her fake weave to the other side and rolled her eyes at me. What was that all about?

The cafeteria was crowded, but we managed to grab an empty table. Darrin reached over and gave me another kiss.

"What was that for?" I asked looking up at him smiling.

"I'm glad to see you. That's all. How's your back?" Darrin asked, reaching in the bag and pulling out a foot-long steak and cheese sandwich. I reached in and grabbed my food as well.

"Oh it's better. It's just bruised now." I grabbed the salt and pepper and seasoned my chicken salad.

I looked around, which was something I tended to do lately, always scoping my surroundings.

"Hey I got a hold of Stan. He said he managed to break the password on the CD and he copied it to another CD for us. He's going out of town again, so I just told him to mail it to my house before he leaves," Darrin stated, right before taking a big bite of his sandwich.

"That's great. Maybe I can finally find some answers now." I really thought that was some good news. Maybe I'm getting closer to something.. "Did you ask him what was on it?"

"No, he was in a hurry when I talked with him, so we'll see when it comes."

I looked down at the time on my cell phone. I promised I'd take Nevilla to the movies, but before doing so, I had something else on my mind. I wanted to tell Darrin, but I didn't want to give him the opportunity to tell me it was a bad idea. I actually didn't want anyone to know what I was up to.

"What's on your mind?" he asked sipping on his drink.

Damn, was he reading my mind or what? "Ah. Nothing."

"Hey what do you think about us moving in together?" Darrin asked leaning forward taking my hand. I was shocked. I almost spit out my food. I would have definitely thought I'd be asking that before him.

"Well, let's talk about it tonight. I actually gotta go honey. I promised I'd take Nevilla to the movies." I really wasn't avoiding his question, but I was so shocked by his question that's all that came to mind. I thought it was a really good idea. I have to admit I was falling in love with Darrin. I just haven't told him that yet.

"Okay. You know I love you right?" He kissed me on the hand. Darrin smiled at me, and I smiled back. For the first time, he told me he loved me. I was feeling so happy right now.

After lunch, Darrin walked me to my car. We hugged each other and then I got in the truck and pulled off as I watched him walk back to the building in my rear view mirror.

Chapter 36

I went over to Sharon's apartment to pick up Nevilla. Of course, knucklehead was there. I stared at Terry, and if looks could kill. They were both cuddled up on the couch watching a movie. I could tell they were up to something, but I wasn't quite sure what. A layer of newspaper was spread on top of the coffee table. Looking toward Nevilla's room, all was quiet. A strange feeling rose within me. Sharon was fidgeting too much. Reaching down, I snatched up the newspaper. I couldn't believe it. There was white shit everywhere, along with two razors.

Sharon stood up and grabbed the paper from my hand. "What the fuck are you doing?"

I didn't utter a word. I frantically shook my head and I looked down at her stomach. She was already about six months . I looked over at Terry, who couldn't look me in my face.

I walked back to Nevilla's room. I remember back when Sharon and I were doing that stuff all the time. I couldn't help but to fault myself that she was still doing dope. If Mama only knew, she'd be too quick to call social services and take Nevilla. But I would never tell Mama. I searched my mind for a solution, but there was nothing. I opened up the door to Nevilla's room. It was so pretty and clean. I would have dreamed to have a room like this when I was a little girl. Uncle Leon helped her put her room together. It was a Care Bear theme, colors of pink and lavender were everywhere. She had most of her Care Bear's sitting across her bed and dresser. As soon as she saw me, she smiled.

"Auntie, can I spend the night?" Nevilla was taking clothes out of her closet and placing them on the bed.

"Well sure, I'm sure your Mom won't mind. We can even go to the movies if you like," I said, sitting down in her rocking chair, trying not to think about Sharon in the front room.

I reached over and helped her pack a pair of jeans and shirt into her Mickey Mouse bag. I noticed there was a picture of Uncle Leon and Nevilla standing together in the front pocket of her bag. Uncle Leon was bent down at knee level and Nevilla was standing with her hand on his shoulder. I'd never seen this picture before. They were both smiling.

"When did you and Uncle Leon take this picture Nevilla?" I asked turning it around. I noticed she was wearing a black jacket with silver buttons going down the front. It was a really nice picture.

"A long time ago, Auntie." Nevilla grabbed her coat from her closet.

I looked at the picture one last time and placed it back into Nevilla's Mickey Mouse bag.

"I'm all ready." Nevilla grabbed her bag from me. I smiled at her and followed her out of the room, looking back into her room closing the door behind me.

"Mommy I'm spending the night at Auntie's," Nevilla said, with her coat and hat on.

Sharon was so doped up, she was in a daze. I snapped my finger to get Sharon's attention.

Sharon looked up. "Okay baby, have fun." Sharon didn't acknowledge us when we left. I felt sorry for the baby inside her.

I took Nevilla's bag and placed it in the trunk. I sat for just a minute to warm up the car, and then off we went. I looked up and to my surprise, Sharon was looking out the window. She was waving at us.

We stopped by the gas station so I could fill up the truck and get a newspaper.

"Nevilla the movie doesn't start for another hour and a half. I need to make a stop before we go, okay sweetie?" I rolled down my window and lit a cigarette.

"Okay Auntie."

I hope what I was about to do would help. I didn't know if Nevilla knew what a psychic was. I know it was a little extreme or awkward but I was getting desperate. I got on the highway and got off at Brownsmen Road.

Looking at the directions , I drove a couple of streets down and didn't see the street I was looking for. I finally realized I had to drive down a long narrow dirt road. I soon came upon a small house with a sign outside that read: Sandy's Psychic and Tarot Readings. I'd never been here, but I was told this woman was good. I looked over at Nevilla. She was looking through a kid's magazine.

"Okay, here we are, lets go." I was surprised Nevilla didn't ask me where we were going. She looked up, glanced around and got out. I took her by the hand and we walked up to the door, which resembled a tarot card with writing and symbols on the front. I rang the bell.

A woman appeared, wearing a scarf with different designs tied around her head. I expected an older person, but she was young, maybe even younger than me. She had the greenest eyes I'd ever seen. They were big and bright. She smiled at us, and welcomed us in.

"You must be Rahkel." Then she looked down at Nevilla. "And you must be Nevilla."

"Yes that's right," I said. "It's nice to meet you Sandy."

"The pleasure's all mine ladies."

I felt a cool breeze as soon as I entered her house. It seemed as though people were surrounding me. It was a strange feeling. It wasn't a bad feeling, just strange. I looked around and saw tarot cards lying everywhere. I saw a painting on the wall of a woman talking to the glitter-filled sky. There were two black cats off to the side as well, one lying on the couch, the other on the floor. Beads hung down through the entrance of the kitchen. I ran my hands through the beads; they were shiny and very smooth.

Sandy had on a long silky gown—so long, you couldn't see her feet—pulling it up as we walked up some stairs, careful not to trip

"Watch your step," she said.

I grabbed onto Nevilla's hand. "This is a nice place you have." We came to a large table, and she pulled a chair out for me. Nevilla held tight onto my hand.

"Thank you. Nevilla would you like to sit here?" Sandy pulled out a chair close to her.

"No, I want to sit by my Auntie." Nevilla pulled the chair from Sandy and slid it closer to me and sat down. She was practically sitting on my lap.

"There's nothing to be afraid of. The spirits here are very calm and nice. They are only provoked by evil." Sandy sat down and placed a shear cloth over the table.

Spirits. That sounded sort of freaky. I was starting to wonder if this was the right thing to do; to bring Nevilla here. Maybe I should have come alone. I looked over at Nevilla and she continued to stare at Sandy.

The psychic started out by telling us to take three deep breaths. I was relaxed almost instantly. I looked over at Nevilla, I think it relaxed her as well. She wasn't holding onto my hand as tight anymore.

Sandy pulled out two blue, liquid-filled candles from a glass cabinet. She sat them on the table and lit them both. I couldn't figure out how the candles had liquid inside them. She went to another cabinet and pulled out a small jar of some sort.

"What is that?" I asked, wondering what she was about to do.

"It's my favorite potion. It sets the mood before I begin my sessions."

She placed two drops into each candle. The smell was intense. It smelled good, but it was strong, then all of a sudden, the smell went completely away. I turned around, because I felt something, almost like someone was behind me. There was nothing but the clock on the wall ticking away. It was shaped like a cat. A tale hung from it, swaying back and forth. Its large eyes moved left to right.

"No one's there," Sandy said looking up at me with those green eyes. "A lot of people think that. Well there may be a spirit or two." She smiled at me.

"Well let's get started shall we?" Sandy shuffled her Tarot cards. She asked us our birthdays. I watched her hands as she placed cards on the table. She wore a beautiful ebony ring on her finger. She must have seen me looking at it. She held the ring up to me. It started to change colors. I touched it and it immediately turned blue and it was very warm. I pulled my hand back.

"What does that mean?" I asked.

She looked at me and said, "You are confused right now because you do not know the truth. But you will find out that the truth is not far from you. And you will be shocked by it."

Spooky. I sat back and looked down at Nevilla. She looked at me and shrugged her shoulders.

"Can I touch it, Auntie?"

"Can she?" I looked up at the Psychic.

"Go for it young lady."

Nevilla reached and touched Sandy's ring. It immediately turned gray with a black spot in the middle.

Nevilla pulled her hand back. "Her ring is cold, Auntie."

"What does that mean?" I asked.

"My dear, this little one has strong powers. Someone is looking out for her. And she knows something but is not telling, but unfortunately I do not know right at this moment what it is." The psychic continued to place more cards on the table. I looked down at Nevilla, and she shrugged her shoulders again. Then I looked back at the psychic.

"Shall we begin?"

As Sandy closed the shear white curtain behind her, I saw a faceless man in the painted sky on the ceiling. I shook my head and blinked my eyes.

"Yes, let's begin," I said.

"Would you like me to tell you why you see images in the sky?" Sandy reached out her hand to me.

I was speechless, I can't believe she knew and how did she know? I reached out my hand to her. Her hands were so soft, silk like. I looked into her green eyes. They were so mesmerizing.

"It is because you possess the power of imagination. Your past has everything to do with what you see. When you find out your past, you will be able to have a comforting future. And you will no longer see pictures."

I was curious about her answer. I wasn't really sure what that meant, but it was interesting.

I wanted to know more, but I glanced at the time on my phone and I did promise Nevilla I'd take her to the movies. Not including I was paying by the half hour for this appointment. So I decided to move on to my real concerns.

I wrote down a list of three questions on a piece of paper and slid it to Sandy. I didn't want to ask out loud in front of Nevilla. I nonchalantly motioned my index finger to the side of my lips. On the paper, I wrote: I want to know about the strange things that have been happening to Nevilla. I also want to know if she was there the day of my accident. Lastly, who murdered my Uncle Leon?

Sandy didn't look at the paper. I watched her as she turned it over and placed the palm of her hand over it.

I started to say something, but she put her finger over her lips and picked up a card that had a butterfly on it, and then looked toward Nevilla. She reached out her hand to Nevilla. Nevilla looked up at me as to confirm if it was safe.

"Go ahead sweetie."

Nevilla slowly reached her hand out to Sandy. "You are such a beautiful child. You love your Uncle Leon very much don't you?"

Nevilla nodded her head.

"Tell me more about the man dressed in white."

Nevilla pulled her hand away from Sandy and shook her head.

I looked at both of them and then back at Sandy with concern in my eyes. "What do you mean, the man in white?"

"I see a man. His entire body is painted white. Nevilla knows this man very well."

I looked down at Nevilla. "What is she talking about Nevilla?"

"I don't know, Auntie." Nevilla looked confused as well.

"Okay well anyway, what about the second part of my question?" This was getting weird and I was starting to feel fearful. I looked behind me up at the cat clock. The tail seemed to be swinging faster.

Sandy picked up another card. This one had different colored stars on it. Sandy reached out her hand to Nevilla again. Nevilla was hesitant.

"One more time Nevilla and then you'll be done." I could tell Nevilla was getting uncomfortable and so was I. I felt bad for having her come here.

"Take a deep breath child." Nevilla did as Sandy asked. There was a long silence. I could only hear the ticks of the clock behind me. Then Sandy released Nevilla's hand. A warm breeze swept through the room; so much so that I felt it in my hair. I touched my hair and looked around the room. What the hell?

"Did anyone feel that?" I asked.

They both just looked at me.

"She is blocking the information. I cannot answer your question." Sandy picked up all the cards and started shuffling them again.

"I wanna go, Auntie, please. I thought we were going to the movies?" Nevilla whispered to me.

"Okay Nevilla." I looked at the time and we'd already been here an hour.

"Okay Sandy what about my last question?" I exhaled as I looked down at Nevilla, wondering and anticipating what Sandy was about to say.

Sandy stopped shuffling and pulled a card from the middle of her deck. It had a picture of the night sky. She laid it on the table. She asked me for his birthday, which I gave her and then she reached her hands out to both me and Nevilla. She asked us to close our eyes for exactly one minute. That minute seemed liked five minutes. I felt something behind me again, but I kept my eyes closed until the minute was over.

"My dear I don't believe your Uncle was murdered," She stated calmly. "And who is this woman whose name starts with an 'S'? You all have something in common: you, Nevilla and this woman whose name starts with an S." She said with a voice that seemed to change tone. It scared the shit out of me. The tone of her voice went from sweet to a lower pitch.

"What do you mean? My Uncle is dead," I blurted out. "And what's wrong with your voice?" I was wondering if I should run out of there right then and there.

She closed her eyes and then opened them . "What about the woman who's name starts with an S?" She asked again. Her voice returned to normal.

"Are you talking about my cousin Sharon?" She nodded her head. "Okay so if you don't think he was murdered then what are you saying?"

"I'm sorry dear, but that is the only information that I have at this moment." She raised her hands into the air, and I felt another breeze come into the room.

I could feel Nevilla yanking on my jacket. "Let's go, Auntie."

"Okay, okay," I said back to Nevilla. "Sandy, I'm afraid we're gonna have to go. I really appreciate your time. How much do I owe you?"

"Fifty. I always take off ten for first time customers."

I paid her and she walked us to the front door. We waved at her as she stood in the doorway. As soon as I stepped out of that house, I felt relieved and free.

"Nevilla," Sandy called. We both looked up. "When the time comes you must tell the truth." Sandy walked back into her house and closed the door behind her. We both looked at each other and got in the car quickly.

Driving to the movies, I looked over at Nevilla. She was reading her magazine.

"So what did she mean by telling the truth Nevilla?"

"I don't know, Auntie, she was a crazy lady." Nevilla flipped through another page in her magazine.

"So if there was something going on with you, you would tell me right, sweetie?"

"Of course." Nevilla didn't look up from her magazine.

I looked ahead at the road. I spent my thoughts thinking about what Sandy said. Her words kept repeating in my mind: "*I don't believe your Uncle was murdered.*"

Chapter 37

It was Sunday and Mama wanted me to go to church with her. I really didn't want to but what could it hurt? After all I've been through this may be exactly what I need. Maybe prayer would do me good. Last night Sierra arrived from Langston University, in Oklahoma . Tony paid for her travel. She's only taking two online classes right now so she figured she could take the break. And plus Mama's been begging her to come up here for Christmas. And since Christmas was only a week away, I was glad to see her as well.

I managed to get both Janetta and Sierra to go with me to church. Janetta's working as an Office Assistant downtown. She said she likes it.

Sierra, Mama and me were on our way to pick up Janetta from her apartment. When we pulled up, I asked Janetta where was Gary.

"Girl, he met some woman on the Internet and moved in as her roommate."

I was surprised to hear that, but oh well, whatever works.

Janetta was decked out, wearing a fur coat, hat and a nice dark blue dress with three-inch heels to match.

"You make me feel underdressed, girl," I said jokingly, wearing a black skirt and a light blue top with my leather coat.

"Please girl, you look fine. But you know how I do it anyway. It's a must that I look good." We both started laughing. "Who knows maybe I'll meet a Christian brotha'."

"Nice to see you, Janetta." Mama looked happy that we all were going.

"You too, Ms. Williams." Janetta sat in the back seat with Sierra who had on a black skirt as well, with a silver blouse and black boots.

When we arrived at the Rose Christian Center, the parking lot was full. That's when Mama whipped out her handicap sticker, which I hung from the rearview mirror. I was glad we were able to park in the front; it was cold, and I didn't want to walk too far.

"Praise the Lord. Today is gonna be a really good service," Mama said as we were walking up to the entrance. Bless Mama's heart she was so excited. Sierra and I looked at each other and smiled.

Halfway through Bible service, Darrin texted me and asked me what I was doing. I text him back, telling him I was at church. He asked me to pray for him. Not sure if he was being for real or funny.

Mama looked over at me and made a face. I nodded at Mama and put away my phone. Boy did this remind me of when I was a little girl, when a pinch would follow that look. Those pinches hurt so bad. I remember those days, going to church with Tony and Mama, and Mama was pregnant with the twins. Tony always found a way to get me in trouble.

While my mind should be on the sermon, it wandered to Tony. He still wants me to come out to California for a visit. But I don't know about that. I haven't spoken to Daddy in a long time and I think it would be awkward. Tony was adamant that Daddy and I should squash our differences, but like I always tell him, when the time was right, I'll come.

As the choir sung their praises, I couldn't help but glance around, to see if I saw anything out of the ordinary. We all stood up, clapping our hands. I saw the light flashing on my cell phone which was in my purse. I waited until we sat back down and grabbed it. I couldn't believe it. It was Adam Rowdosky. I waited until the phone stopped ringing to see if he would leave a voicemail. He did. I excused myself immediately and went to the bathroom. I looked in the mirror and took a deep breath. I could feel my heart starting to beat a little fast. I sort of felt bad about blaming him for ruining my car, and trying to kill me. I wondered if he was still interested in the house.

I listened to the message. He wanted to make an offer on the house. He wanted to know if I could meet him, his wife and kids at the food court at the mall later on today. I put the phone down when I saw Mrs. Nelson come in. I pretended to wash my hands. She was one of Mama's elderly friends and the last thing I need was for her to go back and tell Mama that I was on my cell phone in the bathroom. I wouldn't hear the last of it. I left the bathroom and went outside. I went by a tree and smoked a cigarette. I looked around to make sure no one was watching me.

I decided to give him a call back. I did want to get Uncle Leon's house sold and since he was still interested in the house, I was ready to sell it. I was glad he wanted to meet at a public place. I still had my suspicions. The mall was probably the most public place there was, and that made me feel at ease. He said there were no hard feelings about me giving his name and number to the police. I replied with an "Okay."

I finished my entire cigarette and flicked it in the frost bitten grass. After church, I dropped everybody off. While backing out of Mama's driveway , Sharon pulled up behind me in her Jeep with Nevilla.

She got out and hurried to my car and tapped on the window. "Could you keep Nevilla for me? Please?"

I opened the door. "I have an appointment. Why can't you keep her?"

"Me and Terry are going up to Belterra Casino Resort. Come on now."

"So forget my appointment, while he goes up there to gamble all your money," I said. She was really starting to irritate me.

"Not now Rahkel. Please just do this for me." She sounded so desperate. I frowned at her, wanting to say something I'd probably regret later.

I looked back at the Jeep and didn't see Nevilla, only to find her already at my passenger door looking in. I got out of the car and looked up at Mama as she was about to go inside.

Mama looked back at me. "Don't look at me. Me and Sierra are going to play Bingo with some ladies from church. No kids allowed." Sierra shrugged her shoulders.

"Fine," I snapped, feeling frustrated and put on the spot. I looked towards Nevilla. "Come on Nevilla get in."

Nevilla smiled and opened the door..

"So when are y'all coming back?" I wanted to know. I was so tired of Sharon putting Nevilla off on me, to go be with sorry ass.

"Probably Tuesday, maybe Wednesday. Auntie will keep her. Drop her off after they come back from bingo."

Giving Sharon an I'm-sick-of-your-shit look, "You owe me," I said, climbing back in my car.

"Anything you want." She was already running back to her jeep.

"Rehab," I yelled back at her.

She looked at me and rolled her eyes.

As we left, I called Darrin and headed to his house. I told him about me meeting up with Mr. Rowdosky. He said it would be best if I met him alone and that Nevilla and him would sit a few tables away at the food court. I agreed. I was glad he didn't convince me not to go.

While at Darrin's, I called Mr. Rowdosky. He was happy to hear from me again. He said that he was definitely interested in the house and wanted to make an offer. He said his wife and kids were with him. I really wanted to meet them.

Darrin and I took separate cars. He and Nevilla in his Suburban and me in the pickup. The mall was crowded, which was to be expected since Christmas was right around the corner; last minute shoppers. Nevilla took Darrin to the toy store. He said they wouldn't take long. Yeah right, Nevilla in toy store was like Janetta at a buffet. That's my girl and all, but she can eat her ass off and still look good.

I looked around as I walked through a busy crowd as a man dressed up as Santa Claus handed out candy canes. I took one. Glancing at the massive clock, covered with green wreath and red poinsettia leaves, that hung in the middle of the mall, I had five minutes, so I went to meet Mr. Rowdosky at the food court. I found an empty table and sat down. I took off my coat and left on my hat and scarf.

Five minutes turned into ten minutes and no Mr. Rowdosky or Darrin and Nevilla. I called Darrin on his cell phone.

"Where are y'all at? I'm waiting." I looked around me to make sure I didn't see Mr. Rowdosky.

"We're on our way now. I bought Nevilla a pink teddy bear. She nearly begged me so I couldn't resist." He's such a sucker.

"You didn't have to do that." I looked up and saw Mr. Rowdosky coming in my direction, smiling. "I gotta go, he's coming. Hurry up," I whispered, quickly hanging up the phone.

I pulled the contract and other documents from my bag and placed them on the table. I had an extra pen on the table for him. I didn't see his wife or kids with him though. I looked out of the corner of my eye and saw Darrin and Nevilla coming. The table next to me was taken so they sat at a table across from us on the other side of the food court.

"So where's your wife and kids?" I asked as he pulled out a chair to sit down. He wore a brim hat with a blue ribbon .

"They're shopping. My wife can never pass up a good sale. They should be coming. I told her where we're at." Adam kept fidgeting and looking around.

I looked over his shoulder and noticed that Darrin and Nevilla found a table by the plants. Nevilla was eating on a candy apple. I typed up the contract so the only thing Mr. Rowdosky had to do was look over it and sign by the yellow sticky Post-Its. I was surprised he didn't ask to take a second look at the house or to inspect it in any way. Not that anything was wrong with Uncle Leon's house. I even asked him if he and his wife wanted to take another look at the house, but he denied the offer.

I excused myself while he was looking over the paperwork and made a beeline to Darrin and Nevilla . I smiled at them as I passed and went into the restroom. I looked in the mirror and took a deep breath. I wanted a cigarette bad. I took off my hat and combed my hair. When I came out of the restroom, I noticed Mr. Rowdosky starring my way. But as I got closer, I realized he wasn't looking at me. He was staring at Darrin and Nevilla. His eyebrows curved inward . When I walked up to him, he was still looking there way. I looked back and forth between the direction of his stare and Darrin and Nevilla. Darrin had his back against us and Nevilla was focused on her candy apple, not looking at us.

I pretended to cough when I came directly up to the table, and this distracted him and directed his attention back on me.

He excused himself and got coffee from Starbucks. When he returned, he asked, "So are you here with anyone?" as he sat down.

"No, why?" I asked, raising a brow. What a strange question.

"Just wondering. Well here you go, everything is signed. And I have a cashiers check for the twenty-thousand-dollar down payment that I'd like to make."

I was shocked. He only needed to give me five thousand. I didn't understand why he gave me twenty. I reiterated this to him, but he insisted this would lower his monthly payment and that it was a tax write off for him.

"So where did you park?" I don't know why I asked that. But I did.

"We took a taxi. My truck is in the shop right now. It broke down yesterday," he said as he sipped the last of his coffee.

He got up, shook my hand and said he was going to go look for his wife and kids. I smiled and watched as he walked off. I looked at the twenty thousand dollar cashier's check I held in my hand. Well this was easy. I started to walk over to Darrin and Nevilla, but changed my mind. I suddenly got a funny feeling and stopped in my tracks. I turned on my heels and followed Mr. Rowdosky, staying behind him but far enough so he couldn't see me.

I looked back at Darrin and Nevilla. Darrin was looking at me, trying to figure out what I was doing. I pulled out my cell phone and called him.

"I'm following him. He's about to leave. I want to see something. Follow me." I hung up with Darrin and looked back at them to see if they were getting up. They were. I really wanted to see how his wife and kids looked. I was being noisy.

While following Mr. Rowdosky, he'd turn around, but I stopped a few times pretending I was looking through the glass of stores and stopping by stands. He headed for the exit, while looking around one last time before leaving the mall. I stood for a moment, to see where he was going. He climbed into that same old gray Chevy pickup truck which was parked not far from the entrance.

"That liar." I began running the opposite way, because we'd parked almost on the other side of the mall. When I turned around Darrin knew exactly what I was doing and he grabbed Nevilla by the hand and we all started to run. I heard Nevilla ask him why we were running. He told her I had somewhere to be and that I was running late.

I hurried outside and unlocked the car door and took off immediately to the other side of the mall. I didn't look to see where Darrin and Nevilla were. I figured I'd call them later. I thought I'd missed him by the time I got to the other side of the building. But I looked at the traffic light at the end of the street and he was there behind five other vehicles. I put the pedal to the metal and took off toward him. As soon as I reached him, the light turned green.

However, by the time I met up to it, the light went from yellow to red. I went through it anyway, screeches and all. I could hear the tire Darrin had in the back of the truck slide to the other side. I looked in my rear view mirror and another car that was almost at my back bumper honked at me. I didn't care. I swerved around another five cars before I caught up to Mr. Rowdosky. But I made sure I didn't get too close. I left two cars between us.

I looked in my rear view mirror and, of course, I didn't see any sign of Darrin.

We came upon a hotel. It was one of those rinky-dink hotels, with crack heads and hookers lurking around. Next to the hotel was a strip club. I turned off my car lights and watched him walk up a flight of stairs and into a room. I looked up at the sign. Although it read: Hotel Inn, three of the lights were out, so it read: Ho Inn. I chuckled to myself and looked around. There was a man and women off to the side, they appeared to be high off drugs. Within four or five minutes, Mr. Rowdosky emerged from the room.

I followed him onto the highway. I wondered where we were going now. If he was going to South Bend, that was an hour away and it was the opposite of where we were going. But of course, that story about him moving out here to be closer to his sister was probably a lie as well.

After about twenty minutes of driving, I called Darrin on his cell phone.

"We're stuck in traffic, baby; a bad accident."

"I followed old man Rowdosky to a flea bag hotel, and now we're on the highway."

"Call me as soon as you get to where you're going."

"Okay, I will."

"And, hey…"

"Yeah."

"Be careful. I don't want anything happening to you. And don't approach him alone"

"Okay, I'll be careful. And I don't plan on it.," I said, hanging up the phone.

After ending the call with Darrin, Mama called but I let it go to voice mail. Not now Mama. She probably was only calling to tell me that she and Sierra were back from bingo.

I tried my hardest not to get so close behind him. He finally got off the highway. We had to have been driving for at least an hour and a half. We were headed toward a wooded area. I was skeptical as to whether I should go any further, but something told me to keep following him. I looked in my rear view mirror and there were two cars behind me. They were far behind me. I didn't even know where we were. We kept driving, passing a street sign that read: Blue Spring Road. It couldn't be..

We kept driving. I pulled over to the side when he pulled into a gas station. As he got out of his truck, and went into the station's convenience store, a man walked past Mr. Rowdosky's truck, where he dropped a piece of paper on the ground and kept walking. The man was tall, old, skinny and dressed in denim overalls. He got into the car at another pump across from Rowdosky.

I called Darrin while sitting there, but his voicemail came on immediately. "Damn it!" I blurted out.

I looked around. All I could see were woods and the gas station directly in front of me. Coming out of the store, Mr. Rowdosky stuck a piece of gum in his mouth and dropped the wrapper on the ground, beside his truck. He pretended to pick it up, but he picked up the piece of paper that the skinny man dropped instead. What was that about? I sat up straight in my seat.

Rowdosky got back into his truck and I followed him. I wondered if this was the same Blue Spring Road my Uncle was murdered on that the police mentioned. It had to be. This was either a coincidence, or something shady was going on. I was afraid he might spot me, because we were the only two vehicles on the street, so I kept my distance hoping at the same time not to lose him. We passed a sign that read: Welcome to New Amsterdam. I think I heard about this town. There's only one person who lives here. It was so dark. I wanted to put my bright lights on, but I didn't.

I saw another car coming onto the street. I let them go in front of me. I tried to call Darrin, but it went directly to his voicemail. Suddenly, the car in front of me made a U-turn and went back in the opposite direction. What in the hell was going on? I passed a sign that read: Dead End. I pulled over, parked and turned off the headlights, because at this point there were several big trees ahead of us and nowhere else he could go. I made sure both doors were locked. Mr. Rowdosky came to a stop himself ahead. I pulled out my cell phone and tried to call Darrin again. It still went to voicemail. I tried to call him again, and now I didn't have any reception. Nervousness took over, being out here alone. I no longer thought this was a good idea, but I couldn't leave now. I saw a bright light. I think he had a flash light. Rowdosky was headed into the trees. What was he doing? I was already thinking of asking Darrin later if he'd come back out here with me. I thought about Darrin and Nevilla and wondered where they were.

Sitting in the woods, with barely any light, concerned me. I kept looking around me. I needed a cigarette to calm my nerves, so I reached for my lighter. My hands shook uncontrollably, as the lighter fumbled from my hand and onto the floor. Bending to pick up the lighter, when I pulled myself up, the shit was scared out me by a knock on my window. I nearly jumped out of my seat, let alone my skin. It was a police officer. He held a flashlight up to the window. I took a sigh of relief and rolled down the window, just a little. .

"You okay, Ma'am, its sorta dark out here for yah to be all alone," he said with a thick southern drawl.

I looked in my rear view mirror to see his police car, which had his lights flashing and then I looked ahead to see if Rowdosky had come out of the woods yet. I was afraid Rowdosky would see us.

"Yes officer, I'm fine, I was about to leave any minute. I pulled over to look for something," I said, hoping he'd leave.

"Okay, Ma'am, don't stay around these here roads too long, there's crazy people out here ya' know."

"Thank you."

When he was heading back, I saw him look in my back seat with his flashlight. I could hear a dispatcher on his walkie-talkie reporting a domestic violence. He responded to the call, and took off with his lights still flashing. I was hoping Rowdosky didn't see those lights.

I waited for almost another ten minutes before he finally came out of the woods. He had something in his hand, but I couldn't make out what it was. He got in his truck, made a U-turn and turned off the opposite road of the highway. I didn't feel like following him anymore, I was tired and it was getting late. I looked at my cell phone and I had two voicemails. I didn't even hear my phone ring.

I made a U-turn and headed for the highway to go home. As I was driving, I saw someone standing in the middle of the street in my rearview mirror. I turned all the way around in my car, and the person was just standing there. I couldn't tell if it was female or male. I turned back around and pushed the gas to the floor; thirty miles per hour turned into sixty real quick. My heart raced. I looked in the rear view mirror, and whoever it was, was still standing back there.

Chapter 38

Last night, after the night from hell, when I finally made it back to Darrin's, Nevilla was sleeping on the couch. Darrin covered with a blanket and took off her shoes. I told Darrin everything that happened, where we went and the strange incident of someone standing in the middle of the street; even Rowdosky picking up a piece of paper that some lanky man dropped on the ground.

I didn't really know what to think of it, but something wasn't right. Darrin indicated to me that maybe Rowdosky knew Uncle Leon in some way. I was almost convinced as well, but how? I tried to persuade Darrin to go back with me sometime next week. He never gave me a straight answer, but maybe I could convince him later. I'll have to work on it.

I dropped Nevilla off at Mama's house early this morning, before driving to Michigan City to visit Jacob. I wanted to talk to him and make sure he was alright. Actually maybe it was to make me feel alright.

I was standing when Jacob walked through the door. He looked about the same from the last time I'd seen him. His hair was pulled back into a ponytail. I pressed my hand against the window and blew him a kiss.

"So what's up bro?" I sat down on the stool while holding up the phone to my ear.

"You know, same ole' shit, different day. Just tryin' to maintain in here. I got in a fight yesterday. Someone was trying to steal my cigarettes."

"Did you get into trouble?"

"Nah, it was broken up before they got to us." His eyes were tired and a little red.

"Well, not sure if you know but Franklin is dead." I leaned in close to the window. "He was murdered actually," I whispered. Not sure why I whispered it.

"What? Uncle Leon's friend? He was like family. Damn. What happened?" Jacob's eyes opened wide.

"Not sure." I looked down at my hands and all of a sudden it became clear to me and I was sad. "He was killed right in front of me. Police still working on it. But there's been other people who died that knew Uncle Leon. A lot of strange things have been going on Jacob. More than what I can even begin to tell you right here." I was reliving everything again.

"Damn." Jacob put his hands on the metal shelf in front of him. He shook his head and rubbed his hand over his head in dismay. I noticed he had a tattoo on his arm, which I hadn't seen before. It had M and R on it with some type of symbol underneath it. I smiled, because I wondered if it stood for me and Matthew, but I didn't say anything to him about it.

"Jacob, I'm afraid I'm next," I whispered to him through the phone, looking around.

"Don't think like that. The police are working it, right?"

"Yeah," I said with doubt.

He reassured me again, but I wasn't really convinced.

"You know my parole is in February. I'll probably be out of here girl. I'll come and stay with you." Jacob paused. "If that's alright that is." He looked at me waiting for me to respond.

"Yeah I remember you telling me. You know you're welcomed to my house anytime. Mama is gonna be so happy to see you Jacob." The thought of Jacob getting out actually made me feel better for the moment. "Mama says you and Uncle Leon were close when you were little. I don't really remember that," I said thinking back.

"Not really. I don't know why she would think that. If anything, you and Uncle Leon were very close. That's what I remember." He was fidgeting with his hands. "But I do remember a secret he told me. I ain't never told anyone."

"What secret would that be?"

Jacob looked down and smiled. He leaned back in his seat and slouched lower, looking up at me like he didn't know if he should tell me or not. "Well remember that one time Daisy was lost?"

"Yeah that was Mama's favorite dog. He ran away from home and we never found him." I remembered like it was yesterday.

194

"No, Uncle Leon ran over him by accident and duped him in the trash. He made me swear not to ever tell anybody. I was with him when he did it."

"What? Mama would be so hurt."

"Yeah, that's why you're never gonna tell her. But anyway, I know how close Uncle Leon and Nevilla were. I'm sure my little girl was heartbroken after Uncle Leon died. Has she ever told you any secrets about Uncle Leon?"

"No. I don't think so." I thought about it. I began wondering if Uncle Leon had told her anything, especially after visiting the psychic.

After leaving the prison, I thought about what Jacob had asked me about Nevilla and then I started to think about the psychic again. I shook my head.

I turned up my radio and lit a cigarette. There wasn't too much traffic on the road, but I noticed a car behind me. I placed my focus on the road and called Darrin. He was at lunch with his partner. I told him I'd come over after he got off.

After hanging up with Darrin, I looked back in my rearview mirror and the car came up closer. I couldn't see who was driving behind the wheel, but as they got closer I was shocked that they were wearing a ski mask. I had to take a double look. I put my cigarette out and stepped on the gas petal. The street I was on had a lot of curves and the road was narrow with several trees on both sides. There was nowhere I could turn off, at least until I got to the highway, which was at least another fifteen minutes. I thought about turning around, but I didn't want to get into an accident, the streets were slick. I looked behind me again. The car was dark blue. I tried to keep focus. This isn't happening, I kept telling myself. I could feel myself breathing fast and hard.

I kept both hands on the steering wheel as I turned my head around and looked at the dark blue car behind me again. It was starting to come up real fast again. I turned back around and picked up my cell phone which was in the passenger's seat. Right when I was about to call 911, I felt a hard thrust. The car behind had bumped me. Hard enough to make my phone fall to the floor on the passenger's side. I looked in the rear view again. At this point I was scared out of my mind. I looked on the floor at my cell phone and mashed my foot down on the petal. A large snow truck passed us. I honked repeatedly on the horn, but they kept going. I was pacing my eyes from the front of the road to my rear view mirror.

After passing a curve, I was approaching the highway, but the blue car sped up on the side of me and blocked my path making me swerve onto a side street. I could feel myself going into a panic, the roads were slick and I knew it was a matter of time before I slid off the road if I didn't slow down. I tried to lean down slowly to retrieve my phone. I knew this would be the only thing that could save me now. I grabbed it as quick as I could. When I pulled myself up, , I had already come upon a curve. I tried to swerve the truck, but the street was too slick and it was too late; I ran into the trees off to the side. I hit the side of a tree and my head hit the steering wheel. Everything was going so fast. When I pulled my head up, I was dazed and everything was spinning. I was dizzy. I touched my head and there was blood on my fingers. I turned around and didn't see anything or anyone. I tried to start the engine , but it wouldn't start. My adrenaline kicked in fast. I grabbed my purse and reached down for the cell phone and tried to open the door. It wouldn't open at first but I just kept pushing on it. I looked back and saw someone at the top of the street several feet behind me. I gave it one more push and got out the truck. I had no idea where I was. All I saw was snow and trees. I looked behind me and saw the dark blue truck, but now I didn't see anyone. I started running, running for my life. I looked behind me and the person with the mask was running after me. I had tennis shoes on, so I was hoping I wouldn't slide. I ran faster. I jumped over a rock and slid down a hill. I got up and looked behind me. I didn't see anyone. I got up and ran like hell, , but it was hard trying to get through the snow. I didn't want to think of the worst but I didn't see any place or anyone for me to run to for help. I ran and I ran, without looking behind me. Then I saw a cabin off to the side, giving me all the hope in the world. I was praying someone was inside. I looked behind me and I saw someone far away. I think it was the person from the blue car. With all my strength I ran faster, determined to get to the cabin.

I saw smoke coming out of the chimney as I got closer. Someone had to be home. I tripped on the stairs as I ran up to the cabin and busted my lip. I got up immediately and started banging on the door. An elderly white woman cracked opened the door . I pushed the opened, including her and closed it behind me. I locked all three locks on the door.

"Call the police. Someone's trying to kill me," I yelled. I moved the curtain and looked out her window. I didn't see anyone. The woman stood in the middle of the living room with a frightened look on her face.

I went to another window on the side of the cabin, and still didn't see anyone.

I looked at the woman, and then she went over and picked up her phone and started dialing. A man with suspenders and no shirt came into the living room from the back.

"What's going on?" he asked. He had a cane in one hand and a shotgun in the other.

I took a few steps back and watched his every move.

"Someone's after her, she says, but I'm calling the police," the old woman said.

I looked out the window again. Then I looked at both the man and woman, and started to cry. I felt myself about to hyperventilate. I sat on the floor. I asked for a glass of water. The man helped me to a couch. After taking a few sips of the water, I felt better. I got up and went around and made sure all there doors were locked.

The old lady hung up the phone. "The police are on their way, Henry."

They were both looking at me like I was crazy. Here I was appearing to be a crazy deranged black woman walking around in their home.

I sat down on the couch, waiting for the police, fidgeting uncontrollably while the couple stared at me, as if I was something they'd never seen before. The man was still holding onto his shotgun. He then sat down across from me and placed the gun on the side of him.

"So what's your name girl?" he asked, while his wife brought out a cup of coffee for him.

"Rahkel." I wiped my eyes and stood up for a second to take another peek out the window.

"So who's trying to kill you?" the old lady asked.

"I don't know. Some man with a mask." I got up again and looked out the window.

"Well there is a prison not far from here, maybe someone broke out," the old woman said. She looked over at her husband. He didn't reply. He got up and went over to the window, and looked outside.

"No, I don't think someone escape." I placed my glass of water on the side table next to me and pulled out my pack of cigarettes and my lighter. I lit the cigarette. Then it occurred to me where I was. I looked at both of them, with my cigarette in hand already lit. The man didn't seem too happy . "I'm sorry do you mind if I smoke?"

The couple looked at each other. There was a long silence.

"Yes we mind. Please put that out," the woman said.

I did as she said and pulled out a piece of gum from my purse instead.

I got up and walked over to the window and looked out.

"The sheriff should be here any minute dear," the old lady said again. I looked back at the old woman and nodded my head. I pulled my cell phone from out of my purse and dialed Darrin's number while keeping my eyes locked outside.

Chapter 39

I decided to go into work the next day. I didn't want to be by myself. I was a nervous wreck and I'd been smoking a pack of cigarettes a day. I was looking over my shoulder every second. Darrin came to get me yesterday and the police had Darrin's truck towed. I left a message with Detective Matters because I wanted to meet with him at the station. I was up most of the night. I kept waking Darrin up, with every noise I heard. I was scared out of mind. I thought about having Detective Matters put me in police protective custody. This was not at all how I pictured myself dying.

I wish I knew who was trying to kill me. Was it someone I'd seen before? I bet it was a hit man.

Darrin tried to convince me to go to work with him, but I declined. So he dropped me off at my job, and said he'd pick me up afterwards. He said we'd go work out at his gym to relieve my stress. I wasn't sure if I even wanted to do that. He's talking about working out and someone's trying to kill me. I looked a mess when he dropped me off. A nervous wreck was written all over my face.

While at work, every time I went to the bathroom, I asked someone to come with me or at least stand outside of it. Now if that wasn't pathetic, I don't know what was.

At break, as I was about to go outside to smoke, I stopped myself, fearing someone would be out there waiting for me. When I saw Miguel, I was happy. I managed to get him to go outside with me. I told him a little of what was going on.

"That's crazy. You think someone's really trying to kill you, but why?" Miguel asked as we sat on a bench outside.

"Hell yes. And whoever they are, it has to do with my uncle being murdered. I'm going down to the police station again after work. Hopefully they have something new to tell me." I inhaled the smoke long and hard into my lungs. I looked out across the parking lot. "Who's that?" I asked, standing up from the bench.

"That's Ben, the janitor. He's just shoveling the snow." Miguel looked at me. "Calm down, you're making me nervous."

"Oh, okay."

"Hey, If you really think someone's after you, I can help you with that problem." Miguel took a drag and waved to Ben, who was now passing by us.

I looked at Miguel. "You can?"

"Yeah, my uncle owns a gun shop. I could get him to give you one for little or nothing."

I felt a slight fear come over me. All of a sudden, it hit me. So this was what it came down to; me needing a gun.

"I don't even know anything about guns," I said, thinking of the idea of owning one.

"I'll show you. It's easy. And from what you told me, you need one. Don't you want to protect yourself?" Miguel brushed off the ashes he dropped on his scrubs.

I gave it another thought. I guess it's not a bad idea. It didn't take him too long to convince me.

"How late is his shop open today?" I asked, trying not to sound desperate.

"We can go to his house. I'll take you after work if you want. He has another shop in his basement." He flicked his cigarette and stood up.

I thought about it, trying to think about what I would tell Darrin. I finally decided to tell him that Janetta was going to pick me up today, so he didn't have to. I figured I could always go down to the police station after that or maybe even tomorrow.

After work, I waited for Miguel in the lobby. As we walked outside, I couldn't help but to look around. It was already dark. I walked closer to Miguel and put my arms around his. He looked at me and laughed.

We sat in the parking lot, while Miguel warmed up his car. I locked his doors for him.

"We're gonna have to go out to Lafayette, if you don't mind. I know that's almost an hour away, but that's where my uncle lives," Miguel said as he revved up the engine.

"That's fine. Are you sure you'll be able to get me a gun tonight?" I asked, trying to confirm it, shocked by the thought of me even owning a gun.

"Of course, Ma'. Calm down. You will have your gun tonight, believe me. I'll tell my uncle you're a friend of mine. So he'll give you one for about fifty dollars or so."

"Yeah, that sounds good." I was wondering if this was legal. So I decided to ask, even if I seemed naive. "Don't I have to get it registered or something?"

"Don't worry about all that. My uncle has a license. He'll help you with all that. I told you, he owns a gun shop."

We took off. I was trying not to look behind us so much, but I couldn't help it. Miguel kept looking at me, so I stopped. I didn't want to make him feel as uncomfortable as I was.

An hour later, we pulled up to a house in a cul-de-sac. There was a big black dog lying in the front yard. The garage door was opened, and as soon as we pulled up, the dog perked up.

"Come on, Killer doesn't bite." Miguel got out the car. Okay, well with a name like Killer, who could tell?

I followed closely behind him. The dog sniffed my crouch and waved its tail, before jumping up on Miguel.

An older man came into the garage. He had dark features, wearing a beige cowboy hat and tan boots. He spoke in Spanish to Miguel. I smiled, not knowing what they were talking about. I looked behind me and the dog was lying on the ground, staring at us. He was tied to a railing, with a long leash..

"So you are Rahkel? I'm Juan," he said with a heavy accent. I liked how he pronounced my name thought.

"Yes, nice to meet you." I followed Miguel and his uncle through the garage and once inside, he had three locks on the door to his basement. His basement was really big. And Miguel wasn't lying when he said his uncle had guns. There were guns everywhere.

They continued talking in Spanish while I walked around looking at all the guns in the cases.

"*Senorita,* you see any you like?" Juan asked. There was a small refrigerator off to the side. The uncle went over and pulled out two imported beers. .Not the type of beers I'd ever seen before. He handed one to Miguel and one to me. I took it. I wouldn't normally drink a beer anyway, but then again, I wouldn't normally be buying a gun either, so what the hell.

"What about this one over here? It's kind of cute," I said, pointing to a small silver gun.

"Cute? Ma' why you callin' this gun cute? That's a nine millimeter lightweight semi automatic." Miguel got up and came over to me.

"How much?" I took a sip of the beer. It was good and very cold.

The uncle and Miguel looked at each other and started talking in Spanish again.

I looked at the gun and held it up to a mirror that was in front of me. I actually looked pretty good holding a gun. I pretended to fire it and blew at the imaginary smoke coming out of the barrel.

"Fifty," Juan said.

"Okay, I'll take it," I said, not hesitating.

Juan gave me two cases of bullets which he kept in another room in the basement. There were also three locks to get into that room as well. The room had several shelves with cases of bullets.

After listening to Mexican music all night, I realized I'd already drunk three beers. I looked at the time and told Miguel we had to leave. I took my cases and my box that had the gun inside and put it into a bag Juan had given me. He also handed me a receipt. It had the name and address of his gun shop. Miguel showed me a few times how to use it and then how to load it. He said I could go to the shooting range with him if I wanted. I think that would be a good idea.

I told Miguel to drive by my house before he took me to Mamas. By the time we pulled up it was almost eleven and Darrin was sitting in my garage. I couldn't believe it. I told him Janetta was taking me to Mamas. I thanked Miguel and got out. Darrin had already seen me and I'm sure he was wondering who was dropping me off.

"Hey baby. Why are you here?" I asked, trying to play calm.

"The question is where have you been? And who was that who dropped you off?" Miguel was almost down the road as Darrin looked over my shoulder.

"Oh just Miguel, he works with me. Janetta picked me up and then she took me by there because it's his birthday and his wife wanted us to stop by. Janetta had to leave early, so he dropped me off. I figured I'd go to the police station tomorrow." I thought about the lie I just told. It sounded good to me. Darrin looked at me. I'm not sure if he believed me or not, but he didn't say anything.

"Come on baby, let's go inside. I'm glad you're here." While walking up the stairs, I missed a step and almost fell. Darrin grabbed me by the arm. That's what I get for telling a bold-faced lie.

"How much have you had to drink tonight?" he asked, looking into my eyes.

"Not much." I was feeling buzzed and unbalanced. He helped me to my bed and that's all I remember.

The next morning, I woke up with a pounding head and Darrin staring at me. Then he pulled out my bag with the gun inside and the case of bullets. Damn, I was caught.

"What the hell is this?" My stomach felt queasy. I darted to the bathroom and threw up in the toilet. That imported beer didn't agree with me too well.

After wiping my mouth and sipping on some water I looked back at Darrin.

"I bought it." I splashed my face with water.

We spent most of the morning arguing. Then Darrin stormed out of the house. It took me a minute to realize I was at home alone. "That asshole," I yelled out loud, for leaving me here by myself. I turned on and engaged the alarm immediately, locked myself in my room and stared out the window. I called Sharon to come by my house to pick me up. I loaded my gun, from what I remember Miguel showing me, and placed it on the dresser, hiding the box of bullets in my lingerie drawer. When I heard Sharon ring the doorbell, I turned on the safety of the gun and put it back in the box and slid it under my bed. Grabbing my purse, I headed downstairs. We left and I offered to take her to lunch. I still couldn't get over the fact that Darrin left me alone, knowing that I didn't have a ride anywhere, and also considering there's a crazy person out there trying to kill me.

Chapter 40

I haven't spoken to Darrin at all today . He didn't even call me to see how I was doing. I could be dead somewhere and he wouldn't even know. Sharon and I spent most of the day together. She was getting pretty big, or at least her stomach was. I pulled out a cigarette and started to light it, but then I looked over at her and decided not to.

"You can go ahead," Sharon said. "You know I still smoke lights."

"That's alright. Do you have any gum?"

"Yea I think in the glove compartment. It may be old though." Sharon kept her eyes on the road.

I pulled out the pack of gum and noticed a necklace underneath the stacks of paper she had crammed in her compartment. I pulled it out and noticed the black marble at the end.

"You have one of these necklaces too? I didn't know Uncle Leon gave you one of these also." I examined it.

Next thing I know, it was yanked out of my hand by Sharon. "I thought I threw that shit away. She rolled down her window and tossed it out.

"What the hell is your problem?" I yelled. "Your own father gave that to you." I couldn't believe she had done that.

"Yeah, well I've never worn that thing. And now I never have to see it again." I rolled my eyes at her, not understanding what that was about.

After shopping, we stopped by an auto auction to see what they had. I hadn't intended on buying anything at all, I only wanted to look. However the time and price was right. I bought a 1992 black Cadillac for only thirty-five hundred dollars.

There was something wrong with the locks on the passenger side and the lock to the truck was missing, but other than that, it was in good condition. I figured I'd get it fixed.

Sharon followed me over to Mama's house. I showed Mama, Nevilla, and Sierra my new car. They were impressed. I thought about driving over to Darrin's house, but I forgot we weren't speaking. Tomorrow was Christmas Eve. I was excited but at the same time I was a little down. I think this was our first real fight, and I didn't like it one bit. I bought Darrin a nice watch I found on sale, along with a FUBU sweat suit.

I stayed overnight at mama's in the guest room. The next morning I woke up and looked at my phone and Darrin still hadn't called me. That really bothered me. Mama was already in the kitchen. I could smell the bacon cooking. I got up and peeped in the room next to me. Sierra was still sleep. Nevilla was sleeping beside her. I passed by the Christmas tree that Mama and Nevilla had set up. There were ornaments all over it; some of them from when I was a little girl. One of them I remember was from Uncle Leon. It was a picture of two little angels, one of the angels had Matthew's name engraved on it. The other had my name on it.

I looked at another angel hanging from the tree. It had Nevilla's name on it. It read: "*You will always be in my heart. From Grand Daddy.*"

"Mama, where's Sharon?" I had on a T-shirt and shorts I got from Sierra.

"She left early this morning. Something about she was picking up that ol' Terry boy and they were going to visit his mom or something."

"Oh." I sat down at the table. I had my phone in my hand. I kept looking down at it, hoping Darrin would call.

I tried to keep myself preoccupied. Me, Nevilla, Mama, and Sierra drove around running errands and getting last minute food at the grocery store. Mama was going to cook a big dinner tomorrow, and Darrin was supposed to come. I called Janetta to make sure she was still coming. I even asked her to bring one of her many dates if she wanted to and also Gary.

It was almost seven o'clock and Darrin still hadn't called me. I finally broke down and called him after I dropped everyone off at Mama's. I sure wasn't going home by myself.

He answered which surprised me.

2●6

"I thought you would have called me." I said the first thing that came out.

"Well, Rahkel you pissed me off yesterday. So I figured I'd give you a little space and plus I had some work to get caught up on."

"Okay." I didn't really know what to say. "Well, I was going to come by if that's alright."

"Yeah that's fine. Your uncle's CD arrived today. I figured we'd look at it together."

"Okay, I'll be right over." The news was a relief and maybe a break in the case..

I was starting to forget about that CD. I wanted so bad to know what was on it. As I drove over to Darrin's place I speculated that maybe I could finally get some answers.

Darrin greeted me with a hug. I wanted to forget about our fight and move on. This really made me realize how much I cared for him. I sat on the couch. He asked me if I wanted some wine. I nodded.. I took off my shoes and curled my feet under me. I made myself comfortable on his black leather couch. The television was on, but it was commercials, I wasn't even sure what he was watching. Darrin came back with a tall wine glass, a beer and a bowl of popcorn.

He set up his laptop on the table in front us and showed me the CD. "It's been a long time since I seen that CD," I said, taking a sip from my glass.

He put it in and it asked for a password. "Don't worry, Stan told me to use 1-2-3-4. He reset it for me." It worked; I was so relieved.

I noticed there was a file on there labeled Accounts I told Darrin to click on that first. He did. The CD indicated that both Dennis Lowry and Franklin were to each get two million dollars apiece. Then it listed a bunch of bank accounts and passwords.

As Darrin scrolled down, what intrigued me even more than the two million dollars was that Uncle Leon paid Dennis Lowry five million dollars. The description next to the five million dollars stated: Dental Work.

I looked at Darrin. "What do you suppose that means?" I asked, confused.

"Dental work, I guess."

I gave him a funny look. "Very good, Sherlock Holmes. Why would he be getting dental work, and why the hell would he pay five million dollars for it?"

Darrin shrugged his shoulders and scrolled down on the Excel spreadsheet.

"Look right here. It talks about a key your uncle was to give to both Dennis Lowry and Franklin." Darrin pointed at another page on the spreadsheet. "The key you have might be to a lockbox at the National Bank. Do you still have the key?"

"Yeah I do. It's at home." I forgot all about that key in the box.

Darrin went on to read. "Apparently the one Franklin gave you is to a lockbox at the National Bank as well." There was silence as we both kept reading. "It says that there's another key," Darrin stated.

"I have it, I think," I blurted out. It then dawned on me that I still had that key I found behind the painting. I mentioned it to Darrin and he suggested I compare it to the others.

"Look at this," he pointed to the screen, "Charles Simon's name is even mentioned."

"It says partial dental work next to his name," I finished his sentence.

I didn't quite know what was going on, but something was fishy. It turned out that Uncle Leon owed Donald Hamilton a lot of money, and on top of that he was also laundering millions of dollars through his real estate and leasing business. All those receipts in the box were made up just in case the IRS ever audited him.

I was disgusted to say the least. I couldn't believe it, but the proof was right in front of my face. I told Darrin to click on a file that read: Thank You. It was a photo of Nevilla. She was in a pool on a floater.

We went further into the file and we came upon his will. He left me the business, plus a CD account from the same bank, including the house in Florida Kareena so desperately wanted. He left Sharon and Nevilla almost a million dollars a piece and he left Mama the house, which I'd already sold. The list went on, but I couldn't believe that we never knew about this will. I had Darrin print it out. It looked as though it was scanned so Uncle Leon's signature was already on it.

The strangest thing I pointed out to Darrin was the fact that there was a different number at the top left corner of each file we opened. We couldn't make out what that meant. Maybe that was the order they were in.

That night as I laid in bed, I was more confused than ever. I held my alarm panic button in my hand and looked over at Darrin as he was fast asleep. What was revealed tonight had shed a different light on the situation, especially as far as the man I thought I knew as my Uncle Leon. The same man I looked up to and respected. A dark feeling sunk inside me. I smelled conspiracy in the air. Donald Hamilton had a legitimate alibi, but all the recipients were dead. But honestly I really didn't think Hamilton had anything to do with Uncle Leon's death anymore. I didn't have a clue who would want to kill them or me. The not knowing was tearing me apart. I cried myself to sleep silently, trying not to wake up Darrin.

Chapter 41

It was Christmas day, and I woke up with puffy eyes and a bad headache. I looked over and Darrin was sound asleep. I tried to wake him but he was out like a light. I left a note on the nightstand: *Baby, I'm going over to Sharon's, to drop off the presents. Meet me at Mama's house later..* We finally exchanged keys to each others place, which was a monumental thing in a relationship.

When I arrived at Sharon's, I found her on the couch, wrapped in a blanket, watching Lifetime, and eating a big bowl of ice cream. I wanted to tell her about what was going on, but I chose not to. Quite honestly, I wasn't sure who I could trust. Even Darrin at times was questionable. To be honest everyone's questionable at this point. Besides, Sharon probably wouldn't have believed me anyway, and I didn't want to tarnish any memories she had of her father.

As we talked, she baked fresh oatmeal cookies and poured us a glass of milk. This felt like déjà vu. When we were little, we would have tea parties and invite our friends over: Mr. Bear, Ms. Barbie, Ken, and Mr. Rabbit. And we would sit around with oatmeal cookies that Mama baked for us, and pretended our cup of milk was tea or coffee.

"I'm actually glad you came over Rahkel. I have a favor to ask you." Sharon sat down with a cookie and a tall glass of milk.

"What's up?" I reached for the plate of cookies and grabbed another one.

"I wanna go visit Daddy's grave today and I want you to come with me. I just want to drop off something." Sharon's eyes were so innocent. She placed both of her hands on the table and looked down.

"Sure, that's fine with me." I felt sorry for her and was so happy and relieved I didn't mention anything about what I'd learned about Uncle Leon.

For a Christmas Day, the Fairmount Mortuary felt creepy. I'm no fan of cemeteries. Like Sharon, I don't like visiting them alone, especially when I visit Matthew.

Leonard Durman Wilson — *1944-2001* graced the massive gray headstone. We stood before the grave, silent. I looked over at Sharon, watching her. It was cold and nippy, and although she was wrapped in fur, with a huge hood, each time she drew in her breath, and exhaled, her inner warmth escaped her. Removing the hood of her coat, she walked closer to the grave, knelt on the cold snow-covered ground and hugged the tombstone, crying away every pain she felt from losing her father. Bending down, I tried to comfort her, as I looked around at all the graves and tombstones. Sadness overwhelmed me. I looked up into the sky and saw three angels with missing left wings. Then Uncle Leon's face appeared, with a cunning look in his eyes. I blinked my eyes. It was weird, almost as though I'd seen that look before.

Standing, Sharon dusted the snow off her jeans and pulled the hood over her head. Her nose was as red as Rudolph the Reindeer. I pulled a Kleenex out of my purse and gave it to her. In silence, she placed an army metal of Uncle Leon's when he was in the war on top of the tombstone. I thought maybe she should have kept it, but I didn't say a word. It wasn't my place.

The drive back to Sharon's was silent. I didn't know what to do. I honestly didn't know how to comfort her. I still have my parents, although I'm estranged from my dad. I searched my mind for a topic of conversation, but my heart insisted I keep quiet, giving her time to grieve.

Sharon was in the bathroom for a while, which concerned me. As I was about to check on her, she came out talking as though everything was alright.

"So what time are we going over Auntie's house?" She asked straightening up her living room.

"I believe five or six. Are you okay?"

"Yes perfectly fine. I feel like the past is finally behind me." She went to the back again and returned with a basket of clothes.

I was indifferent about her sudden chipper behavior, not really knowing why.

"Tomorrow I'm going to have to take these to the cleaners. I can't believe Nevilla wasted grape juice all over her blue jacket, and on top of that, one of the silver buttons fell off. I hope they can get the juice stain out and fix the button. This was my favorite jacket of hers." Sharon grabbed a garbage bag and placed the clothes inside.

I acknowledged what she was saying and looked out the window, and then it dawned on me. I pulled the jacket out of the bag and examined it.

"Is this the one I bought her?"

"Yes of course it is." She grabbed the jacket back, and put it back in the bag.

"When did I buy that jacket for her?" I honestly couldn't remember.

"What do you mean? You don't remember? It was the day before Daddy's funeral. Remember? Because I had gotten my hair did." Sharon looked at me.

I felt an overwhelming feeling come over me. My entire body froze. Sharon continued to talk, but I didn't hear anything she said. I'm not sure if the room started to spin or if it was my head.

Regaining control, I briskly walked into Nevilla's room. I was trying to find her Mickey Mouse bag.

Sharon came in behind me. "What are you doing?"

I turned to Sharon. "Where is Nevilla's Mickey Mouse bag?"

"It's with her. Why?" Sharon walked into the room, now standing in front of me.

"I need to see a picture she had in there." I left the room grabbing my coat. "I gotta go Sharon. I'm going over to Mama's house."

"Rahkel what is wrong? You're scarring me." She followed me to the front door as I put on my hat and wrapped my scarf around my neck.

"Nothing…Nothing." I tried to make my voice sound as calm as possible although my insides were trembling with the most extreme fear I'd ever felt. "There was this picture in her backpack that I wanted to see. No big deal." I smiled and changed the subject, reminding Sharon to buy an apple pie for Mama's Christmas dinner. "The picture just reminded me that I wanted to make a copy of it," I said lastly, as I went out the door, barely falling on the sidewalk, hurrying to my car.

Pulling off from Sharon's, Darrin called me on my cell.

"Hello?" I answered rather quickly.

"Hey baby, are you still over your cousin's house?"

"Yes. No. I mean, I'm leaving now. Darrin, I have to show you something, but I have to get it first. I can't explain it now. There's something strange, something unreal, something, something..." I felt myself talking really fast with short breaths, unable to think straight.

"Calm down, Rahkel. Where are you? What are you talking about?"

"I'm going over to Mama's. I'll call you when I get there." I hung up with Darrin.

When I pulled into the driveway of Mama's house, I saw Nevilla looking down at me from an upstairs bedroom window. She was truly freaking me out by the day.

When I opened the door, the welcoming aroma of Mama's Christmas dinner smacked me in the face. Mama was sitting in front of the television. I gave her a hug and walked upstairs. The door to my childhood bedroom was closed. I opened it slowly to Nevilla sitting on the bed Indian style with her back turned to me. I walked in and closed the door behind me. I called out to her but she did not answer. I sat on the bed next to her and touched her on her shoulder. It was like I wasn't even in the room. She didn't move; she didn't even blink.

"Sweetie are you okay?"

She stared blankly out of the window with her arms resting on her legs, and face resting in her palms. I looked at the edge of the bed and saw the Mickey Mouse bag. I grab it and started to look inside.

"It's not in there, Auntie." Nevilla slowly turned her head and looked at me, like something out of the Exorcist.

I continued searching through the bag. She was right, it wasn't there. I scooted closer to her. "Nevilla where is the picture of you and Granddaddy?"

She stared out the window with that blank look again.

Frustrated, I turned her face gently toward me, and spoke in a stern voice. "Nevilla, I'm asking you a question. Please answer me."

"The man in white took it," she said quietly and calmly.

My throat tightened as I tried to swallow. "What man in white?" I asked calmly, trying not to show the fear that shot through me like a hot bullet.

"The man in white."

"What man in white? Who is he? Did he hurt you?" I stood up on the side of Nevilla. She was starting to scare me.

Unfolding her legs, she stood up from the bed and looked me right in the face. "*The man in white! The man in white!*" she yelled stomping her feet. "*He took it!*" She shouted even louder. She opened the door and ran downstairs calling out to her grandma. I stood in the middle of the room. I looked around and starred into the full-length mirror at myself. I felt sick to my stomach when I saw an image of Uncle Leon's face in the sky behind me as it reflected off the mirror.

Chapter 42

It's been almost two weeks since Christmas. I dropped Sierra off at the airport some days ago. She was excited to go back to school. I'll miss her though.

Darrin stayed the night at my place again. We traded off at each others place, but I didn't care, so long as I wasn't at home sleeping by myself.

I woke up feeling a little down. Here I am, with no picture, I never told Darrin about it, because I had no proof. I made up something else and told him to forget about it all together. I don't think he really believed me, but he went along with it. I was still scared for my life.

Detective Matters mentioned they may have a break through, but he didn't offer any details. I'll believe it when they capture someone. I was still confused and pretty much thought I was going insane, but kept that thought to myself.

Before Sierra left, Janetta managed to take us out to happy hour. I really wasn't comfortable being out and about anymore, and definitely didn't want to drink too much. Darrin and Calvin met up with us. I smoked seven cigarettes that night as I kept glancing around me.

I called into work, not sure why though, other than I didn't want to go. I'd talk to Nevilla again on a few occasions, but she pretended to not know what I was talking about when I brought up the situation. So I let it go and continued our normal Aunt-Niece relationship.

I convinced myself that maybe I should see a psychiatrist, to talk with. I thought about calling my brother Tony to tell him some of what was going on, but as I dialed his number, I hung up on the first ring. Something about reliving everything wasn't appealing.

I decided to have lunch at a café, alone. They served really good soups and salads. I had my phone in hand in case I needed to call 911, and I had my gun in case someone decided to run me off the road again. I looked at the time and drove a different route so I could pass by Nevilla's school. They should be outside for lunch. I wanted to see her. When I approached her school, I turned off the motor and sat in my car across from the fenced gate that surrounded the playground. I made sure I stayed down the road some, so she couldn't see me. There were a few kids throwing snowballs at each other, while others were building a snowman. I finally spotted Nevilla. She played on the swings for a moment and then went over to the gate. I smiled. I thought about Matthew . She pressed her face up against the fence.

Nevilla placed her hands in her coat pocket as she looked out into the street. I watched as another kid came up to her. He must have asked her to play, but she shook her head at him and turned back to the street. The kid ran off.

I rolled my window down slightly and pulled out a cigarette, which I accidentally dropped on the floor. After retrieving my cigarette, I lit it. When I looked up, a man was talking to Nevilla. I sat up in my seat. His back was turned toward me, so I couldn't see his face. I wanted to get out the car, but I didn't. Not yet. Nevilla was smiling at him, and she reached out her hand through the gate and he grabbed it and kissed it. He reached in his pocket and pulled out a red bear. He looked around to see if anyone was looking. I ducked my head, although they couldn't see me anyway.

When the man turned his head, I believed at that moment I stopped breathing. I was in total shock. I couldn't believe it. It was Adam Rowdosky. If I had heart problems, I would have had a heart attack right there on the spot. I opened up my car door and was about to get out, but that's when I heard the school bell ring. Nevilla looked behind her and quickly gave the man a kiss on his cheek through the fence. She ran and got in line with the other kids to go back inside. I got back in my car and put my head down as he passed by me in his car. I started my car up and followed him. He went to the house I'd sold him. He shouldn't recognize me since I'm in a new car.

As I was about to pull off, he came out, got back in his car and drove off. I was about to follow him, but then I realized I still had a key to the house. I searched my purse and pulled out the key. Watching him make a right at the stop sign at the end of the block, I got out of my car and walked cautiously, and briskly, across the street, around to the back door. The key only unlocked the top lock.

"Damn it," I blurted under my breath. I pulled out one of my many credit cards and jammed it in the side. It worked. I couldn't believe it. There were only a few pieces of furniture in the living room. When I walked up the stairs, I heard a key unlocking the door. Was he back already? I ran as fast as I could to the back door. As I was closing the back door, he was walking in through the front. I didn't have time to lock it back. I put my back against the other side of the door, hoping he didn't see me. The dog in the other yard wouldn't stop barking. "Oh shit!" I whispered. When did they get a dog?

I jumped the fence to the neighbors house on the opposite side, and hid behind there shed. I heard Rowdosky's back door open. I imagined Rowdosky coming outside looking around. After a few seconds, I heard the door close. I took a deep breath. I didn't know how long I should wait. Ten minutes felt like an eternity. Not to mention, it was cold. Then I slowly came from behind the shed. I had on some ankle boots, jeans, sweater and a light jacket with my scarf. I was freezing. I bent down as I walked slowly past Rowdosky's house, trying to hide from the windows. I looked behind me and saw my footprints in the snow. I didn't see his truck or that car he was driving, but it could have been in the garage. I didn't want to take any chances so I went the opposite way and walked around the other side of the block and came back around to my car. I got in and turned my car on immediately. My hands were ice cold. I looked back down at the house and didn't see him. I think I made it. I started my car and headed to Darrin's office.

Chapter 43

I told Darrin everything, even about the picture I'd found in Nevilla's backpack. I even told him about me and Nevilla going to see that psychic Sandy. However, what I didn't tell him was that I was going down to the police station. I wanted to talk to Detective Matters. I knew he wouldn't have liked that idea. But I had to tell them that I was for sure, Rowdosky was the suspect. He was in some way tied to Uncle Leon and I was going to figure out how.

I got off work early and headed downtown. I walked up to the counter and there was a lady behind the wall who had long blonde skinny braids and long purple nails.

"Is Detective Matters in?" I asked.

"No, he's not. Come back around five." She didn't even acknowledge me. She was looking through a stack of paperwork.

"Well, can I wait for him?" I looked up over her head at the time. It was three-thirty.

She looked up at me, with impatience. "No, I said come back around five." She walked over to the other side and took more paperwork out of a drawer.

I had had it with this woman's attitude. How was she going to have the nerve to tell me I couldn't even wait? I rolled my eyes and walked off to the side.

An officer came in shortly with a man in handcuffs. All of a sudden the man started fighting and kicking. The man fell on the ground and as the police officer tried to pick him up, the guy kicked the officer in the face. The rude lady came over and both the officer and her held the man down, while the officer turned the man over and put his club on the back of man's neck.

I took this opportunity and snuck in through the door. I don't know what her problem was, the last guy who worked the counter let me wait around.

I asked the first officer who past me where I could find Detective Matters.

"Oh Miss, he should be here around four or five," he said looking down at his watch. "His office is right over there. His partner Hudson is over there, if you wanna speak to him." He pointed and I walked over to him.

Detective Hudson seemed to remember me immediately.

"How can I help you? It's Rahkel right?" Detective Hudson said, reaching his hand out for me to shake it.

"Well I really want to talk to Detective Matters. Can you have him call me immediately?" I said, looking around in the office.

"Sure can. Are you sure there's nothing I can do for you? I've been working on the case as well, if that's why you're here," he confirmed.

I hesitated for a moment, then I asked him if he could look up a man by the name of Adam Rowdosky. I gave him the social security number that was on the application he'd filled out. I knew they'd already checked on him, but I was hoping something new would come up if I gave him the social security number.

He took the information I'd written on the piece of paper and told me he'd be right back. I waited, looking around. Everyone seemed pretty busy. Within ten minutes, Hudson returned. He informed me the social security belonged to someone by the name of Roger Avery. The last record was almost twelve years ago, and showed that his last address was in Memphis, Tennessee. Who was Roger Avery? Either way he'd given me a fake number. I still wanted to talk to Detective Matters.

I thanked him for his time and left. I passed that woman and I could see out of the corner of my eyes as she was staring at me with much attitude as I walked out the front door. I stopped in my tracks when I got outside and thought hard about the name Roger Avery. I took a seat on the bench and sat in complete thought. I buried my head into my hands. When I looked up, across the way I saw a man walking down the street, wearing very dingy clothes. He was looking down and had a cardboard sign in his hand that read: I'll work for food.

I immediately thought about the homeless guy who came up to me awhile back. His name was? I closed my eyes to look for the answer. "Tim," I said out loud. And his friend's name was Roger, I think. It couldn't be, or could it? The name Roger was so popular. But just in case, I drove to the homeless shelter to find him. It was only down the street from the police station. When I got there the lady in charge said Tim checked out almost a month ago, but that he probably would come back. I was so disappointed. I was about to leave, then I decided to ask her to check on the name Roger Avery. Within minutes she came back and it was confirmed. The lady said the last time he'd been in there was almost a year ago. She said his friend Tim kept complaining that his friend, Roger was missing. I was speechless.

Chapter 44

I had an idea. I woke Darrin up as he lay peacefully next to me. I almost felt bad waking him up. I shook him and he moved a little.

Then he mumbled, "I'm sleep. Leave me alone." He turned over, his back facing me. .

"I know. Wake up." He turned around and opened his eyes slightly. "I want to go out to that place in the woods that I followed Rowdosky to." Darrin turned back over and pulled the covers over his head.

By the middle of the day I convinced Darrin to pass by Rowdosky's house. We saw Adam Rowdosky's truck parked in the driveway. I ducked my head down as we passed by. I didn't tell Darrin I still had a key or that I snuck in. I wanted to come back later.

I also managed to get Darrin to go out to that same spot I followed Rowdosky. I'm sure it had to do with the fact that we had amazing sex this morning. So needless to say he was in a good mood. Something was telling me by going out there I'd get closer to the truth. I was still thinking about that jacket I'd given Nevilla and the picture she'd taken with Uncle Leon. I couldn't explain or understand it.

We stopped outside the small town and managed to find a Subway for lunch. We ate there and left. While we were getting into the car, nonchalantly I told Darrin to look on the side of us. There was a small black older car I'd seen behind us an hour ago. At least I thought it was the same car. I told him not to look until we got inside his truck. When he looked over at the car, there was no one inside, but I wanted him to see if he'd recognized the car. He said he didn't. After putting my seat beat on, I looked around and didn't see anything or anyone out of the ordinary, so we drove off.

We drove up a long road until I saw the same gas station I followed Rowdosky to. Things appeared differently in the daytime. I told Darrin we were close. We continued up the street and parked on the side of the road. Darrin had a flashlight in his hand and a backpack. I saw a car pass us, but it was a lady with two kids in the back. I looked around one last time, before I pulled my hood on my head and followed Darrin into the woods. Darrin called his partner Calvin and was telling him where we were and what we were doing. Good idea, I thought.

I wasn't even sure what to look for. But I searched the grounds for any clues. I listened as Darrin talked on the phone, with the large flashlight in his hand. I didn't tell Darrin but I had my gun in my purse just in case he needed backup. And I knew Darrin probably had his on him as well.

We continued to walk when I saw something that made me pause for a moment. There was a large leaf stuck to a tree. It almost looked as though it was placed there on purpose. I removed it and behind the leaf there was a hole in the trunk of the tree. It was deep like someone drilled into it. I grabbed the back of Darrin's jacket. He stopped for a moment and completed his phone call with Calvin.

"Look at this? There's a hole in this tree. You think that means anything?"

I took my glove off and stuck my finger in the hole. After I did that something started to beep. We both looked at each other and then we looked around us. I couldn't tell where that noise was coming from. And then the noise stopped. We continued to look around. The noise started up again, then it stopped. Finally just a few feet away I started brushing the sole of my boot against the ground where I thought the noise was coming from. The ground felt softer than any other parts of the ground. I brushed away the snow on the ground with my hand to reveal a patch of imitation grass. I pushed down on it with my boot.

"I think there's something under here." I looked over at Darrin. He came over and pushed down with his boot. He took out a knife and cut into the ground. He pulled up the patch of frozen grass and there was a metal box with a combination lock on it. I could tell it was heavy by the way Darrin held it. He pulled it out of the ground and shook the dirt and snow off of it.

"What do you think it is? You think Rowdosky left it here?" I asked, intrigued by it. "I have those keys with me. You think I should see if one of them fits the lock?"

"Yea, but lets not do it here., We'll take it with us. We'll find out when we get home." He picked it up and carried it with both hands, while I carried the flashlight.

As we were headed back to the road, we saw the flashing lights of a police car. He was approaching us. Darrin immediately stuffed the metal box into his backpack.

"Is everything alright folks?" The police officer asked. He had on a bulky coat jacket with long black boots. He also wore a hat, with a flat base. He took out a small light and flashed it in both of our faces.

"We're just taking a small stroll through the woods officer," Darrin said, looking at me and then back at the officer. I nodded and smiled at the officer.

"Well anyway, someone called in saying they saw a Black Suburban off on the side of the road. Is that you're vehicle back there, Sir?"

"Yes it is."

"Well it needs to be moved immediately, before I have it towed." The officer looked at us and signaled with his hand for us to start walking. We started walking back up and the officer followed behind us.

When we got to the road, he asked Darrin what his name was, his birthday, verified his address and patted him down. I thought it was so unnecessary. After that the police officer left.

"Damn, what was that all about?" I asked Darrin as I was walking around to the passenger side.

"Well we are in a small white town. Go figure."

Just when I was about to get into the car I looked back into the woods. I thought I saw movement. I called out to Darrin so he could turn around and look.

"Did you see someone?" I asked looking at Darrin.

"No I didn't see anyone." He turned back around to me.

I opened the car door and got in. "Let's go. This place is giving me the creeps"

Darrin started the car and we pulled off. While passing the gas station, I saw the small black older car again. There was no one inside, but I stared at it in the side view mirror until I didn't see it anymore. I looked over at Darrin. I started to say something, but I didn't. I couldn't wait until we got back home to see what was inside the box. Plus, I was eager to go to Rowdosky's house again.

Chapter 45

Ileft Darrin's house early the next morning. I pretended to go to work, and went over to Mama's house instead. I stayed over there for a couple of hours and kept Mama company. I was contemplating if I should make another visit to Adam Rowdosky's house. To keep me feeling a little safe, I kept feeling on the outside of my purse. The gun was still inside.

"What's wrong child? You seem on edge or something." Mama poured me a cup of coffee.

"No Mama. I'm alright," I lied getting up from the couch. "I have a few things on my mind, but I'm alright."

I helped Mama clean up the house and then I left. I was nervous as I drove to Rowdosky's house. I stopped at the end of his street. I was hoping he wouldn't be home. I didn't see his truck in the driveway. I took a deep breath and finally got out the car. The gun was in the holster, nestled in my back pocket, my cell phone was in my coat pocket with my car keys. I walked slowly and casually down the street. I cut across somebody's yard and went around back, hopping the fence. I peeked through the back door and didn't see his truck or any car in the garage. I looked across the way and saw the neighbor's dog. But I wasn't too worried, because this time the dog was looking at me from inside the house. His bark wasn't that loud. I looked around again and unlocked the top door and used one of my credit cards to slide open the door. It worked just like the last time.

I went to the front window and peeked out, just in case he was coming, then I headed upstairs. I felt on my back pocket for the gun, for security. For a minute, I felt like Angie Dickinson in Police Woman.

I don't know if I was more nervous about the gun being in my back pocket or of Rowdosky coming home. I first walked into what used to be

225

Uncle Leon's bedroom. I browsed the dresser and then searched through his drawers. My heart literally stopped when I pulled out a picture of Nevilla. I couldn't believe it. It was tucked under clothes. I looked at it and then put it on top of the dresser. I went over to a box I saw on the side of the bed and opened it.

I pulled out a gray hat. I examined it and looked on the inside. It had the initials L.W. I think I remembered Mama giving this hat to Uncle Leon for a birthday present. I put it to the side and pulled out a picture of Sharon when she was a little girl. She was sitting in the tub with a sad look on her face. I pulled out another picture of me. I was laying on Sharon's old bed, I didn't have any clothes on. I couldn't believe my eyes. My chest literally started to hurt, and I began breathing very deeply.

One after another I pulled out pictures of me, Nevilla and Sharon. It was very hard to believe what I was looking at. I didn't remember taking any of these pictures. Most of the pictures consisted of us either being naked, with our underwear on or posed up on the bed. I was in complete disbelief. I started shaking uncontrollably. I was disgusted. I got up and ran to the bathroom across the hallway and threw up in the toilet.

Back in Rowdosky's bedroom, I placed all the pictures back into the box. I even found the picture I was looking for that I'd seen in Nevilla's Mickey Mouse bag. I kept taking deep breaths, borderline hyperventilation. I put my hand up to my head, as I stood up with the box in my hand. When I opened the closet, and to my surprise, different hairpieces and wigs were hanging on coat hangers. I also saw some of Nevilla's clothes and little girl's underwear in a laundry basket. In the corner I saw Nevilla's Mickey Mouse bag.

"Oh my God." I turned around. I wanted to get out of there as quick as possible. I couldn't take it any longer. I was very distraught. I felt dizzy almost as if I was going to pass out.

When I got to the top of the stairs I saw Adam Rowdosky standing in the middle of the front entrance. We both stood, frozen in time, looking at each other.

"Rahkel, baby, so it comes to this," he said, as I slowly walked down the stairs toward him. I was at a loss for words. "I knew you were getting close. I just didn't know it was this close."

With the box in hand, I couldn't stop shaking. I took deep breaths because I could feel that I was going to start hyperventilating any minute now. I couldn't believe what was being discovered right in front of my eyes.

"Uncle Leon?" I asked. I walked closer and reached my hand out to touch his white face.

He nodded his head.

"*Why? Why?*" I screamed hysterically stepping back. I dropped the box on the floor and the pictures scattered across the room. I placed my hand over my mouth. Tears streamed down my face.

"I didn't want to hurt you. I've never wanted to hurt you, Sharon or Nevilla. I just wanted to get away. But somehow you have been preventing that." He paced the room, and then he walked toward me. "They were all getting in my way." He rambled on, at first not making sense. "Dennis Lowry, he exchanged that homeless man's teeth with mine. The same man they found burned in my car. I was starting not to trust him. And Franklin, he was going to tell you what was going on. I couldn't allow that." He came right up to me and pointed in my face. "I couldn't allow him to mess up my plan. Don't you see? And Dr. Simon, I just didn't like him."

Unable to move my feet, I couldn't move. My body felt heavy, as if someone had poured plaster over me, still as a wall. I didn't know who this man was that was standing before me. I just listened, terrified for my life and deeply confused with disbelief. I thought about my gun in my back pocket.

He continued to pace the floor. "Charles Simon was just stupid. I tried to cut him into the deal, and then he tries to take over my business. And Rahkel my dear." He paused. I took a heavy step backward, as he moved in closer. "You just kept trying to find the truth. You wouldn't leave it alone. You got yourself in too deep. You should have just left my death alone."

"Uncle Leon," I called out to him in a sympathetic voice. I started to reach behind me to feel on the gun.

"You were my favorite besides Nevilla." He kept coming closer and I kept moving back. That's when I saw Nevilla appear from the front door. My eyes grew big.

She stood there with her hands in front of her, with a blank look on her face. I called out her name before I was hit in the head with a baseball bat that came out of nowhere. The last thing I remember was hitting the floor.

Chapter 46

I woke up in the back of a car. I had no idea how long I'd been out. My head was pounding in pain, and my vision was a little blurred. But, I was able to see that Leon was driving. My hands were handcuffed behind me. I looked to the side of me and Nevilla was beside me, staring at me. She didn't seem normal at all. I wondered if he'd drugged her.

"So you're awoke are you?" Leon or Rowdosky said, looking in the rearview mirror at me.

"Where are we going?" I asked feeling dazed. A few drops of blood fell from my head onto my white coat. Leaning forward, I wiped my forehead against the back of the front seat. I looked outside, behind us, on the side and in front. I didn't know where we were or where we were going. I was riding in the same black car I saw when Darrin and I drove to New Amsterdam.

"We're going somewhere special," Leon said. He looked in the mirror and smiled at me. I couldn't believe this was happening. I can't believe a man I adored so much and loved was full of evil and was about to kill me.

"So you must be the man in white," I said. Nevilla looked over at me after I said that, but didn't say anything.

"The man in white?" he asked.

"Never mind. What about Nevilla? You have me. Why don't you let her go?" I pleaded, wondering exactly what his plan involved.

"Nevilla's going with me, probably out of the country. Anything is possible with over fifty million dollars. As far as you, we've had our fun when you were young," he grinned.

"Why did you do those things to us when we were young?" I had to know. I was so hurt and afraid for Nevilla. He didn't answer me. He looked into my eyes in the rearview mirror and laughed. "You can't do this!" I yelled. I struggled, trying to free myself.

"I can do anything I want, Rahkel. I became Adam Rowdosky didn't I?"

I don't know why but I started thinking about Matthew, and then Mama. The thought of being killed didn't sit right with me at all. I was overwhelmed with fear. I looked down at the door handle. Nevilla was still staring at me and then she looked out the window. I was very worried about her. Well at least he won't kill her I hoped, but thinking about what he has been doing and what he will continue to do to her was worse than being dead.

"Do you want to know why she's like that?" Leon asked as he turned around slightly and then looked in the mirror.

I didn't respond. I was trying to feel for my gun. I was surprised to find it was still in my back pocket.

"She's hypnotized. It worked with you too when you were little, but I don't think it ever worked with Sharon." He started to laugh. I was so disgusted. "That Sharon has done a pretty good job with keeping her mouth shut. I guess money will buy anybody." He laughed more.

"Does she know about you now, about being Adam Rowdosky?" I asked hoping and praying she wouldn't keep that a secret.

"Hell no! Of course not.." .

"Does she know what you've been doing to Nevilla?" I asked, wanting to know. I swallowed feeling a large lump in my throat, praying Sharon wasn't that stupid.

"Enough talking okay?" he said with a stern, serious look on his face.

I started calling out Nevilla's name but she didn't even flinch.

"Shut up!" he yelled, startling me.

Just then my phone rung. It was still in my coat pocket. I had a feeling it was Darrin. I looked at the time on the digital radio up front. This would be about the time I would be getting off work; about four. And Nevilla would have gotten out of school at three, so I know Mama and Sharon are worried. Leon turned around in his seat and then pulled over the car. He got out and opened my door and stuck his hands in both my coat pockets, pulling out my cell phone. He made sure I was looking and with force he threw it into the woods. He got back in the car and drove off.

As we were driving, I looked out the window helplessly. Nothing could have prepared me for this. I imagined this as a nightmare, but I wasn't waking up. I really didn't know where we were going. I had to be strong and think, but tears still fell down my face. I couldn't die this way and I couldn't let him take Nevilla with him. I was determined not to. I said a small prayer and then sat up against the back seat and felt the gun in my back pocket. I couldn't wait for the opportunity to use it. It was only a matter of time.

Chapter 47

I was already at Rahkel's house, and tried calling her several times, but got no answer. It's not like Rahkel to not answer her cell phone. An eerie feeling came over me, so I looked under her bed. And, as I suspected, the gun was missing. Fear shot through me, Rahkel doesn't know the first thing about shooting a gun. I feared for her. I rummaged through her lingerie drawer for her bullets. They were gone too. "Shit!" I yelled in frustration, slamming the dresser drawer. "Rahkel, where in the hell are you, baby?"

After calling her a few more times, I drove over to Ms. Williams', maybe she'd heard from Rahkel.

Arriving at Mrs. Williams', Rahkel's car was nowhere in sight. As much as I tried to push it out of my mind, I thought the worse. When Mrs. Williams' opened the front door, she seemed happy to see me.

"Mrs. Williams, I can't get a hold of Rahkel. Have you heard from her at all?"

She stepped back and opened the door wide, welcoming me in. "Yes, she came by here earlier this morning. She said she was off work today. I thought maybe she picked up Nevilla from school, because Sharon called me and said she didn't come home. Is something wrong?"

"Damn!" I yelled, catching myself. "Oh, sorry Mrs. Williams. She told me she *was* going in to work."

Following her inside, she went into the kitchen to call Rahkel. "She's not answering her phone."

"I tried too. I don't have a good feeling," I said, pacing the living room floor thinking what to do next.

There was another knock at the door. It was Sharon, hysterical, with Terry in tow. "I can't get a hold of Rahkel. If she would have picked up

Nevilla she would have called me or came by. Did either of them come by here, Auntie?" Sharon glanced my way and acknowledged me.

"No, Sharon, Nevilla's not here. Where do you think she could be?" Moving out of the kitchen and into the living room, Mrs. Williams limped toward the sofa.

"Don't worry, we'll find her. Maybe she's with Rahkel." I flipped open my cell phone.

"But we don't know where she's at either," Mrs. Williams' said.

"Y'all don't know where Rahkel's at?" Sharon asked, confused and distraught.

Dialing Calvin's number, I gave Sharon and Mrs. Williams my business card. "Here's my number. Call me if you hear from them. I'm gonna go search for them right now."

Both Sharon and Mrs. Williams were in tears, and Terry did his best to console them. He's a joke anyway, but I have to give the brother cool points for making an attempt. My heart went out to them, but hell my baby was missing. I had to stay strong. I needed to find my woman.

Calvin met me at Adam Rowdosky's house. Rahkel's car was parked at the end of the block. Walking over to the car with caution, I peeked in and opened the driver's side door. Her purse was on the floor, on the passenger's side. Right then I had an inclination that something was wrong. I snatched up her purse and sifted through it, looking for something, anything. Spotting the three keys, I put them in my pocket.

"Let's roll," I said to Calvin, walking back to my truck.

"What are you doing man?" Calvin asked.

I reached in the backseat. "Me and Rahkel found this lock box in the woods. We believe Adam Rowdosky left it, and I wanna see if any of these keys will unlock this box." I looked around to make sure I didn't see anyone.

The third key I tried opened up the box. There were plane tickets inside for two people: Roger Avery and Susie Avery. There were also passports, money, bank account papers and other stuff.

I looked at Calvin. "This is unreal. He's using fake names. Who is this son of a bitch?""Yeah it is. I wonder what he's running from." Calvin said.

232

"We're about to see. Are you ready to do this man?" I stood with strong vengeance looking toward the house.

"Yeah I'm with you." Calvin pulled his gun out, cocked it and stuck it in his vest.

Both of them got out the car and briskly walked up to Rowdosky's house. Calvin walked behind me, looking around. Like a couple of cat burglars, we carefully and slowly walked to the back of the house. I pulled out my gun, so did Calvin. With him on one side and me on the other, I gave him the signal to kick the door in and enter, while I was right behind.

After casing the place, and searching each room, no one appeared to be home. Calvin went upstairs, while I was in the kitchen looking through drawers before going into the living room.

"Darrin! You've gotta see this," Calvin yelled from upstairs.

I hustled up the steps to Calvin. "What's up?" I said, looking at papers strewn everywhere.

"Look at this, man." Calvin picked up a picture of Rahkel when she was a little, which was lodged in the side of the bed.

Taking the picture, I examined it. Anger rose within me. Rahkel was naked from top to bottom. Turning the photo over, Rahkel's name and the date was written on the back.

"That is one sick motherfucker," Calvin announced.

There was also a photograph of me and Rahkel coming out of my place. As well as a current picture of Nevilla.

"That fuckin' asshole. I can't believe this. He must have Rahkel and Nevilla." I threw the pictures on the bed and rubbed my head in dismay.

"Look at this." Calvin held up a wig, a pair of glasses and piece of paper with the name of an airline and the date written on it. "That's one sick fucker." Calvin looked down at the picture of Rahkel on the bed.

Realization hit me. I looked over at Calvin. "You know what this means don't you?"

"What's that?"

"I'm almost positive that Leon Wilson is Adam Rowdosky." I picked up the pictures and stuffed them in my coat pocket.

Chapter 48

After passing the gas station, I realized we were driving to New Amsterdam. I sat up in my seat and looked over at Nevilla who was fast asleep. My wrists were hurting and still handcuffed behind me and my headache had returned. I didn't say a word. I knew he was probably going for that box. Suddenly, I thought about Darrin. I wondered where he was and if he was looking for me at all. Leon pulled over to the side of the road in a parked area. I turned around and didn't see anyone around, just trees for miles. The roads were still a little slick and it was snowing again.

Leon faced me before getting out of the car. "I suggest you stay inside. If you open your side door, the entire car will explode." He smiled, climbing out of the car, shutting the door. I didn't know whether to believe him or not, but I wasn't taking any chances. After all he's done, he would kill me in a heartbeat. I looked over at Nevilla.

"Nevilla wake up!" I yelled. She moved a little bit, but not much. I scooted over to her with my hands still behind my back. I shoved my body into her, but not too hard. "Nevilla, please wake up."

She wiped her eyes and looked around. "Where are we Auntie?" I was so happy she was back to normal. Or at least I thought.

"Somewhere far princess. Why don't you climb up front and open the door on the driver's side."

"You know about Granddaddy?" Nevilla asked looking around in the car.

"Yeah I do, but don't worry about it. The only thing I care about is us getting out of here."

"I had to lie Auntie, he said he would kill you if I told." Nevilla's face frowned up and she looked scared.

234

"Nevilla it's all right," I reassured her. Little did she know he was going to kill me anyway. "Don't think about that, just try to get up front and open up the driver's side door."

Just when Nevilla was about to climb up front, Leon opened my door and pulled me out by the shoulder of my coat. Out the corner of my eye, I saw some type of remote in his hand. I fell to the ground and he pulled me back up by my hood.

"Where the hell is it?" he yelled.

"Where's what?" I slipped and he pulled me back up by my coat. He slapped me hard in the face, instantly numbing me, and it stung really bad. I could hear Nevilla from the inside of the car banging on the window and crying.

"Don't hurt my Auntie," she yelled.

"You know what the hell I'm talking about. *The damn metal box*! You tell me now or you're dead, Rahkel. I'm not playing with you. And no one will ever see Nevilla again." His eyes set fear in me. So I complied.

"Okay, Okay." I regained my balance and felt on the back pocket of my jeans. The gun was still there. "A friend of mine has it," I said, trying not to give too much information away.

"What, your boyfriend Darrin?

How did he know about Darrin?

"Oh yea, I've been watching you and him." Leon opened up my door and pushed me inside. "Get in. We're gonna call him."

Leon slammed the door and got behind the wheel. He turned to Nevilla and pulled out a necklace. It had a large black marble at the end. What was up with this necklace?. Me, Sharon and now Nevilla had one. Except, Sharon tossed her out the window… Oh my God, he used it to hypnotize us!

He took her hand and started talking another language. I think in tongues or something. It freaked me out. After he was done, she became calm, with a blank stare. Then she sat back in her seat. She appeared spaced out. Then she turned her head toward the window.

Leon looked over at me and slapped the shit out of me. I fell towards Nevilla and my hair covered my face. I had no idea what that was for. "I should kill you now. If it wasn't for that box, I would."

I felt so helpless. I couldn't even defend myself with my hands behind me. My tears stung the cuts on my face as they fell. I wondered what was in that box that made him so angry. I also wondered if Darrin had opened it yet.

Leon began laying out his plan. He first told me to call Darrin from a pay phone, and have him meet us at a designated parking lot. He was to come alone. He let me know that if Darrin brought anyone or if anything funny went down, then with just a click of a button Leon would explode the hospital that Jamie was in and kill me. I couldn't believe he knew Darrin's sister. He claimed to have planted five bombs around the entire hospital. He'd been following me the entire time after his death. This man was crazy and desperate. I had no idea who this man was. He wasn't the Uncle Leon I knew.

Leon drove to the gas station I had followed him to. We sat in the car while Leon drilled me with the plan, again. Afterwards he opened up my side of the door and took the cuffs off, while he held a gun against my back. We walked towards the payphone. He was right up against my back. He let me know if I said anything other than what we talked about, he'd shoot me. I looked back at Nevilla and she was watching us.

Darrin answered on the first ring. I was so happy to hear his voice I started to cry. I did exactly what Leon asked me.

"Please do exactly what he says." Those were the last words I said. I was trying not to sound too panicky.

"Everything will be okay, baby. I know Rowdosky is your uncle."

At that point Leon snatched the phone from me.

Darrin and Leon talked on the phone for at least five minutes. I thought about the gun in my back pocket, but he was pushing his gun so tight up against my back, I didn't want to take the risk.

I overheard Leon say he had someone at the hospital watching his sister and could call the man at any time to have him kill her directly, if Darrin didn't do exactly what he wanted.

I couldn't wait until I had the opportunity to use my gun. I wouldn't hesitate at all.

After the phone call, I asked Leon if I could use the bathroom. At first he wasn't going to let me go, then he reconsidered.

"You're not using it here, let's go over into the woods. You can use it there," he said. He walked me down a slant hill. He put the handcuffs back on me immediately and helped me unbutton my pants and pulled them down for me. He watched me carefully as I squatted in front of him.

"Why are you doing this?" I said looking up at him trying to keep my balance. I felt a cold breeze brush against my ass. It was hard to squat when you have your hands behind you. A few times I fell on the ground.

"Rahkel don't ever say I never loved you. But this is about me, and I really don't care about anyone right now. I owe a lot of people a lot of money and I will not go to prison for anyone." He looked around and then back at the car. "I'm too old for prison. This is an opportunity to start my life new with Nevilla."

I tried to pull up my pants, but wasn't able to. Leon helped me and turned me around as we started to go back to the car.

"You have a smart boyfriend. I can't wait to kill 'em," Leon said, as he let out a loud evil laugh.

He started up the car and we drove off.

Chapter 49

amn!" I yelled, banging my fist against the wall, after hanging up with Leon. I grabbed my keys off the counter and looked over at Calvin. "He's got Rahkel and Nevilla. And this crazy asshole has bombs posted around the hospital where Jaime's at."

"Let's do this man," Calvin said as he headed for the door. He un-cocked his gun and placed it back in his jacket.

Inside the truck, I reached in the glove compartment and pulled out another gun, this one smaller, and attached it to a pocket on my ankle, underneath my pants.

"We're gonna have to go and get your car. I want you to follow me. And stay back a ways. I have to show up by myself."

Calvin nodded and I pulled off.

Feeling anxious as I drove, I kept thinking back and forth between my sister and Rahkel. Trust, I will take Leon down the first opportunity I get. Angry and afraid, more so for my sister and Rahkel, than myself, I banged on the steering wheel and made a right turn. I looked in the rearview mirror confirming Calvin was not far behind me. I drove under a bridge and turned into an empty parking lot to meet Leon.

Dialing Calvin's number, "This is it," I confirmed. "Keep going and turn into the third entrance by the dumpster ahead."

Beads of sweat formed on my forehead, and the adrenaline rush I was getting right now was what I liked most about this job. But never in a million years did I think my job would involve the ones I love.

I parked in the middle of the lot. There was no one around, except a few trees and a frozen pond off to the side. I looked in the rearview and saw the vague view of the top half of Calvin's car.

"Where are they?" I mumbled.

I pulled a picture of my sister from my wallet and said a small prayer.

Chapter 50

The plan was set. As we were driving I kept thinking about Darrin. Then I thought about Darrin's sister that I'd only met once. I couldn't believe Leon brought her into the picture. We stopped by the hospital on our way to meet Darrin. I had no idea why and eagerly wanted to know what Leon was up to now. We parked in the underground garage and he got out the car and opened my door. He took out another pair of handcuffs and placed them on my ankles and placed some duct tape over my mouth. He took Nevilla with him. Then he took out a suitcase from the trunk.

I had no idea what was going on. I felt totally out of control. I tried to get up front, but I couldn't. So I sat there waiting. I saw a woman walking about three car spaces in front of me. I started banging my head on the glass, but she didn't see me, and plus that hurt.

After about ten minutes, Leon was back and he had Nevilla with him. He took the duct tape off my mouth and the handcuffs from my ankles. I didn't ask any questions, but instead thought about how I was going to get the gun from my back pocket. He'd changed into overalls and a baseball cap.

I tried to focus. We were coming to the finale and I had to think smart. There were no words exchanged the entire drive. I looked up front because he had Nevilla in the passenger seat now. She was also in different clothing, including a shoulder length sandy brown wig on her head. He must still have her hypnotized, because she didn't react or say a word. She just stared forward

I can't imagine how my wrists looked right now, and my head had started to bleed again, but I didn't think about the pain, I remained focused.

I wondered what plan Darrin had because I was sure he had one. We pulled up to the parking lot, and I saw Darrin's Suburban parked in the middle several feet ahead of us. I was somewhat relieved when I saw him. He opened his car door and got out. He was holding the metal box in his hand.

My heart immediately accelerated. This was it. There's no backing down, there's no time to be sad or afraid. This was it.

Leon parked the car, reached underneath Nevilla's seat and pulled out a gun. He cocked the gun and turned to me. "Your boyfriends a dead man," Leon said and got out.

I was terrified. I called out Nevilla's name but she didn't turn around. I tried to bring my arms under my butt and under my legs. I was struggling. I looked up and I think they were talking. I continued, but to no avail, it wasn't working. I could feel my heart beating faster. I definitely wasn't the most flexible person and I think my arms had fallen asleep by being in the handcuffs all this time. They felt numb. I almost couldn't feel them. I looked up at Nevilla again, she blankly stared straight ahead. I yelled at her without being too loud. Then I moved my body up closer to her and nudged her. She didn't bulge or even blink. I had to get out of the car in order to bring my arms under me, but how was I going to do that?

"Nevilla, don't you hear me? Wake up! Snap out of it!" I screamed and cried again. I turned on my other side and sobbed. I knew that wouldn't help, but I felt helpless. I wasn't being strong at all. I'm not sure why, but I called out Matthew's name. I thought about him at that very moment. Then, all of a sudden Nevilla turned around.

"Auntie what's wrong? What's going on? Did you just say Matthew?" She looked really confused.

It was such a relief to hear her voice. "Nevilla, you got to help me. We have to get out of here." I made her bring Leon's seat up and get in the back with me.

One last try. With all my strength I managed to get my arms under me in front. There was hope. I looked up at Leon and Darrin. Darrin had placed the box on the ground and was taking a few steps back, still talking, with his hands in the air.

Damn it, I should have grabbed the gun first.

"I'm scared," Nevilla said.

"I am too, but we have to be strong. Grab the gun behind my back. I knew at any moment Leon was going to make his move and reach in his pocket to get the gun. I heard Darrin yelling for me to get out the car. I looked up and saw Leon reaching inside his pocket.

Nevilla had my gun in her hand and climbed up front and opened up the passenger's side door. I yelled at her to give it to me. But she wasn't listening. I saw both Leon and Darrin look at her. She held the gun up with both her small hands straight ahead. Darrin tackled Leon to the ground. Nevilla began walking closer and closer to them. I froze for a moment and then made my way up front. I managed to wiggle my body half way out the car. Leon turned around and pointed the gun at me. And just like that I'd been shot.

Chapter 51

Nevilla!" Darrin ran towards Nevilla. She dropped the gun after firing at Leon and stood there. He picked her up and they ran back behind his truck. Leon dropped to the ground. He went back to Leon and removed the gun from his hand. In the other hand he had a pager, which read: One Page Sent. Darrin wondered what that meant. Calvin drove up in the parking lot and got out with his gun in hand and ran towards Darrin.

"Calvin watch Nevilla." Darrin handed Nevilla to him and ran over to me. I laid on the ground completely limp for a moment. Then I slowly opened up my eyes.

"Am I dead?" I asked in a weak voice.

"No, but you've been shot. It was in your shoulder, but we need to get you to a hospital." He checked my chest and I had a vague heartbeat. He picked me up and carried me over to where Calvin and Nevilla were. He pulled out his phone and dialed 911. Darrin went over to Leon's body and found the keys to the handcuffs.

"Watch out!" Nevilla yelled. Leon was slowly reaching in his pocket. Darrin was too quick and pulled out his gun from his ankle and made a clear shot to Leon's head.

Nevilla slowly began walking over to Leon. Darrin tried to reach out for her, but he had me in his arms and the gun in the other. Calvin ran over to Nevilla and stopped her, but she resisted. She continued to walk and stood over Leon's body and stared down at him.

"That's for Matthew," she said.

I wondered what that meant. She reached in her pocket and pulled out the necklace with the black marble at the end and placed it on top of his body. She then ran over and hugged me.

"Be careful Nevilla. She's hurt," Darrin said.

242

After Darrin removed the handcuffs, the ambulance arrived and the EMTs lifted me into the ambulance. I couldn't help but look down at Leon. Although my vision was a little blurry, I could see the paramedics zipping him up in a black bag. I couldn't believe it was over. Was it really finally over?

Nevilla rode in the ambulance with me and Darrin. Calvin followed us to the hospital. We were on our way to the same hospital where Jaime was. I felt weak as the oxygen mask was placed over my nose and mouth. I kept falling in and out of consciousness on the way to the hospital. Nevilla was leaning forward staring into my eyes, holding my hand. She had tears in her eyes, which made me cry as well.

Chapter 52

I feared the worst as we got closer to the hospital, as I followed behind the ambulance,. I was thinking it would be blown up, due to the 'one page,' but it wasn't.

I jumped out of my truck and ran into the hospital, taking the stairs four flights up to Jaime's floor. Running, I almost knocked down a man walking with an IV bag hanging from a metal post. "Excuse me, Sir," I yelled back at him.

When I busted through the doors of Jaime's room, she was standing over a man with a fire extinguisher in her hands. She looked up at me. "This man tried to suffocate me. He got what was coming to him," Jaime said.

Relieved, I chuckled and shook my head. The man was moaning on the ground, with his hands on his head. Two police officers came rushing into the room seconds later. They helped the man up off the floor. I turned the man's head toward me, looking into his blood shot eyes. He was still a little out of it from getting clunked on the head.

"Who had you do this?" I asked him, now serious.

The man had blue scrubs on and a name badge he'd stolen from a hospital attendant. The man lifted his head and smiled at me. Then after the police handcuffed the man he finally decided to speak. "Who's Rahkel, I've heard a lot about her. Tell her hello for me," he said, with slurred speech before laughing hysterically.

"Get him out of here," I said to the police.

As the police were carrying him out, the man was yelling that he still hadn't gotten his money from Rowdosky and that he wanted to be paid now.

I made sure my sister was alright and asked a nurse to come in and sit with her. One of the police officers went over to Jaime and began asking her questions. Detective Matters showed up and I notified him of possible bombs surrounding the building. I wasn't too happy to see him, but I knew he was here to help. They brought in a swat team. Not long after, they'd found the five homemade bombs in the basement of the hospital, which they safely removed.

After all was done, I went to Rachel's room to kiss my girl and make sure she was alright.

Chapter 53

Eight months had past since Leon's official death. I remember waking up in Darrin's arms after I'd dozed off. We were at my house sitting on the couch, resting after returning from working out at the gym. I thought about Leon and became terrified, but then realized he was really gone. However, every once in awhile I would still look over my shoulders. It was finally over. I had to keep reminding myself of that for a while. I still had eerie feelings in my mind about the pictures I found and exactly what happened to me when I was a child. I believe what disturbed me the most was what Nevilla told me when I was at the hospital, the day we were kidnapped. We were alone in the hospital room for a few minutes.

"It's okay, Auntie," she said. "I finally told the truth. Grandpa killed Matthew." I looked at her in disbelief.

"What do you mean? He died in a car accident, Nevilla," I said, slowly trying to get my words out. I was in pain and there were IV's in my arm.

"He took the seat belt off Matthew when you were inside the gas station. I remember Auntie." She looked up at the ceiling, thinking. "And then he did something to your steering wheel and your gas pedal. He said we'd be in an accident, but not to be afraid."

I said nothing, only listened to Nevilla's words, which were unbelievable. I didn't think it could get any worse.

"Grandpa had been trying to hurt Matthew every since Matthew saw him touch me." She rested her arms on my hospital bed looking sadly into my eyes.

Those words played over in my head and that's when I went into an unconscious state. I remembered the doctors rushing into my room. My pressure rose and then I blacked out. Later, when I woke up I saw Mama, Sharon, Darrin and Janetta standing around my bed.

I can't believe Sharon never told anyone what Uncle Leon did to her when she was younger, especially me. Now I know why he'd been giving her all that money and taking care of her like she was helpless. He paid her to keep quiet. But she had to have some kind of clue of what he was doing to Nevilla. I can't forgive Sharon for that.

Nobody really talked about what happened. The only ones I'd been able to talk to were Janetta and Darrin. I once talked with Mama. But Mama feels so bad about all of this. She blamed herself, but I reassured her that nobody blamed her at all, because she didn't have a clue what was happening to us as little girls.

I told Sharon what Nevilla told me about Matthew and even tried to talk to her more about what Leon had done to Nevilla. Sharon would change the subject or walk out the room every time I brought it up. I have tried my best to remember back when Sharon and I were little, but the only thoughts of Leon I have were positive. I finally decided to talk with a psychologist, but not even that made me remember the horrors I'd encountered as a child. It was concluded that I suffered from a repressed memory and post-traumatic stress disorder.

Nevilla was much better now and she never talked about Uncle Leon at all. I convinced Sharon to let me take Nevilla to counseling, which I was glad she agreed to. Nevilla and I were attending counseling sessions once a week. It has helped immensely. Sharon refused to go.

Sharon finally had her baby, some time ago. A beautiful baby boy, born a crack baby. He was premature and had to stay in the hospital for four weeks after he was born. Sad to say, he died two months later. The fact that she and Terry continued to smoke that stuff after the death of her son was very disturbing. I finally had to get social services involved, because Nevilla was curious one day and tried that stuff. They placed her in rehab. I didn't want to but I didn't know what else to do. They gave me and Mama custody of Nevilla until Sharon could get herself together.

I finally broke down and decided to take Tony up on his offer to go to California and visit Daddy. I have a different perspective on life and wanted to make amends with my father. This entire experience had changed my life. Darrin wanted to be with me when I finally confronted my dad, but I thought it best to swallow the big girl pill and go it alone. I'm glad I did too.

As soon as Tony and I got to the front door of Daddy's house, I took a deep breath, because I was nervous and didn't really know what to expect.

Tony grabbed my hand and I squeezed it, as there was a brief silence. "I'm glad you came, Rahkel. He's gonna be happy to see you." Tony hugged me and I smiled.

Phillip, Daddy's partner, greeted us at the door and welcomed me in. He gave me a kiss on the cheek. I hadn't seen him in years. He was shorter than Daddy and had sandy-blonde hair. There was dinner prepared on the table, set for four with candlelights.

Daddy appeared from the back room. Tears welled in my eyes as we rushed towards each other and hugged. I was happy to see him and it was obvious he was happy to see me. Finding out the truth about Leon made me want to be closer to my Daddy.

"I'm glad to see my girl. You've grown up so beautifully, Rahkel."

I smiled at him.

It was a really good visit and we talked a lot. I got a lot off my chest. We laughed together and cried together. It was a wonderful five-day visit. When he dropped me off at the airport, he promised he'd keep in touch and I promised the same. He made me promise I'd come back next year to visit. I agreed.

I can now say things are getting better. Darrin proposed to me a couple of days ago, which I gladly accepted. I already told Janetta she's gonna be my maid of honor. And on top of that, next month it's confirmed that Jacobs getting out of jail. I was really excited and so was Mama.

What kept me going was that I have a wonderful man in my life who loves me and I love him. The past was the past and it will stay that way. I still think of Matthew from time to time and I still get sad especially since I know the truth. I could never forget about my baby. As far as Leon, I would never wish death upon anyone, but I am definitely not sad that Leon was gone. I'm sad about what we had to endure. Honestly, it hurts me even more to know what he did to Sharon and Nevilla, because I was the only one that didn't remember my past.

Darrin and I sat in the living room. The television was on as we sat on the couch with his arms wrapped around me. I looked up into his eyes as he pulled my hair back, caressing my face. I knew right then we'd be together for the long ride. Without Darrin, I'm not sure how I would have gotten through all this.

I looked down, and admired my diamond ring he'd bought me, and then noticed the light from the sun behind me reflecting, coming in through the blinds. It was really bright in the room. I didn't know if Darrin noticed or not, but I turned my head and looked out the window. The sun became less bright as I stared outside. I looked up into the blue sky and I didn't see anything in the sky, no image, no picture, nothing at all; and it has stayed that way.